PRAISE FOR *BEING MARY RO*

"A charming book."
THE SUDBURY STAR

"I cannot imagine anyone not enjoying *Being Mary Ro*. The material is suitable for mature young readers, contains small sketches (by Melissa Ashley Cromarty), and is an excellent first novel for Ms. Linehan Young."
THE MIRAMICHI READER

"We're only halfway through the novel when Mary pulls the trigger. The strength and courage required to shoot the pistol is the same strength and courage that afterwards allows Mary to travel to . . . and pursue an independent career as a . . . I'm not telling. Find out for yourself. Read *Being Mary Ro*. It's first-rate entertainment."
THE TELEGRAM

PRAISE FOR *THE PROMISE*

"A well-written story that many will want to read in one night . . . just because the plot is that good."
EDWARDS BOOK CLUB

"Ida Linehan Young . . . evokes a time and a place and a strong female lead. She has also well-positioned this book to pilot into a follow-up. Her knowledge of, and research into, the processes pre-20th century household labour, or the state of the justice system after the 1892 fire, pay off." — THE TELEGRAM

the Liars

the Liars

IDA LINEHAN YOUNG

FLANKER PRESS LIMITED
ST. JOHN'S

Library and Archives Canada Cataloguing in Publication

Title: The liars : a novel / Ida Linehan Young.
Names: Linehan Young, Ida, 1964- author.
Identifiers: Canadiana (print) 20200199188 | Canadiana (ebook) 2020019920X | ISBN 9781771178013
    (softcover) | ISBN 9781771178020 (EPUB) | ISBN 9781771178037 (Kindle) | ISBN 9781771178044 (PDF)
Classification: LCC PS8623.I54 L53 2020 | DDC C813/.6—dc23

© 2020 by Ida Linehan Young

PRINTED IN CANADA

MIX
Paper from
responsible sources
FSC
www.fsc.org **FSC® C016245**

This paper has been certified to meet the environmental and social standards of the Forest Stewardship Council® (FSC®) and comes from responsibly managed forests, and verified recycled sources.

Cover Design by Graham Blair

FLANKER PRESS LTD.
PO BOX 2522, STATION C
ST. JOHN'S, NL
CANADA

TELEPHONE: (709) 739-4477   FAX: (709) 739-4420   TOLL-FREE: 1-866-739-4420

WWW.FLANKERPRESS.COM

9 8 7 6 5 4 3 2

Canada Council   Conseil des Arts
for the Arts   du Canada

We acknowledge the financial support of the Government of Canada through the Canada Book Fund (CBF) and the Government of Newfoundland and Labrador, Department of Tourism, Culture, Industry and Innovation for our publishing activities. We acknowledge the support of the Canada Council for the Arts, which last year invested $157 million to bring the arts to Canadians throughout the country. *Nous remercions le Conseil des arts du Canada de son soutien. L'an dernier, le Conseil a investi 157 millions de dollars pour mettre de l'art dans la vie des Canadiennes et des Canadiens de tout le pays.*

Dedication

The local store was the heart of every outport community and kept the life in many over the years. Any time I refer to a store in any of my books, I model it after my own great experiences in the little community of North Harbour, St. Mary's Bay. Although we had many shops and even a snack bar for a summer or two, in my lifetime in the community, for me the heartbeat of North Harbour was at Sebastian (1933–2012) and Josephine Walsh's store—Seb and Jos(e) to everyone who darkened their door.

Seb grew up in North Harbour with my mother, who was just a month older than him. He worked for a time in Argentia and St. John's before returning home to fish. He ran a small shop out of the pantry at their homestead with his sister, Margaret. He met and married Jos (Collins), a teacher from Freshwater, Placentia Bay. Jos took over the main duties associated with the shop in 1960 and became a strong female influence for many of our generation. Seb started fishing full-time, first in a little motorboat, then a bigger skiff, before getting his first longliner in 1970, the year the youngest of his seven children was born.

Jos settled into life in North Harbour, made many friends, and raised their family. She was the reason we could buy a bottle of cola, a bag of flour, felt and tar for the roof, fruit (plums, apples, oranges, and grapes at Christmas), toys, paper glue and scribblers, trendy clothes for school, shoes and rubber boots, panes of glass for the many shattered windows, sheets and blankets, turkey necks, bread, milk—you get the picture. If you could name it, Jos would stock it.

She made up the bill at the end of every month, because most of the community shopped there on credit. I'm sure there were many families, including our own, who carried a balance month over month, and year over year, but were never denied anything (including cash, if needed), no matter how much was owed. I'm sure, though it wasn't spoken, there were many times we didn't go hungry because of the generosity of the shopkeepers.

Nobody went there too early or left there too late. Sometimes it was standing room only, a multitude of conversations, laughter, raised voices, hushed whispers—but no matter what, it was always the place we wanted to be. Even a crowd of loud teenagers were welcome. I have very happy memories associated with the busyness of the "shop."

As a sign of the times, more people had access to vehicles, roads were built and improved, people commuted, the community opened up, and the "shop" evolved. Alas, in 2003, after more than forty-three years in business, the shop closed, and Seb and Jos began their well-deserved retirement. People adapted, as people do, and the significance of the community shop was lost on the younger generation who aren't as "enclosed" now as we were then.

However, fond memories flow of my first taste of Pepsi, my first candy, my first school shirt (it was a mosaic of pink and purple hues on a polyester print), my first homemade pizza, and so many more firsts that happened because of the "shop."

Several years ago, I was privileged to speak at their fiftieth wedding anniversary. However, I didn't have time to prepare and didn't get a chance to tell them how grateful and thankful I am to have been reared up by a "shop" such as theirs.

I would like to formally recognize the influential strength and perseverance of two of the greatest shopkeepers—Seb and Jos Walsh—as well as their entire civic-minded family, who do so much for the community of North Harbour, always my hometown.

❧

For family and friends who so fully support me. For Sam and Parker, who don't know what that means yet but who lift me up with love.

❧

For Georgette, who finds the most fascinating things for me to write about and who keeps me out of trouble or gets in trouble with me.

❧

For my secret book club, who provide solid counsel for my plot.

❧

For Clyde, who couldn't wait!

Prologue

Newfoundland is a large island in the northwest Atlantic Ocean, off the east coast of Canada. During the late nineteenth century, the island was a Dominion of the British Empire (together with Canada, New Zealand, the Irish Free State, and Australia). Until it joined Canada as a province in 1949, it was self-governed and had its own currency and coinage, defence, anthem, postal service, and banking system.

In 1890, the population of the capital city of St. John's was approximately 25,000, but the island's huge coastline (9,600 kilometres) had an additional 50,000 inhabitants attracted by the productive cod fishery. These livyers were scattered throughout hundreds of tiny communities in coves and bays around the coast. Typical communities had between forty and 200 residents—by design, the numbers could sustain a reasonable inshore trap fishery.

Labrador, the continental part of Newfoundland, had an additional 7,886 kilometres of coastline and a settled population between 1,200 and 1,300. The Innu and Inuit peoples migrated seasonally between the coast and inland. They were referenced as Eskimow, Esquimeaux, Esquimoe, or Eskimo in journals and newspapers of that period.

Several year-round Moravian Missions were established to educate indigenous peoples in their native language. They were located in Nain, Hopedale, Hebron, Zoar, Ramah, Makkovik, and Killinek. The posts also attracted "white" settlers.

The population and marine traffic in Labrador dramatically increased between early spring and late fall when the coast was seasonally settled by "green fishermen" taking part in the Labrador fishery. "Floater fishermen" also fished the grounds. However, they returned to the island of Newfoundland to process their catch.

In the spring, merchants traded provisions for furs trapped over the winter. During the fishing season, the merchants' ships collected dried salt cod, salmon, and fish oil in exchange for provisions. In Labrador, most of the commerce and trading was conducted between the fishermen and the Hudson's Bay Company's ships out of Montreal, or with the Moravian Missions, who bartered with Europe. On the island, cod was shipped to Britain, Canada, and the United States through Boston and New York.

After first snow, coastal settlements in Labrador were isolated and cut off until spring thaw. Residents survived on salt cod, farm animals, merchant provisions coming from Europe through the Moravian Missions (tea, flour, molasses, beans, etc.), as well as caribou, seals, and seabirds hunted during the winter and early spring.

Travel amongst settlements was rare. However, sleds led by dog teams were the most popular means of transportation during the long, harsh winters.

The Moravian missionaries tried to convert the Innu and

Inuit to Christianity and attracted indigenous encampments near their posts during the winter. The indigenous were vulnerable to diseases introduced by European travellers who came to the Missions and by the enterprises involving those who were prosecuting the fishery.

Civil law was rarely practised, except for the most heinous of crimes. Those brought before the courts would generally be tried at Twillingate, Harbour Grace, St. John's, or, on rare occasions, in Labrador. Executives at the Moravian Missions would sometimes act as justices for lesser crimes.

1

Somewhere near Nain, Labrador, 1880s

Hesitantly and with great care, she set the plate of hot stew on the old wooden table. His dark eyes leered at the spot where her outstretched arm had brushed his shoulder. She held her breath and slunk away. He looked to his supper. His arms tensed, and his knuckles whitened on the fork and knife he held upright on each side of the chipped dish.

"Why is the caribou burnt?" he said too quietly, his teeth gritted and jaw strained. "Why weren't you paying attention?"

Her body flexed to run, but the air seemed to solidify around her and his stare held her fast. "I'm sorry," she stammered. "I thought you liked it browned."

"Browned, yes. But not burnt!" he roared. With deliberation and drawn-out movements, he laid the utensils down one by one as he stared at her. His muscular arms bulged and pulsed as he gripped the edge of the table.

Terror was a swollen river cresting upon her. "I'll take it back," she said, almost as if the words could save her. She could change the meat in the black iron pot with other pieces that were not as brown. That should satisfy him.

With one swoop of his big arm and the speed of a pouncing lynx, he cleared off the table, pushed back the chair, and landed a blow across her face that whipped her head back and split her lip. She didn't see it coming to brace herself. She lost her footing, stumbled backward, and tripped over the second chair in the small two-roomed sod hut. Its leg twisted and broke under her, and she crumpled, tangled in the wood, against the unforgiving earthen wall.

Before she could recover, he grabbed a fistful of her dark hair and pulled her upright in front of him. She clutched the strands to relieve the pain in her scalp while using her arms, bent around her face, to protect herself. He struck her about the head twice more with his free hand before landing an elbow to her midsection, all the while cursing her stupidity and uselessness. He released her and she doubled over in pain, unable to catch her breath.

She scrambled away from him but became trapped against the dirt-packed wall near the shoddy stone fireplace. In the dimness of the room, she tried to make herself as small as possible under the protection of her arms and legs as he rained down his blows. Then he seized her hair once more and dragged her from the ramshackle shelter she knew as home.

Stumps, low bushes, and loose rocks on the rugged path tore at her bare heels, ankles, and calves as he stomped along. As much as she tried, she could neither stand nor right herself. He was going too fast. She clutched her hair to lessen the strain and struck out at him with her other fist. Her arm couldn't reach far enough to land a blow. She screamed in agony as she tried to keep up, but there was no reprieve. It only angered him more.

She was dragged up across the headland to the edge of the cliff, where he stood her on the precipice of death once again.

She thought, *It must be two hundred feet down to the rocks.* But after almost a year, this view didn't intimidate her. She'd become accustomed to it. She thought back to how terrifying it had been the first time he'd hauled her to this bluff. That time she'd been sure he was going to fling her over. She'd flailed and screamed and begged and cried and said she was sorry, though for what she did not know. When he was sure she was sufficiently frightened, he took her back to the sod hut. He always took her back. He carried on with whatever he was doing, as if nothing had happened, reassured she was discontented in his cruel entrapment.

She didn't quite know how to deal with the beatings. Sometimes she would fight back, and sometimes she would try to hide. There were times she held her tongue to the point she believed she'd forgotten how to speak. She silently spewed her hatred for him behind his back, and when she was alone, she would tell the trees or the grass or the birds how much she hated him. When she'd tried to leave, she'd gotten too cold, or too wet, or too hungry. The wilderness, her solitary friend, continuously betrayed her. She'd come to believe she deserved what he doled out.

He reminded her often that she should be grateful he was a good provider. But when he went fishing or hunting, she prayed he would not come home. She'd be left alone. She didn't know if that would be harder, if women knew how to survive, but there were times she thought it couldn't be as hard as things were now.

Ezra, the man born to a mean white fur trader and an Esquimeaux woman, had a reputation like that of his father. He had no care for the law nor his wife. His mother had been brutalized by his father, who ran off after she had disappeared. Ezra scrounged around from family to family for food and lodging in the settlement on the outskirts of the Moravian Mission in Nain. By the time he was thirteen years old, he was all but banished because of the cruelty he showed to both the children and animals in the village. He was given food when he was hungry but had learned to depend on his wits and hunting skills to make him an independent, anchorless sort with regard for nobody. His brutality was remarkable, and most people steered clear of the mean man he'd become. But unlike them, she didn't have a say in steering clear.

In flights of fancy, she wondered if there was something different. For as long as she had memories, she was hiding or running away, all the while listening to the screams and pleadings. She understood that things were the same for her mother. She supposed it must be like that for all women. If it weren't, then somebody would undoubtedly have helped her mother or would help her. But no one would interfere with a man's business.

She often blamed herself for her mother's death. She'd stood up to her father. She'd stood up to him for her, so he wouldn't trade her at fifteen years of age for a quintal of fish and a bottle of cheap stilled whiskey. People were afraid of him, too. No one stopped her father. A man's business.

And now, because she was Ezra's wife, that same business was handed out to her.

The last time she went to the general store, she had heard the chatter inside, but when she entered, a hush fell over the entire place. Mr. Making motioned to her from behind the counter, and the others shuffled aside to let her pass. No matter who or how many were waiting to be served, or for what reason they were in the store, there was whispering and a knowing. No one wanted to be responsible for what would happen if she were delayed. A servant of hopelessness, she would have welcomed a delay, a kind word, or a smile. The beatings happened anyway, but her isolation would have been lessened and her desolate spirit lifted.

Now here she stood at the cliff, waiting to be dragged back to the house once he saw she was terrorized enough and remorseful enough for her failings as a wife. Her future was in his grasp, always in his harsh grasp. *Just push me,* she thought.

A fish hawk screamed from the overcast sky, its cry foretelling what was to come. Her throbbing face mellowed. Her breathing calmed. The sting from the cuts, scrapes, and scratches about her legs and feet eased. The soothing breeze tugged at the long black tresses ensnared in the drying blood on her temple and lips. The grass where she stood seemed to paint itself several shades greener and the water below several shades bluer. She looked down at the rocks and silently pondered the remnants of her miserable life, which smeared clouded pictures across her mind. Not one recollection was a good one. Not one made her smile.

The ocean, pulsating, mesmerizing, and soothing, summoned her as its frothed lips salivated and drummed on the rocky shore. Its voice was deep and turbulent and welcoming. She stopped fighting him.

Sensing the change in her, without care, he slung her over the edge. She didn't look back. The fish hawk shrieked once more as its steep dive matched her own. The rocks welcomed her into their granite bosom. The sea devoured her.

Once the ocean was finished with her, the waves spat her ashore near Nain four days later. The community was riled and demanded action for the murder of the young woman. A few of the brothers from the Mission confronted Ezra, but there were no consequences for his actions. The good Christians of the settlement all gathered for a service. She was buried in the community graveyard. A scrap of wood carved with the name Ruth Taktos served to mark her final resting place.

Ezra watched from the trees on the hillside. There was a sombre yet harmonious chorus of voices in the chapel. When the people left, he did, too. He grinned—a man's business.

2

Holyrood, Conception Bay
Present day, late spring, 1895

John MacDonald, his tall frame straight and stiff, gazed around Carroll's crowded store in Holyrood. He could not shake the uneasiness he felt whenever he was amongst people. A consequence of hiding, he supposed. Always watchful, always waiting, expecting a mortal outcome that didn't favour his own longevity.

He tended not to say much. Folks said he wasn't a friendly sort. But when Beatrice was around, he was a different man. She was a salve on an open wound. She let him forget. Maybe she would be the distraction that would lead to his downfall, but because of her, he didn't care. Without Beatrice, there would be too much remembering. That wasn't always good for the soul, he allowed. Especially one like his.

His time with Beatrice was precious to him. He didn't want her remembering "bad" things about the man she called her father. He was not entirely sure why, but for some reason, that mattered, especially if something were to change. He wanted her to be able to look back on her childhood as a pleasant one.

He knew what it was like to be somebody else's rubbish—thrown out in the gutter to make his way in filth and squalor. Beatrice had been, too. But she wouldn't know. She wouldn't feel that shame, not as long as he could help it.

His eyes followed the young girl, Caddy, as she paraded from the mail desk to the store counter. He liked her. She couldn't be any more than fourteen or fifteen, he reckoned. She had a way about her, a boldness for living, that didn't sit too well with people.

She made a great fuss of opening the *Harbour Grace Standard*, cleared her throat, and waited for the chatter to cease. There was still one conversation going on, so she *ahemed* once again. Despite the gravity of the situation, he lowered his head and smiled into the collar of his jacket.

Then she started to read out the article titled "Prisoner Escapes."

"About a quarter to eight o'clock last night, Police Inspector CARTY received a telegram from Brigus stating that the Eskimo charged with the murder of his son at Nain, Labrador, and who escaped at Scrammy, from custody, on board the SS Panther, *had arrived at Harbour Main from HANNON, and that while being conveyed by the said HANNON from Harbour Main to Brigus, to be handed over to the police authorities there, he made his escape at Gasters, Salmon Cove. On receipt of this information, the Inspector immediately sent dispatches to the police in Holyrood, Brigus, Bay Roberts, and Harbour Grace, instructing them to leave nothing undone that would be likely to lead up to his apprehension. At eight o'clock, some of the horse police were sent from St. John's in search of the fugitive, followed shortly after by a detachment on foot. Up to the time of our ongoing press, his recapture had not been effected."*

When she finished, she carefully folded the paper and laid it on the grey oilcloth covering the counter.

"I'll be locking my door tonight," said Mrs. Fewer. "Jim, I don't know that you should go fishing till he's caught."

"That's right," said Mrs. Crawley. "A dangerous fellow like that, you don't know what he could do."

"The murderer could be watching us right now," said Mrs. Hickey. "Good thing Charl is here to bring me home."

"Seen the police go through today on the train," said Mr. Quinlan.

"The ones on the horses will be about soon enough," said Mr. Healey.

John made his way to the counter as the chatter continued and folks moved toward the door.

Caddy smiled. "What can I do for you, Mr. MacDonald?"

"You're sure that's yesterday's paper, Caddy?" he asked. "Never heard anything today, did you?"

"A couple of officers are staying up to Veitch's," she said. "They were in here just before supper, and I heard them talking. He's not been caught yet." Caddy regarded him for a moment, searching his face. "You see anything?"

"No, no," said John. "The missus is scared, that's all. We're out on that lane by ourselves."

Caddy nodded, his explanation acceptable, at least so it seemed. "I'm glad we live across the way. Lots of people around. I didn't tell Ma about it."

"Good thing not to worry her," John said. He tipped his hat and wished her a good night. Out in the fresh air, he kept his head down, eyes hooded beneath his cap, and made quick steps. He passed the train station and the hotel before heading up the hill toward home.

Alice would be anxiously waiting for news, and Beatrice would be ready for bed by the time he got there. He didn't like to see Alice fretting about the situation. So much had changed between them. Yet somehow so much had stayed the same.

John had a job to get Alice to lie down that night. She was on the verge of hysteria before the sun rose and calmed her some.

John brought Beatrice to school and made a quick trip to Carroll's for the mail. Though they had only recently begun to receive one letter at the end of each month, it was an excuse to find news. The trips made him vulnerable, but he wouldn't see Alice suffering.

Back at the house, John had no different news for Alice. Her voice quivered and a shadow passed over her eyes as the situation sank in. Red-faced, she reached for the chair and crumpled there. He went to her side and placed his hands on her shoulders.

"You're sure it was Ezra?"

"Yes," he said.

She inhaled sharply. "What are we going to do now?" She hung her head and wept into her hands. John knelt in front of her and pushed some long black strands of hair behind her ears. The misery of worry had settled on her features.

Awkwardly, she eased into his embrace. Reflex made him stiffen before he could stop himself. He forced himself to relax. Her arms encircled him, and she cried into his shoulder. He slowly put his arms around her and held her.

"We do nothing. Nobody knows where we are. We left all that far away."

"But he's so close," Alice said. "Harbour Main, it's hardly a day's walk."

"He'll get caught," John said, his voice surer than his thoughts.

"What if he doesn't? I'm scared, John. It's not just us anymore. We have Beatrice to think of now."

He glanced at the clock on the wall. "It's time." He gently eased her away. "I'll go get her from the schoolhouse. Will you be all right?"

"Beatrice will always come first. I'll be fine," Alice said. She wiped her eyes with the tail of her skirt, then straightened her back. He admired her strength. She didn't know it, but she kept him strong. She held him in the present as much as Beatrice did.

John felt her eyes on him. His tall, stout frame was hunched just a bit. His dark hair was thinning around the temples. He turned at the gate when he heard her voice.

"We must be watchful and ready."

"I know," he said. He turned once more toward the coast. John walked this two-mile route twice a day. He wasn't as sure in his thinking about being found out since Beatrice started school. He was taking more and more chances of being recognized. He was almost daring somebody to recognize him. Maybe then it would be over. But the thought of something happening to her, especially because of him, was worse than the thought of being exposed. Today his step was quicker than most others, though, because of the threat to Alice.

If it weren't for Beatrice, they would have stared at changing seasons through the window of the house. Even if staying hidden was probably best, both he and Alice wanted more for Beatrice. They wanted her to be schooled. She was their miracle in all this. Something John was sure that he didn't deserve. The little girl had given them so much happiness despite their circumstances. In truth, it was the child who probably kept them both sane. It was the child who stopped the running. It was Beatrice who kept them together. She made them believe they were a family. Those were dangerous thoughts for a man like him.

School would soon be out for the summer, and they could stay in the isolation of their farm until the vegetables were ready for sale. It was one of the things they had to do to survive. That meant something different now. Living here, though self-exiled, seemed normal. That's what he told himself when he remembered he had to do things he hadn't imagined he would ever do—things that were wrong, according to the law—things that could turn Alice against him. But he would do them now if there was a threat to his family. He just didn't want to have to do them again. He walked out of the tree-lined lane a short time later, high above the schoolhouse in the distance on the point of land jutting out into Holyrood harbour. The white church steeple glistened in the sun behind the small one-room school. Its bell tolled the beginning and end of the school day as well as the call to prayer on Sundays when the priest was visiting.

There was a lot of activity in the area in the last few months. The train brought people, people brought prosperity, and prosperity brought trouble. That was the part that worried him. He was uneasy about remaining here.

They hadn't been thinking straight when they'd arrived here on the train. That was when Beatrice came into their lives. That was when they went from running to hiding.

"Good day, Mr. MacDonald."

His thoughts were broken by a short, round woman. "Oh, Mrs. Byrne, I didn't see you."

"On your way to the school, I see."

"Yes, it's almost that time."

"Indeed. I'm on my way to the church with the linens for Sunday. I'll keep you company, if you don't mind."

"Of course not. But I'd be happy to drop them off if you have something better to do. After all, I'm going that way."

Mrs. Byrne hesitated before agreeing to hand him the basket. She gave him instructions, then turned and went back the way she came. John was glad not to have to listen to her ramblings while he was so distracted. He made fast work of the extra chore and returned to the lime-washed wooden fence post near the gate leading to the schoolyard. This was where Beatrice would meet him.

He scanned the harbour, his daily musing. There was a multitude of small fishing boats along the shores and around the wharves. There were plenty of two- and three-masted schooners anchored off or coming and going. He wouldn't be part of any of that commerce ever again.

In the distance, a crowd of people waited for the train on the wooden platform. They would be heading to the capital, St. John's, or to some of the communities in between. He wouldn't be part of any of that travel, either.

Most days, he and Beatrice were halfway back to their turnoff when the train passed. Beatrice sometimes tried to outrun it or asked him to stop and wave at the people, depending on her mood. She wouldn't notice his bowed head as she was waving and giggling. She was a jolly child, for sure.

Construction had already begun on wharves and cribbing directly below him on the beach. Big logs came in on the train, and men pulled rocks from a nearby quarry in order to keep them in place. Holyrood would be a large port soon enough. Easy access to the train and deep waters were all the freight boats needed, and it was all here.

John put his foot on the rail of the fence, his elbow on his bent knee and his hand under his jaw as he watched the activity. He looked out at the boats once more. Sometimes he missed being part of that world, but some things were more important than company. When the church bell rang, the most important one ran toward him shouting "Daddy." That was all he needed to sustain him—that and Alice.

John walked hand in hand with the blonde-haired child who put a touch of contentment in his world. He couldn't believe she was seven. They guessed her age and had made up a birthday a few days after they got her. The name Beatrice had been sewn into some of her clothing. They didn't change that. She gave them life just as sure as her mother had given birth to her and etched the words "This is Beatrice, she was loved" into the blanket that enwrapped her. Alice kept it until Christmas past, when she returned it to the mother who bore her.

In the beginning, he told himself that Beatrice and Alice were a means to an end. A hiding place of sorts. But over time, his cold heart had warmed to the little blonde-haired beauty who called him Daddy and the raven-haired woman she called Mommy. The three had become a family, at least in the eyes of the few who made their acquaintance.

Only he and Alice knew the truth. At least about Beatrice. He sometimes wondered if he really knew everything about Alice. Alice didn't know about him. She hadn't asked. His truth was a twisted mess. But somehow the child had made it okay. John couldn't admit it, but he had grown to love Alice. He wouldn't tell her. He couldn't tell her. She wouldn't forgive him for his sins, and he wondered if he would ever care to forgive himself.

Beatrice chattered away as they listened to the sound of the train whistle in the distance. She skipped along the beach. This little child had changed him. He sometimes worried that she'd broken him, that he wouldn't be able to do what needed to be done because of her. But because of her, he might be able to do it more easily. He might find out sooner than he'd thought because of the prison break in Salmon Cove. He would do what he had to do for Alice.

Just last summer, a man, Danol Cooper, had come. John remembered being surprised in the barn. He thought he'd finally been found out and was almost relieved. The uneasiness of always looking over his shoulder, always waiting, was a heavy burden and made him suspicious of things that weren't always real. But when the man had stared at Beatrice, he knew it was about her and not him. Then he felt guilty for feeling relieved. He and Alice were going to run again. But Cooper had found where they were hiding and would probably have found them again if they had done so. That could have led to other truths being unearthed, and he couldn't risk disclosure.

In the end, though the child had been left with them instead of being returned to her mother, John had ultimately chosen his own welfare over hers. Though the child was fixed in his heart and he wouldn't change anything about that, he now carried another guilt. He had chosen himself over Beatrice. What kind of man did that make him?

He didn't force himself to remember his past acts like he used to do. His new family eased the bitterness that had consumed him for so long, and Beatrice kept it from festering. Maybe he was satisfied that Lavinia's justice had been served.

The courts had failed, leaving him responsible for that judgment. There was no fairness in the consequences to himself. He was running ever since. Well, until Beatrice. Though in many ways he was still running, he was staying put in a situation that he was more than happy to live with. The one before this had been bleak and lonesome.

His mind wandered back to Alice's predicament. The more he thought about it, the more it bothered him that Ezra was so close. Maybe Alice was right. It couldn't be a coincidence—he didn't believe in them. Perhaps it was time to make a decision about Beatrice. Maybe he, too, was too easy to be found. He shook his head. This was about Alice and not about him.

But after having the opportunity to do the right thing for Beatrice and choosing his own well-being instead, he wondered if he'd really changed at all. Maybe he was a coward. Perhaps the selfish, lawless, street-living, good-for-nothing boy, and the bitter, murdering young man couldn't be changed despite his efforts to believe otherwise. Just because he didn't think about it like he used to didn't make it untrue.

3

Beatrice smiled up at him as she skipped along. "What do you think, Daddy?"

"About what?"

"I just asked you. Do you think we can ever go on the train?"

"We'll talk to your mother about that when we get home," John replied.

"Really?" Beatrice's voice rose in surprise. "Really, Daddy?"

"We'll talk to your mother," he repeated, attempting to sound stern. "Now, let's beat that train to the road." He quickened his step, in preparation of racing her. Beatrice squealed and ran ahead of him.

All the way back to the house she questioned him about where she could go. John warned her not to mention the train to her mother until he had a chance to talk to her about it.

Alice was waiting at the door when they returned. Beatrice hugged her and went in ahead of him. He brought her books and lunch pail and laid them on the table.

"Go change your clothes," he said to Beatrice.

"Are you going to talk to Mommy?"

"Go and change out of your good clothes," Alice said as she stared at John.

When Beatrice disappeared through the door on the opposite side of the kitchen, Alice grabbed John's arm. "What is it?" Terror swam in her eyes.

"Sit down, Alice," he said as he guided her to the chair. "I've been thinking on what you said about Ezra being so close. I don't like it."

Alice put her face in her palms and then massaged her scalp with her fingertips. When she finally looked up at him, she asked, "What do we do?"

"Hear me out, Alice." John sat next to her and took her hand. "What if we sent Beatrice back to her mother?"

With a sharp intake of breath, Alice shook her head and pushed his hand away. "No. No. No."

"Hear me out, Alice," he repeated. He took her hand once more and squeezed it. "I don't mean forever."

She stared at the door through which her daughter had gone. Slowly, she squeezed his hand in return.

"What do you mean?"

"That Cooper fellow. He said that if he could do anything for us to let him know. The mother said the same thing in her letter. We just need to contact that lawyer in St. John's."

"But we could lose her, John. We can't. At least *I* can't lose her."

"Now, Alice, that's not fair." John didn't want to raise his voice to her, but he felt gut-punched from her words. Alice was hurting. "I love that little girl as much as you do. What do you think will happen if Ezra finds you here? If he finds Beatrice here?"

"Oh, John, I didn't think of that. Oh God, John. You're right, we have to get her out of here. Ezra could kill her." Alice jumped from the chair, and he stopped her before she reached Beatrice's door. Beatrice was singing some sort of children's rhyme, her voice carrying through the thin walls.

Alice pulled from his grip, and he grabbed her again. "Alice, stop it. You'll frighten her." He held her in place until he saw calmness in her eyes. "We'll go tomorrow."

Alice nodded. "We have a lot to do."

"We do," said John.

They both turned when the door opened. "Did you ask her, Daddy?"

"He did," Alice said.

"We are going on the train tomorrow," John said.

Beatrice jumped up and down and squealed. "Where are we going?"

"Do you remember when there was a man here last year? He stayed for toutons?"

"Yes, he talked funny."

"Don't say that," Alice said.

Beatrice looked down at her hands. "I'm sorry, Mommy."

Alice looked at John.

"Let's get some supper and then talk about it," he said.

"Do you have lessons?" Alice asked.

Beatrice nodded and shuffled through her books. "What about Penny?"

"What about her?"

"She's my best friend," Beatrice said. "Can I tell her tomorrow?"

Alice and John looked at each other. John shrugged. "I don't see why not," he said.

4

Erith Lock stared at her reflection in the tiny mirror. She couldn't see the white dress even from her tippytoes. She had to take her friend Maggie's word that she looked just fine. Maggie, a proxy for the mother she hadn't known, had fussed between her and the stove the whole morning. Arguably, she would have spent more time with her, but her daughter-in-law and Erith's dear friend, Agnes, had shown up at dawn to help ready the feast and to dress the bride.

Her heart did a somersault, her belly heaved, and her hand shook as she focused on the image before her. Agnes had pulled her hair back from her face in a loose knot. She wouldn't allow her to tie it too tight because it brought back unpleasant memories of not so happy times.

Little Annie had picked purple asters from the meadow, while Tommy and George had plucked some ferns to add to her bouquet. How she loved those little ones—well, not so little now. Her heart gave another thump to remind her of Beatrice. Not that she could ever forget her. She'd grab some white daisies from the laneway to add to the purple bouquet. That would be for her baby, whom she hadn't seen since she was a few months old. Erith had something to be thankful for, though. Beatrice was alive, when for so long she'd thought her to be dead!

Danol's voice and the merriment of the children as they greeted him wafted through the walls. Danol Cooper, her husband-to-be. What was he doing here? She was supposed to meet him shortly at the church.

Maggie's raised voice penetrated the wooden door. "Danol. Danol! I can't let you go in there."

"It's important, Maggie. I have to speak to Erith."

Erith heard the urgency in his voice. Her stomach rolled once more, and she staggered toward the sound of the man she would soon marry. Clothing whooshed against the wood, and the door rattled as somebody—she'd bet Maggie—put her body against it.

"I don't care. It will have to wait," Maggie said.

"What's going on?" Erith called.

"Erith, honey, I need to speak to you."

"You'll have to do it through the door," Maggie said. The woman's clothing sighed on the wood as her plump body moved against the door. Knowing Maggie, she probably had the rolling pin.

"Okay, that's fine." Danol's voice rose as if in acceptance. "It's important, Maggie. I wouldn't be here if it weren't."

"Where's Father Desmond?"

"He's outside in the wagon. He said he fancied a walk to the church," Danol said.

"Oh, for heaven's sake. Why didn't he come in?"

"We don't have time, Maggie. I have to speak with Erith."

"Danol Cooper, if you take one peek at that woman, I swear, I'll—"

"Maggie, please! It's very important," Danol interrupted. "Please move aside."

Erith smiled as she listened to the sparring outside her door, until she picked up on the impatience in his voice. That was not his custom. Something was wrong. What could Danol want that was so important? He'd been underfoot for the last month since she'd agreed to marry him. He hadn't even bothered to go on a freight run and instead chose to send his crew. It was the crew who'd fetched the priest from St. John's. Danol said he wanted to make sure he wouldn't be late for their wedding.

Her palms began to sweat, and she took a gulp of air. "Danol, what's wrong?" Erith couldn't stop the tremble in her voice. She reached to turn the key in the lock, but then she hesitated. This could be Danol's way of sneaking a kiss. He and the children had been pretty foxy, especially this last week. It could be a ruse of some sort. But he wouldn't intentionally worry her.

"Danol, you're frightening me," she said. Maggie's footfalls went out the hall.

"I don't mean to, Erith. But I do have news."

She turned the key and opened the door a crack, remaining out of sight. There was a soft thud as he rested his forehead on the jamb.

"What is it, Danol?"

"It's about Beatrice."

Erith yanked on the door and it flew back, striking the wall with some force. Danol straightened his tall frame, and his brilliant blue eyes met hers. "It's not bad news. At least I don't think so. I received a letter from your solicitor about the Mac-Donalds. They want me—well, us, if that's what you want—to come pick up Beatrice. It says they have to deal with urgent business and need a place for Beatrice to stay for a month or two. They would only entrust her to us."

Erith gasped and reached for Danol to steady herself. He gathered her in his arms. "Want to go? Of course I want to go— more than anything! We'll leave right now. Let me pack a bag. What about the children? How soon can we leave? My God, Danol—what could be wrong?" Tears brimmed in her eyes as she buried her face in his coat to quell the frantic feeling rising inside.

A small, firm hand rested on her back before she heard a calming voice. "It doesn't sound like Beatrice is in any kind of danger. Don't worry about anything, Erith. Peter and I will take care of things here." Her friend and confidante, Dr. Mary Nolan, spoke behind her. Mary Ro looked beautiful. Her red hair was bundled beneath a small, light blue hat edged with creamy lace pinned off-centre on her head. Her blue dress with a pale trim flowed to the floor on her slender body.

"I told Mary Ro and Peter on the way here," Danol said. Erith glanced from one to the other. Quickly, Maggie and Peter rushed down the hall toward them. Peter, a striking picture with his dark, perfectly trimmed hair contrasting with his light grey suit, reached for his wife. Mary instantly nestled in the crook of his arm.

"There's no reason not to go ahead with the wedding," Mary said. "The men need time to provision the boat. They must get water and supplies." She looked at Erith as if waiting for her to agree. Mary's green eyes were wide and expectant while Erith absorbed what she and Danol had said. After a long pause, Mary added, "Father Desmond is ready whenever you are."

"How can we get married? What of the guests? The food? The children?"

"That's why you are going ahead with the wedding," Mary

replied. "The children have been so excited. You can't disappoint them. Having the wedding won't delay you from seeing Beatrice."

Mary turned Erith to face her. Her tone was soft as she spoke. "I know you are confused. But I also know how much you were looking forward to today. It is not selfish to get married. You deserve to be happy, Erith. There is nothing wrong with that."

Danol gently pulled her back to him. "Erith, I will do as you wish. However, I won't pretend that I won't be greatly disappointed if we don't get married today. I love you. But there can't be a wedding if your heart is not in it with mine. I won't force you to marry me. I want you to be happy. I'll respect your wishes." His eyes locked with hers. He bent and softly kissed her lips. The earth seemed to shift beneath Erith. "I will wait for you forever, Erith Lock. I hope you know how happy you have made me and how much I love you," he whispered in her ear as he squeezed her tighter.

Erith hugged him fiercely. "I know that." She slowly let her arms fall from around his neck. Her palms grazed his cheeks, and their eyes met and held. How easy this had become—how love and kindness had changed her. Her heart seemed to leap in her chest, and she drew in a deep breath to calm herself.

"We can take a wagon as far as Whitbourne and catch the train tomorrow morning," Danol said. "The crew of the *Angel Endeavours* should be able to meet us in St. John's in a day or two, and we can bring Beatrice back here by sea."

"I'll keep the three children here until you return," Maggie piped in too cheerily, her toothless grin strained, and her troubled eyes betrayed the sweetness of the sentiment.

"With Agnes and Patrick's help, we'll take care of the food and the wedding guests," Mary said matter-of-factly. "There is not one person here in North Harbour who wouldn't do anything for you or to protect you. You've already seen that. I'll explain the situation. It won't be a problem. The children will be cared for, whatever you decide to do."

Erith had so much to be thankful for: three beautiful children who, though they were no blood relation, were as much her own as was Beatrice; a loving partner who wanted to marry her and help raise the children; wonderful friends who were worried about her; and a community she could count on. "I need a little time," she said. "I'll be ready in a few moments." Danol's heavy sigh of relief would have been funny in other circumstances. She reached for his hand. "I'll be right along. I promise."

He grinned. "I'll be waiting at the altar." His face grew more serious. "Are you sure? We can wait. I can go myself. This should be a happy day."

"I'm sure, Danol. I'm sure. It is a happy day. We'll have the rest of our lives to celebrate."

Erith rested her back on the door, and the crowd shuffled out the hall. The murmur of voices disappeared to the kitchen. "I will not cry," she whispered to the walls. "Today is a happy day." And in fact, it was. Danol had been like a wondrous child since she'd agreed to marry him. He talked of him staying around instead of spending a life at sea. He wanted to have a larger family. He wanted to bring her to England to meet her mother's people. So many plans and so many reasons to be happy. He was a good man.

And now she would see her Beatrice. The picture Danol had given her only a few months ago was nestled in a hidden pocket in her dress. She took it out and rubbed her thumb over the beautiful face of her baby. Well, not a baby any longer. She was eight now. Erith would see her as early as tomorrow. Tomorrow! A whirlwind of images popped into Erith's mind. She crossed the room to the mirror and then peered at the picture once again. Slowly, she reached to untie the ribbon and pins that were holding her wild and wiry hair. She glanced from the mirror to the picture and back again.

Beatrice would know. She might not know tomorrow, but she would know sometime. That wouldn't be fair to anyone. Everything she had done, every decision she'd made, had been for Beatrice.

The windowpane rattled and the tiny branch of a lilac tree swayed in the breeze, intruding on her reverie. A knife on the sill drew her attention. She remembered Danol had brought it to help Annie cut the ribbon for a wedding gift she was wrapping. He must have forgotten to take it back to the kitchen. It would do the trick.

She returned to the mirror. Maggie called to her from the kitchen. "Erith, will you be ready soon?"

"Yes," she said in a low voice.

Erith stared at her reflection, and at once her eyes filled with tears. She grabbed a fistful of hair before she could stop herself and laid the back of the blade on her neck just below her ear. She shuddered. Beatrice would know. Without thinking, she pulled the hair and began to cut it away. A handful came free, and she tossed it aside on the floor. She seized onto more. She could hardly see with tears.

Maggie gasped behind her. "Erith, what have you done?"

Almost blinded by the stream of tears running down her face, Erith traced Maggie's approaching form in the mirror without turning around. Maggie's rough hand covered hers on the handle. "Help me, Maggie."

"Oh, Erith, my child. Your beautiful hair."

"It's like Beatrice's."

"I know. I know." Maggie's voice wavered. "Danol Cooper doesn't know what he's getting himself into." She chuckled through her tears, and Erith burst out laughing. Maggie hugged her from behind. "I'll get the scissors and a sheet to cover your dress. We must hurry. They'll be waiting."

Within a few moments, Erith was sheared. She patted her head several times. Her short hair felt odd through the tips of her fingers. Maggie handed her a handkerchief to dry her eyes. She took one last glimpse. Today was about Beatrice before it could be about herself. That would not change.

Erith grabbed her bouquet from the table while Maggie put the veil under her arm, and they rushed out the door, heading toward the church. Thoughts of Beatrice, her family, and the man she would soon marry flowed and churned inside her until she was almost giddy.

"One thing at a time, Erith. One thing at a time," she whispered to herself as she stooped to pick a bunch of daisies. She paused for a moment and turned toward the gravestones of her mother and father. They would want her to be happy. She smiled.

Just beyond them was the grave of her stepmother, Kathleen Lock. Erith guessed she would not be resting quietly today, nor would she be keen to see Erith married. A draft of wind blew through her short tresses, cooled her scalp, and caused her to shiver. The cruel woman who'd raised her had no say in anything to do with her now. With Maggie urging her onward, she straightened her back and continued along the lane to the white church above her on the hill.

She felt safe and strong with Danol. The echoes of resonating waves of blackness and loneliness had quieted. Erith hoped they would disappear as she looked forward to life with him by her side. She trusted that Danol would help her face whatever was to come. As his wife, she wouldn't have to be alone any longer.

And she would see Beatrice again.

5

Somewhere between Nain and Zoar, Labrador
Spring, 1887

Her husband was dead. Ezra had shot him. There was no doubt it was with intention. He'd murdered her spouse.

Philip fell before she heard the report. He almost dragged her to the ground with him. She staggered, but her legs kept her upright when she let him go. She followed the sound, thinking her father-in-law had somehow stumbled and the gun had gone off. Her gaze fell on the man, his stance that of a hunter, his grin that of somebody who had felled a great pointed bull.

She shook her head, thinking it was a mistake. But there was no mistaking the gaping hole in her husband's back, nor the sticky, warm droplets that had hit the side of her face and the blood that had spattered all over her sealskin coat and moccasins.

Terror held her fast. The breath went out of her, and her legs gave out beneath her. She dropped beside Philip and waited for her turn to die.

He startled her when he closed his bear-paw hand over her mouth.

"Nobody will hear you," Ezra said in a quiet whisper. She

stopped screaming. She hadn't realized she'd made a sound. He pulled her away onto a rocky embankment. Her legs refused to work, and she collapsed onto the bedrock.

He sat cross-legged beside her. His black, piercing eyes stared at her while she caught her breath.

"You shot my husband," she stammered as she gulped for air. Fear inside her was calming as anger took over. "You killed my husband," she said, mustering a little more strength.

"Yes, now we can be together."

"What?"

"We can be together."

"Together?"

"Yes. You wanted me to shoot him so we could be together."

"What?" she asked again.

"You accepted my courting."

"Ezra, I don't understand."

"I came courting when Philip was gone."

"I didn't see you when Philip was away."

"No, but you didn't tell him."

"How do you know?"

"He would have said. He has a big mouth like his mother. She's gone now, too."

"What have you done?"

"You know it's what you wanted."

He was so matter-of-fact. Nancy almost believed he saw nothing wrong with what he had just done. Maybe he didn't. She had heard the rumours. He'd killed his first wife, thrown her from the cliff above their house. Now he killed her Philip and possibly Philip's mother.

"You're mine, Nancy. You will always be mine."

"You killed my husband."

"Yes, it's what you wanted."

"Ezra, I never wanted this."

"You did. You kept my gifts."

"I didn't say anything to Philip so he wouldn't be angry." She regretted that now.

"You wanted this."

"You must be mad. I never wanted this."

"You wanted this. You're my woman now."

"I'm your woman now?" Nancy repeated flatly.

Ezra grabbed her arm and yanked it. She yelped. He stood, went to Philip, and dragged the body from the path and rolled him into a dry gully. The dead man lay face down and almost hidden beneath the overhanging limbs of a large spruce. Ezra gathered sticks and rocks and tossed them toward the body.

Nancy stared, transfixed. This would be her husband's grave. As Ezra moved to conceal the man she'd married, a cool breeze crossed her cheek. *Run, Nancy, run.* She didn't know if it was the wind or her thoughts that roused her. Her hand fell on a soggy stick as she braced herself to stand. She grabbed it and crept the short distance to where Ezra crouched, his back to her, gathering debris to cover Philip's body.

With all her might, she raised the stick and brought it down upon him. Blood seeped through the matted black hair on his head as he slumped forward. She turned and ran.

First, the running was just to get somewhere else. Away. She feared for her life. Nancy imagined him having her in his sights. She weaved through the naked birch trees to make his line of sight more difficult. She waited for the yawning hole in her back, for the pain to fell her. It didn't come. She imagined the whisper of his sealskins right behind her, and she unwittingly braced for the fall when the tackle came. But it didn't.

A glance from the rise she was traversing caught no movement from Ezra where he slumped near his kill. He hadn't recovered yet. But he would be undaunted—he was an excellent tracker. It was only a matter of time before he'd be upon her.

Nancy determined he would have to work for it. She had to get as far as she could and look for a place to hide. With her heart beating out of her chest, her feet seemed as if they had grown wings. Perhaps Philip was somehow carrying her in spirit. She gasped aloud at the thought. Philip was gone. Her Philip. Her provider.

She could hear Philip's voice on the wind. *Nancy, Nancy.* She followed the sound through the birch and into the spruce. The thick green boughs struck at her and beat at her face. They tripped her, but she didn't fall as she frantically and blindly ran through the brush. Nancy held up her arms to protect herself as she scampered through the forest. She grabbed the nettled limbs to keep herself upright as she plunged forward. Every step was away. At least she hoped it was.

She had heard stories of people getting lost and circling and being found dead within a few miles of their point of origin. Would she ever be found? Would her finder be Ezra?

Maybe she'd killed him. Her blow could have rendered him unable to move. Was that too much to hope for?

Nancy had always been wary, yet intrigued by him. She had been privy to the hushed rumours about him and his first wife. The poor young girl had been beaten senseless so often that it was a wonder it hadn't happen sooner than it had. She hadn't lasted a year. Then, just a few months later, Ezra had married Philip's mother, a woman more than twice his age.

Philip was livid before the wedding and the most vocal of the three sons. They had threatened Ezra about being harsh to their mother. Then she had turned on them, one by one. When Nancy went to their house with Philip, Ezra had always smiled at her and tried to talk to her. She'd avoided the encounter if possible.

Only for fear of what Philip would do if he lost his temper, she would have stayed away. But she accompanied her husband to intervene if needed. At least that was what she told herself to justify the mystery of the man who, if she was honest with herself, drew her there.

When Philip and his brother were away on overnight hunting trips or gone to Zoar for missionary work, she'd find rabbits or moose or caribou outside the door in the morning. She believed they were gifts from Ezra. She dared not tell Philip. Secretly, she liked the forbidden attention.

Philip's brother Malcolm usually accompanied him on the trip between Nain and Zoar, but he'd had an accident during the seal hunt. A stray bullet had shattered his leg, and he was recovering. Ezra had been at the hunt. She wondered, now, if this had all been planned.

It was thirty miles or so by land between the two Moravian Missions in Nain and Zoar. When the harbours were frozen among the dozens of islands, the trek was much shorter. This time, with an early spring thaw, the ice wasn't safe to walk, so they took the land route instead.

Philip's brother Paul and his wife, Nancy's sister Irene, had just had their third child. Nancy was excited to see the new little one. She'd suggested she take the journey with her husband to keep him company.

The terrain was rugged and rocky, making for slow progress. They had used a night camp south of Makhavinekh Lake, which they had reached early the evening before. They had a simple breakfast of dried seal meat and bread that morning before setting out for Zoar.

Nancy enjoyed walking with Philip. They talked and laughed like they had done when she had first gotten to the Moravian Mission encampment at Nain. She was happy that she had gone with him.

Ezra must have followed them. And now the unthinkable had happened. Now, her breathing laboured, she began to slow. The woods became very dense, and the trees closed in on her. The whoosh of rushing water meant a river was close. She slowed a little and picked her way toward the sound.

Nancy. Nancy. Philip was whispering her name. She followed the voice. It wasn't Philip—it was Ezra. He had come to the river, upstream from her. He was standing at the edge of the rock face, high above her position, and was calling her name. She panicked. He would climb down, and that would be the end of her. He scowled as he raised his gun.

Huge boulders were like sentries around her in the narrow gorge. She was bordered by sheer cliffs and a steep climb through the trees. The water rushed by a short footfall away. Nancy was trapped.

A fleeting thought went to Ezra's first wife, and Nancy could see herself on the cliffs above and Ezra pushing her off. She now realized she had been a fool not to tell Philip about Ezra's gifts, and along with Philip, she would pay for that stupidity.

The sky darkened, and a gust of wind rushed violently along the edge of the rock face. She thought her name was whispered once more—*Nancy*. The wind whipped through her clothes, so she shuffled her feet to hold her position and wait for the gunshot. A loose rock shifted beneath her, taking her off balance. She fell backward, flailing her arms to stay upright, and screamed as she toppled and plunged into the icy dark flow. Nancy caught a glimpse of Ezra leaving his lookout, but he was out of her sight when she hit the water.

She tumbled and twisted and swirled in the deep pool that had formed at the river bend before she was spat out into the main current and hurled downstream. A battered and limbless log bobbed boldly beside her. Nancy grabbed for the closest yellowed knot, but the tree pulled away from her and she went under a second time. Cliffs narrowed into a chute and the tree hit a submerged rock, halting long enough to turn and allowing her to catch up. She grabbed it one more time and flung herself over the top between the slippery spikes. Grabbing hold of one, she managed to pull her body forward to balance on the slick, wet surface.

The water's movement sped up as the river narrowed. Nancy kicked her legs to try and guide her makeshift raft through the rough currents that formed near the next bend. She was bobbing on the white crests of river waves and moving fast when the land fell away. The river widened between great stands of thick green forest, and the rushing water emptied her into a lake.

Nancy's clothing dragged at her, its weight trying to pull her from her roost. The current slowed, and she drifted to shore.

Her mind went to Philip. Philip was gone. Surely, after causing Ezra all this trouble, she'd be gone, too. But today it would be on her own terms, if only she could make it. She kicked and guided the log toward the far shore.

Nancy's energy was fading as the cold slowly claimed her. She tried to make herself move, but her legs stopped obeying. With what little effort she had left, her gentle movements were enough to ground the log about half a mile from the mouth of the river. She dragged herself ashore and stumbled underneath the low-hanging limbs of ragged spruce, curling into a ball be-fore rolling onto her back.

Bedraggled and soaking wet, she lay prostrate, shivering, waiting for death. Her end wouldn't be swift nor merciful, but it would be of her own doing and not that of Ezra at the top of a ravine. She'd be as alone in death as poor Philip was in his. Out of sight, Nancy hoped Ezra wouldn't find her.

Her gaze grew hazy, and warmth crept through her veins as if she were resting by a blazing fire. She stopped shivering. *Nancy, Nancy* was in the stillness. But she was confused. It wasn't her name. It was the brush of the trees shifting, then a hollow snarl. She was too weak to save herself. She hoped death would take her before . . .

Too late. The hot breath on her cheek, the soft growl, the wet nose, sent shock through her. Panic welled in her, but her body wouldn't respond. She was unable to help herself.

"Get away."

Was it her voice or somebody else's?

"Get."

Something yelped. She squeezed her eyes shut, and she struggled to pull herself into a ball. Hands were upon her. She was being tossed, and moved, and covered, and picked up. Was this how it ended?

She moaned.

"Hold on, Lavinia. Hold on." It was a man's voice. It was Ezra. No, not Ezra.

She was weightless and drifting. Fragrant fir limbs swept a soft touch across her face. Warmth penetrated through her clothes. She faded in and out. Breathing became a struggle. She couldn't tell if the raspiness was hers. Nancy tried to con-centrate, but the fog persisted and finally took her.

6

The crackle and hiss of burning wood awakened her. A weight was on her. Nancy pushed and met little resistance. She squirmed and opened her eyes. Chopped logs lined the ceiling above her. She was roused by a whimper somewhere nearby through the wall, then a growl. She was naked and warm. Was this death?

Pushing herself up on her elbows, she glanced around. A young, dark-haired man not much older than her own twenty years was coming toward her. She screamed. A dog barked near her elbow, and the man pushed it out of the way. He opened a door in the one-room shack, and the dog disappeared into the light.

"Where am I? Who are you?"

"I'm John. John MacDonald." His voice had a hint of an accent not common to the Labrador. "Who might you be?"

"I'm Na—" She paused. "I'm Alice." Her middle name. A distinctive *caw* somewhere in the distance finished her name. "Alice Crowe."

If he didn't believe her, it didn't register on his features. His blue eyes showed no sign of malice. Nancy saw her long brown skirt hanging near the open fire and gasped, remembering her nakedness. She huddled beneath the skins that covered her.

"They're dry now. I'm sorry I had to remove them. You would have died."

John retrieved the clothing and laid the bundle on the edge of a stump that seemed to serve as a chair. From a pile of chopped wood in the corner he threw a few sticks on the fire and left without saying a word.

Nancy waited until his voice trailed off as he talked—to what she guessed were the dogs—as he moved away from the cabin. She scrambled from under the soft caribou hides, quickly dressed, then found her seal boots, turned upside down on two green sticks near the fire. The warmth was immediate after she shook them and pulled them on over her bare feet.

Sitting back on the skins, she took in her surroundings. The room was small, with just the bunk, a rock fireplace, a couple of stumps, one bigger than the other—she guessed one was used as a table and one as a chair—and a door made from thin strips of wood that swung on rawhide hinges. There was no window, the floor was packed earth, and the seams between the small logs in the walls were stuffed with long-dried moss. The many cracks of light suggested it hadn't been stogged within the last year or maybe two. Surely this could not be home to John MacDonald.

Something rustled outside, and dogs barked. Ezra was here. Panic rose in her gullet. There was nowhere to hide. She grabbed one of the sticks that had held her boot and pointed it at the door. Sweat broke out on the back of her neck as she stood her ground.

There was a quick knock on the door. The rescuer called to see if it was all right to come in. Nancy dropped the stick and slumped back on the bunk. He eyed her from the door, taking notice of the slender wooden limb near her feet.

"No harm will come to you from me," he stated simply. "I'm not in the habit of hurting women."

Nancy blushed. Should she tell him that it wasn't him she feared?

"Who's Lavinia?" A sudden intake of breath indicated she hadn't heard him wrong.

"You stay out of my business and I'll stay out of yours," he said too quickly.

She nodded. "Where are we? How far from where you found me?"

"Half a day."

"Half a day?" she stammered. "You carried me for half a day?"

"Well, I couldn't very well leave you there."

"Why were you there?"

"I was pulling out my traplines. Can you cook? I have a rabbit outside."

Nancy nodded once more. "Is there somewhere close to where you found me where you could have crossed the river?"

"Not on foot now that the ice is thin."

"So, it wouldn't be easy to cross?"

"If you're looking to get to the other side, we'd have to go almost to the coast. Maybe go to Zoar. The Mission boat might be in. I don't have the means to get you across."

"I can't go to Zoar," she said flatly. That's where Ezra would go looking for her. Or would he dare? She couldn't be sure. What would he tell everyone? Would he track her here? Would he kill this man who'd rescued her? "I can't stay here, either." She fell back on the bunk once more. "It's not safe here."

"Why?"

"It's Ezra the Esquimeaux," she said.

"I've heard the name. He's in Nain."

Reluctantly, Nancy told him about the events of that morning. She couldn't believe they had taken place just a few hours ago. When she finished, she burst out crying. She pushed her head into the furs on the bunk.

John was poking at the fire when she sat up once again. She wiped at her eyes while taking big gulps of air to quash the grief.

"It's getting late. We'll cook the rabbit and decide what to do in the morning."

"But what if he finds us?"

"The dogs will know if anybody's coming. I'll keep the gun close. You're safe here."

"That'll have to do," she said. She didn't trust herself to say much more. Panic was saturating her core, and she had to concentrate to prevent it from overwhelming her.

An easy silence followed while he prepared the rabbit to roast over the fire. Nancy didn't offer to take on the chore. He must have skinned and gutted it outside, as only the pink flesh was stretched on the spit. Her stomach gurgled when the smell of the meat wafted to her nostrils.

"There's no oil lamp here," John said. "Just the light of the fire for company."

"I'm tired. It won't be a problem," she said. It had been the same at home. The winter had been full of dark nights until the seals arrived. It was only then that they'd had oil for their lamps.

Poor Philip. He would be cold tonight. No matter what became of her, she wouldn't leave him there. He deserved better.

Sometime later, she cried herself to sleep in the darkness, longing for his warmth by her side.

7

The dogs woke her. Nancy didn't know if it was night or day, but she could see a grey light through the cracks near her head. Her heart raced, and she bolted up from the bunk. There was a caribou hide folded on the ground in the corner of the room.

A man's voice drifted in, talking quietly, yet firmly, to the dogs. His words didn't have an air of urgency. It wasn't Ezra. It was morning.

The room was warm. There was a leg of rabbit and a piece of dried bread on a tin plate laid near the fire. She turned toward John as he entered the room.

"There's some water on the stump," he said casually as he nodded toward the door. "The dogs are out front in the trees. Stay to the back of the cabin and you should be fine."

Nancy grabbed the edge of her skirts, lifted them, and headed outside. The dogs barked, and he whistled for them to be quiet. The morning air was cold and crisp. She quickly attended to her business, washed her hands, and splashed her face with the tepid water in the tin pan by the door before heading back inside.

She shivered as she imagined Ezra's eyes watching her. Uneasiness crept through her, and the hair stood up on the back of her neck. Of course, the dogs would know if he were there, but she was happy to get inside just the same.

They split the fare in silence. John wiped his hands on his pants and got up.

"You can't stay here. Trapping is done, and I'm leaving."

"I want my husband found and buried," Nancy said. "He didn't deserve to die. Ezra also said that he'd killed Philip's mother. I don't know if that was true or if it was to frighten me, so I don't know if anyone will be looking for me."

"And Philip's mother is Ezra's wife. Is that what you said?"

"Yes, she's twice his age. They've been married for almost two years." Nancy grimaced when she thought of being married to such a vicious man. Philip and Malcolm had gone up against Ezra more than once when they saw bruises or black eyes on their mother, but in the end, she had turned on them. Perhaps it was to protect them. Nancy didn't know.

She was responsible for this tragedy. It was her fault Philip was gone. Her own foolishness. She'd have to right that wrong.

"I'll take you to Zoar. That's as much as I can do," John said. He left the cabin.

Nancy was torn—she couldn't stay there. She had some idea about how to survive, but not by herself. Philip had taught her how to hunt and fish, but he was the provider, she the helper.

John was rummaging outside. There were two hollow thuds on the cabin wall. She could see the darkening and lightening through the seams in the logs as John MacDonald moved in and out of shadows. The tin pan rattled, and a few more sounds signalled a man packing up his belongings.

He returned and took the plate that had held the rabbit,

then left again. Water splashed, and tin rattled once more. He stood in the doorway and motioned for the caribou hide that had kept her warm the night before. Rolling the pelts, he tied them with a string of rawhide and left again. A few moments later, he called for her.

Nancy grabbed her sealskin jacket and followed the sound of his voice. The dogs bounded toward her through the trees. John was behind them with his load secured to a wooden rack on his back.

"Let's go."

The dogs ran ahead, and on occasion, he whistled them back. Nancy settled into the drone of the day as she marched behind him. The whoosh of the branches on their clothes, the buzz of early mosquitoes, the hollow clink of metal scraping together in the pack, crows scavenging for food in the distance, and the crunch of their feet on the thawing tundra kept her company. Her mind was occupied with thoughts of Philip, always culminating with his body discarded in a rocky washout. Sadness built within her as she trudged onward.

The sun was high in the sky when they came upon a narrow trail. John pulled off his pack and took a seat on a large rock nearby. He didn't speak, and she got the feeling he had forgotten her.

"You'll get wet there," he said when she was about to lower herself onto a grassy hummock. He motioned toward another rock. "Rest there."

He whistled for the dogs, and they returned. Nancy recognized the breed as sled dog huskies and remembered seeing the sleds leaning against the north wall of the cabin in the shade of the trees.

They were on a rise overlooking the ocean and the numerous islands that were cloistered between Nain and Zoar. The sky was grey and reflected on the sea of pack ice in the distance. There was no telling where one ended and the other began. The ebb and flow of the current had loosened the ice around the shore. Blue water added a splash of colour to the lifelessness of the view. Scattered spruce kept their heads low to the terrain, trained by the icy winds and harsh winters on the exposed coast. From this distance they were no more than dots, but up close they bent over as if growing along the land instead of skyward.

Though spring had come early, the timing wasn't right to put the dogs out on the islands for the summer. Though some dogs stayed around the villages, most mushers had an island for the dogs where they could run free and hunt until the snows came once again. However, late spring storms had been known to lay a thick cover, and today the sky was ripe for just such a thing.

Behind her, in the distance to the west, white-cloaked hills mixed with a foggy haze that married the sky to the land. Sparse patches of trees nested to form green and grey pockets around lakes and rivers edging on the even greyer tundra. Nancy believed there was nothing beyond what the eye could feast on. She hadn't been outside the Mission in Nain except for the year before, when she went to Zoar for Paul's wedding, and last spring, when she'd accompanied Philip north to the sealing camps to collect pelts.

Now she'd go to Zoar again, to bring news of Philip's murder. If Ezra was there, she'd risk being arrested by the missionaries, should he claim she had counselled him to kill her husband. She risked death if he laid in wait for her near the Mission.

8

Zoar was situated on a narrow peninsula sheltered by several islands to the east. The linear settlement was strung along the coastline with a low but steep ridge peppered with ragged black spruce at its back. Like many of the settlements along the coast, without intimate knowledge of the location, it would be hard to find.

John MacDonald had traded furs at Zoar for winter staples. He'd been welcomed but didn't stay despite the offers to winter there. He took his bearings from various landmarks, as well as the sun's position in the sky, to lead them to Zoar.

Though barely perceptible in the grey of the day, he saw the curls of smoke as they drew skyward on the horizon from the chimneys in the settlement. The buildings themselves would not come into view until they crested the ridge. He stopped for a moment, and the woman he knew as Alice butted into him before he could turn. She muttered an apology and stepped back.

She scanned the skyline and pointed toward the smoke. He nodded.

"We're almost there," Alice said.

"The snow is not far off," John said. "We should hurry."

They made good time before the first of the heavy wet snow quickly rendered a white spell on everything it touched. Near the village, John whistled for the dogs. He pulled tethers from his backpack and secured the dogs to a nearby tree, where they quickly circled and lay down for a rest.

Alice didn't complain as they continued on to their destination. The snow was rapidly accumulating and made descending the ridge a bit tricky. John reached for her hand to guide her down the hill. She hesitated and then took it, though she was probably sure-footed enough to make it on her own. The wind picked up, and snow beat into their faces as they crossed the threshold of the community. John tucked her in behind him as he closed his coat tighter around him. Dogs barked in the distance—he guessed they were tied out beyond the houses. They were near the church when they came out of the trees. Snow was stuck to every part of him, and he regretted not tying the top of his boots tighter about his calves.

"Do you know where you're going?" John asked.

"Paul's is over there," Alice said, pointing toward the general area of the smaller wooden units close to the three-storey trading post.

He took her hand and pulled her along through what had turned into a raging blizzard. Her hands were bare and cold under his. John would have been in a shelter long before this to wait out the storm, but there was nothing he could do about that now. He'd see her to her destination and head to the post for a night's rest.

In the shade of the trading post, they got a reprieve from the icy wind and made better headway to Paul's. The houses were all similar box-shaped wooden structures. They stopped at the third. John, relieved to be clear of the company, turned and prepared to hurry back the way he came, as Alice stomped and brushed off her clothes in the porch.

John was tempted to return to the woods, but it was too late to be foolhardy. Instead, he brushed himself off and laid down his pack just inside the door of the warm dry goods store. He moved to the reddened pot-bellied stove and rubbed his hands together before extending them out over the heat.

A balding man in his early fifties came around the counter and offered his hand. John shook it. "MacDonald, what brings you in this evening?"

"Came for a few supplies," John replied.

"Thought you might have the mail," the man said. "Been a while since it came in. Nobody runs it like you." He laughed. "Word is the boat can get to Hopedale but no farther north yet. She'll try for a few more days before heading back to Makkovik to wait."

"Ice is breaking up."

"The Esquimeaux say there's a lot coming down the coast. I'll listen to them," said the man. "Thought it was going to be a short winter, but not by the looks of it out now."

"It'll blow itself out by the morning," John said. "Speaking of that, I was hoping to hole up somewhere around here tonight."

"Three beds are spoken for out back, but there's two more."

"That'll do."

They agreed on the price, which John promptly paid. He pulled a stool near the fire and sat and dried the insides of his boots and coat and picked up some items to replenish his pack. Settling up with the storekeeper, he returned to the fire. This was going to make him soft, he allowed. He wondered how

Alice had made out, then mentally reminded himself that it was none of his business.

John could see through the window that darkness had come early with the storm raging outside. He was about to head to the storeroom and turn in for the night when the door opened and a man rushed in, closing it firmly behind him. He came right to John.

"MacDonald," he said. "Paul, Paul Martin."

John didn't speak. He wasn't the sort to start or join in conversation. The storekeeper looked up from a book and waved. "Paul." Paul waved back.

"Need to see MacDonald, Henry." The storekeeper nodded and went back to what he was doing.

"I've seen you before," said Paul.

"Been around the post a few times," John replied.

"You brought the mail from Hopedale a few times. If I rightly recollect."

"Yes," John said. "When the boat couldn't get through." John had been hired several times each year to bring the mail along the coast. He didn't care what the conditions were like. He managed to make the trek no matter the weather. The nights were long and cold, but it kept him away from people. It wasn't the people, really, but the fear of being found out.

"I want to speak to you about where I can find my brother."

"I don't know that," John said.

"I know," said Paul. "If you can tell me where you picked up . . ." He paused for a moment. "Where you picked up Alice, it might give me a better idea."

John explained in great detail where he had found Alice in relation to the trail. He gave Paul his best guess as to where his brother might be located based on what she had said.

"Me and the missus were wondering if you could carry Alice to Hopedale and put her on the boat," Paul said in a hushed voice. "We'd pay you, of course."

"I'm not in the business of people."

"Look, mister," Paul said, his voice shaking just a little. "Alice is in trouble. If Ezra finds her, she won't survive. You know what I mean."

"That's not my problem."

"I'd go myself only for I have to find my brother's body," said Paul.

John caught a glimpse of three men coming for the storeroom. He thought he recognized one but couldn't be sure. This wasn't the first time he'd seen ghosts of people from the Island. He saw them when nobody was there. He'd heard the Esquimeaux say it was common in folks who didn't belong on the lonesome land. It had driven some people foolish. He quickly turned his back to the three who were making their way toward Henry.

"All right," said John. "But we leave at first light, and I'm coming with you now." His heart began to race. He jammed his feet into his boots and grabbed his coat and pack.

"Yes," Paul said. "Of course." His jaw had dropped with the turn of events.

John would be out of the store before Henry realized he had gone. Out on the step, he pulled on the sealskin mitts and followed Paul through the blinding snow. The wind whipped and tore at his face, and he held his mitt to his brow to see where he was going. It was nearly pitch black, but Paul had a rope that guided the way. John had to force himself to concentrate after seeing the men inside. He could easily get turned around and lost on a night like this, even with the houses so close.

Paul shouted something at him, but he couldn't make it

out. John followed him into the porch. "We don't have much room, but you're welcome to the floor."

"The shed's fine with me," John replied.

"You'll do no such thing," Irene said. Alice sat at the table. Her red, sad eyes fixed on him. He felt a warmth go through him that wasn't from the fire. It was surprising, and he was not sure he liked it.

Paul was talking again, but John wasn't listening. "So, you'll take her."

"Could you say that again?" John asked.

"Alice is afraid of Ezra, and with good reason. She has to get away from here," Paul repeated. "He is a dangerous man. She'll go to the Island from Hopedale. So, you'll take her?"

"I have the dogs," John said. "But no sleds."

"I have what you'll need. We don't have much money, but we'll give you what we got."

John looked from Paul to Irene. "I was planning to go to Hopedale. The sleds will be fine. I'll get them back to you."

"We have to pay you," said Irene.

"I'm going anyway. No need."

It was settled. Irene had a ptarmigan soup on the stove and bread sliced on the table. She offered, and he gladly ate.

The storm raged well into the night. John settled on caribou hide near the door. Paul took the daybed, though he offered it to John, and Irene and Alice slept in the room with the children. Whispers carried on the air after they went to bed.

Paul jammed a large spruce stick into the fire and turned down the damper in the metal stovepipe. It was drafty, but

John had slept in colder places. He remembered spending part of a winter in an abandoned sod hut the first year in Labrador. He only came out to hunt for food and get firewood. After a particularly bad snowstorm, he was immured, and it took him two days to beat his way out from under the snow. An Esquimeaux man came upon him when he was looking for his hunting party. John had been cold and scared and hungry. Truth be told, he was ready to die.

The old Esquimeaux took pity on him and brought John along with him. John stayed with the man at an inland camp with a dozen other families for the rest of the winter. He learned some of the language, sledding, and most importantly, he learned how to survive. John came to hold the people and their ways in the highest regard and also to respect the land.

He made a name for himself at the traplines. John gave over all his furs to the camp folks, who traded them for supplies. When spring came, the old Esquimeaux, whom he called Joe, gave him his dogs and sleds. He said it was a fair trade for all the furs. John refused, but the old man made the excuse that the dogs were too young for him. They needed a young master, and that was John.

When John awoke the next morning, the entire camp had scattered to the seal camps on the coast. John was alone with the dogs and a pair of sleds. This time he knew what it took to survive. He trapped some more and ventured out on occasion to sell the furs and pick up supplies at stores in the Moravian Missions on the coast.

That summer he built a crude shelter that would be the centre of his traplines. It lasted a good many winters, and nobody had been inside the cabin until he'd come across Alice and brought her back there a few days before.

9

John slept fitfully and woke just before dawn. The wind had subsided, and he wondered, not for the first time, what he'd gotten himself into. Paul snoozed on the daybed, and the fire had long gone out. John crept out from beneath the caribou hide and slipped out into the porch. There he made quick work of tying the rawhide in his seal boots, pulled on his coat and mitts, and slung his backpack on his back. He opened the door and kicked out the snow that had piled there.

Twilight gripped the land in a crisp cocoon. Nothing stirred on the white powdered ground. John's breath created a haze ahead of him and clung to his face as he trudged through knee-high snow. Ice formed on his cheeks and in the two days' growth that had formed on his chin. He wasn't inclined to be bearded, finding the hair too itchy to his liking. He suffered the consequences on mornings such as these.

With great care he picked his way around the houses and toward the store, being mindful of humps where the snow might be covering something that could trip him. From the store he veered to the west and bypassed the church. He climbed the hill without incident, using the tree limbs to pull himself along. Several times he had to hunch over as the trees dumped their branches on him and cold water trickled down his neck.

Once he cleared the ridge, daylight was closer, and he took his bearings from the landmarks he'd been careful to remember the day before. John headed southwest and waited until he was a reasonable distance from the village before he'd signal for the dogs. He crossed the vast expanse of snow, its smoothness deceptive to the untrained eye. When he reached the treeline, he gave a soft whistle.

The snow moved as the white and grey dogs uncurled from their frosty beds. They yawned, shook the snow clear, and pranced around their tethered territory. John untied them, and they bounded back and forth across the land, digging their heads beneath the snow as they went, rushing toward him and then veering off to either side at the last moment. They pawed each other and wrestled in the white powder as he took some seal jerky from the pouch in his pack. John sat cross-legged in the snow as he contemplated his next move. He could easily be miles from here before anyone knew he was gone. He could go back to his solitary existence and forget he'd ever crossed paths with Alice. One of the dogs nuzzled him, looking for food. He fed the pack and watched them tussle over the last few morsels.

He thought of Lavinia and what her last days must have been like. Would that be Alice? Did he care? Had he been away from civilization so long that he'd become cold-hearted? Was there just enough humanity in him to go back for her, or was it too late?

John saw movement in the pre-dawn that settled the dilemma for him. A lone figure had followed his tracks, startling him at first. A ghost? A man from the trading post? But the small and slender figure wasn't a threat to him—or maybe she was the biggest imperilment of all. It was Alice, who had followed his footsteps in the snow.

The dogs ran out to greet her, but he whistled them back. Alice fell sideways a few times as she misstepped on a hummock but managed to right herself before hitting the ground. John should have gone to meet her, but he was mesmerized by her outline as the sun rose behind her. She looked golden and unearthly as she fractured the morning light that surrounded her like a halo.

The dogs shifted querulously beside him. They, too, were uncomfortable and seemingly unable to move. His eyes strained as he watched her kick snow ahead of her as she trudged toward him.

"I thought you were gone," Alice said.

"So did I," John said under his breath as he stared at her face. Her chest heaved beneath the sealskin coat, and the air crystallized in front of her with each breath. The dogs whimpered again, anxious to play. "I came for the dogs." He made a circular motion with his hand, and the dogs leaped up and began to canter around once again.

Alice continued to stare at him as he sat in the snow. "I came for the dogs," he repeated as he pushed himself up to stand in front of her, almost touching. She looked up at him but didn't move, and he had to step back to avoid her. "The sled is no good without the dogs."

John whistled again and began to retrace his footprints. He didn't look back to see if Alice was coming. As he was trekking down the ridge, he noticed places where she had fallen on the steeper part. He had the thought no sooner out of his head when she struck him from behind and nearly took him off his feet. Reaching out for the nearest limb, he grabbed her arm as she passed him. He shuffled his feet a few times before he managed to right himself and then dragged her to stand in front of him.

One of the dogs struck the back of his legs, and he lost his footing. His feet shot out from under him. There were arms and legs flying as he and Alice tumbled down the ridge and landed in a pile of snow at the back of the church. She was partially under him when he found which way was up. He pushed his head up out of the snow and quickly stood, taking her with him.

Alice spat snow from her mouth and brushed at her face so she could see. "Are you all right?" John asked.

She stomped a few times, twisted her arms around in the air, and moved her head from side to side. "Nothing's broken," she said as she walked away from him toward Paul's house. He brushed himself off before following her.

The long and narrow sled was swept off and leaning against the porch when John reached the house. Alice must be inside. The dogs' harness was draped over the rail at the back. Paul's tracks were all around, where he had dug out the sled and retrieved the ropes from the shed.

Paul came out as John was getting the dogs tied into the harness. The lead dog, a female, was a mosaic of browns, greys, black, and white. He had a specific order for the other six. He'd learned from trial in different positions over the last two years where on the line the dogs liked and worked the best.

Paul was quiet as he threw several caribou hides on the sled base. He had tied food in another, smaller tanned pouch, which he laid near the back.

"Alice will be right along," Paul said. "She's saying her goodbyes to Irene."

John didn't answer but nodded that he understood. Paul

grabbed some rawhide string for the shed and tied down the pelts to the cross boards.

"The runners are good and strong. The sled's only had a few seasons on it," Paul continued as he worked. The snow crunched under their feet as they moved around the sled, getting it ready for the journey.

"The dogs look fit," Paul said. "Think they can make it in two days?"

"Should be," John said.

"You won't have any trouble from Alice. She's toughened to the Labrador. She was the best thing that ever happened to Philip."

John was pretty sure that Philip was dead because of Alice. But that wasn't his business. He would take her to Makkovik and be rid of her there. That would be the end of it. He'd be on the lookout for Ezra on their journey. "I'm almost out of shot," he said, patting his gun.

Paul went into the house and returned with several shells. "This is what I have."

"That should do," said John. He wasn't in the habit of missing a target.

Alice and Irene came out behind John. Alice hugged her sister. Irene swiped at her eyes.

"You be careful," Irene said.

"I will," said Alice. She hugged her sister tightly. "Goodbye, Irene. Thanks for doing this for me."

"We'll make sure everything will be all right, won't we, Paul?"

Paul went to the step. "I'll bring him home, Alice. Don't you worry." Paul squeezed her arm, and she hugged him.

"Philip will get his proper resting place?" she asked.

"He will."

"I'm so sorry this happened," Alice said. She started to cry.

"We'll bring him home, Alice," Irene promised. They hugged, and Irene whispered something to her. Alice nodded and wiped her face. The tears had almost frozen there.

"Going is the safest thing to do," said Paul. "You know that better than anyone." Turning to John, he said, "Thanks for taking her. Alice has some money." He held up his hand when he saw that John was about to interrupt. "Alice has some money," he repeated. "I'll give you some time to get out over the ridge before telling Brother Hayward what happened."

"And then what?" Alice asked.

"Brother Hayward will get some men to go with me. We'll find him."

Paul asked Alice to describe the area again where she had been on the trail. Once he had the details, he shook John's hand.

Alice refused to ride. John shrugged. It was of no consequence to him if she couldn't keep up. He turned the dogs toward the trail that circled around the ridge and followed a gradual incline to the top. Grabbing the rail of the sled, he pushed it along on the snow while the dogs took off running. This was what they loved. They barked excitedly as he signalled for them to go. Dogs tethered on the other side of Zoar barked their displeasure at not being able to join them. Within minutes the whole community would be awake. John was happy to get out of there before the settlement came to life.

He didn't look back, and when the trail looped around at the top of the hill, he saw that Alice was close behind but a little out of breath. John slowed the dogs and then stopped them with another whistle. He motioned for Alice to get on the sled. She nodded and ran up beside them. John grabbed her arm, and she jumped on. She untied the hides, leaving one beneath her, and laid two over her legs. John's pack was behind her, resting on the steering rail that John held. She leaned back on it, and he got the dogs going once again. They yipped and barked their delight and set out across the barrens, south, toward Makkovik.

John felt the wind on his face and buried his chin inside the neckline of his sealskin jacket. The hood was pulled tight, and the fur from an Arctic hare that circled his face kept his brow from freezing. The sealskin clothes had not failed him yet. He'd fallen in rivers and gotten caught in freezing rain and regular spring downpours, but the clothing had kept him warm and dry.

With the new-fallen snow glazing the frozen terrain, they glided smoothly behind the dog team. There was something cathartic about running behind the sled, pushing off the ground, and springing back up on the runners, while holding on with all his strength so he didn't wind up on his face in the snow waiting for the dogs to return. Or worse, the dogs not returning and having to march along the trail until he caught up to them. But this morning the dogs were swift, and the exhilarating feeling came from just moving his body into the bend of the winding track to keep the sled from upsetting.

Times like this, he was wrenched back to glimpse younger and happier times. He believed they had been good before his father died. Before his mother remarried. Before his nightmare began.

John didn't like to think of those days—if they were even real at all. The memories were overwrought with the torturous life he had lived after his father's death. Even now, he didn't know if the times he dreamed of were not just that. A dream. Something he'd made up to keep from going insane.

He forgot about Alice until she signalled she needed a break. Near midday, he guided the dogs to a thicket of black spruce under a darkening sky. They would be hungry and thirsty by now.

Alice went off into the woods while John made his way to the nearest rise to search the country they had just come through. He knew Ezra to have a reputation as a hunter and an expert tracker, so he wouldn't easily be seen even in the whiteness of the land.

John looked from west to east. A squall blew in off the ice and passed through the terrain farther north. The wind had shifted, and it looked clear to the south. Seeing nothing alarming, John decided to make a quick fire. He'd warm the woman, make some tea, heat the dried caribou, and give the dogs a chance to run loose.

The dogs danced around Alice as she made her way back to him. "Isn't that dangerous?" she asked when she saw the smoke rising through the trees.

"Nothing's stirring," John said. "We'll be all right."

With the tin kettle in hand, he scooped up snow near the base of the tree behind him and strung it on a stick. He took out some tea and a mug.

Alice untied the rawhide string from the package Paul had given them. She dug down in the sack and took out a mug and a spoon. After rummaging some more, she pulled out some of Irene's sliced bread.

Looking around, she found a small limb sticking out of the snow. She pulled off the sprigs and cracked it off before shoving it into the bread and holding it over the flame. Before long, curls of black smoke rose around the browning slab, and she pulled it back toward her and turned it over. She laid the slice on the sled and gestured for John to take it.

"That's for you. Oh, wait. I have some partridgeberry jam here, too." Alice dug down again and removed a small crock filled with dark red jam. The top was covered and tied with a thin piece of rawhide. She laid the jar on the sled and went to work on another slice of bread.

John hung strings of meat over the stick that held the kettle. Steam was rising from both as the flames danced and licked the bottom of the tin.

Alice sat on the edge of the sled with her feet buried in the snow as they ate and drank in silence. While she waited for John to finish his tea, she pulled her knees to her chest, folded her arms over them, and rested her head there, watching the dogs bound.

John couldn't see her face, but he watched her just the same. He was taking his last swallow when the dogs started to growl. First one, then the others. Their teeth bared as a slow rumble emanated from deep in their bellies.

John threw the dregs from his cup. The dogs were reticent to come when he signalled. He whistled louder and shouted to them in the language of the Esquimeaux. They slunk back to their positions on the line, tails low and thick.

Within moments, Alice had the sled packed while John got the dogs on the leads. Each one snarled and growled, fur raised, staring toward the trees. John tried to calm them. Then he caught a movement in the trees. It was subtle, and he wasn't sure at first.

"Is it him?" The terror in Alice's voice was palpable.

The dogs were restless, whining, and pulling on the lines. "It's a polar bear," John said. "Maybe cubs, too. She's coming fast, probably very hungry."

He grabbed the back of the sled and repositioned it to give the dogs a clear path across the frozen land. They were barking, agitated and anxious to move. He couldn't risk them running in different directions. Unsheathing his knife from his belt, he hauled down on a couple of low-hanging green branches, breaking some and cutting others at the same time. He grabbed the stringy dry moss dangling close to the trunk.

"What are you doing?" asked Alice. Her eyes were fixed on the woods, where the sounds of the bear, crashing limbs and bawling, were getting louder.

John laid the moss and then a green bough on what was left of the flames. They ignited. A crackling noise was followed by thick black smoke that rose into the air. John gave Alice the reins while he grabbed some more limbs. He threw several more on the flames before turning to the sled.

The fire roared and devoured the wood and blazed toward the sky. He glanced at the bear and kicked at the sticks so that they were partially hidden behind the now raging inferno. He figured he had time for one more try with the limbs, which he quickly added to the burning pile.

Turning, John scooped up Alice about the waist, hoisted her over the handrail, and deposited her on the sled. He whistled for the dogs to go, dug the balls of his feet in the snow, and pushed on the wooden rail to give them a good start. The dogs were anxious, and somehow in the commotion the lead dog had tangled with the one behind her. Before he could act, Alice leapt from the seat and pulled the second dog back and to the side. She dragged on the lead dog until she could slacken the rope. It was no easy feat when the dogs were worked up. She pushed the second dog under the line that was tangling her, freeing both.

John had snatched the rifle and loaded it, ready to defend them. But to his amazement, Alice had the situation handled rather quickly. The lead dog took off, and Alice fell sideways into the snow when the second rope twisted around her feet. She managed to kick it free before it tightened. She was trying to get up from her prone position when the last dog passed her.

John, with one arm wrapped around the back rail holding the gun, and his feet on the runners, reached out and grabbed for Alice's arm with his free hand. He managed to whip her up out of the snow. She made two running strides while he grasped her coat. He yanked hard and landed her onto the sled, holding tight so she didn't shoot off the other side.

He looked back. The bear was standing on her hindquarters, batting at the smoke and flame, two year-old cubs barrelling in behind her. One was close to the fire when the mother's powerful jaw clamped down on the back of its neck and flung it aside. She roared her displeasure and batted at the other one with a swing of her powerful head. Hopefully she would be confused by the fire and wouldn't venture too far from her den with the cubs.

John had been distracted by Alice and missed the signs. But that was his fault and not hers. The dogs picked up speed as they hit the open barrens. He loosened his tense grip on the rail, let out a long, deep breath, and let the dogs do what they did best—run.

Not unlike him, in many ways. Seems like that's what he did best, too—run. It hadn't been a plan, it hadn't been thought out, it had just been done. He had no idea how empty it would be when he started.

First, fear and anger had driven him, then survival. Now he didn't know. He only knew his life was empty. The first feeling he'd had in a long time was just now. Fear for the woman who accompanied him and the need to protect her.

He mulled over his "becoming." He hadn't thought about that in quite some time, either.

10

St. John's, eight years earlier

In many ways, Teddy White envied his friend John MacDonald. Teddy's father had been killed by the police at a voting rally when Teddy had just passed his tenth birthday. His mother had remarried soon after and, despite his mother's less than sincere efforts to the contrary, his stepfather threw him out on the streets before he turned thirteen. His family moved away sometime after that, and he was on his own.

Teddy ran with a gang of others like himself, stealing money and food, trying to evade the constables, sleeping on the streets or in barns or wherever they could find shelter. He had to be tough. Sometimes he believed himself to be more an animal than a person when he was hungry and hadn't eaten for days.

One day his friends had accosted a young, dark-haired girl who had a basket of bread on her arm. She wasn't making it easy for them.

"You go on and get out of here," she shouted, her stance straight and defiant. "This is for the mistress, and she'll have my hide if I don't get it back to her."

Three boys faced her as she backed up to the stone warehouse wall just off Duckworth Street. Two boys moved in on each side of her while the other stayed in her path in case she ran. One boy moved to her left, where she clutched the basket in her hand, and tried to grab some bread.

"We won't take it all," he said.

"You won't take any," she returned. She swung her right arm around and struck the boy across the face before quickly putting her back to the wall again.

Teddy had just received a few coins for mucking out the horses' stalls at the stables at Government House. He was going back toward the docks when he saw the commotion. The girl must have tried to take a shortcut between the buildings. He admired her courage as she refused to back down from the bigger boys.

"Now, lads. What've we got here?" Teddy asked casually.

"We just want a few pieces of bread," the taller boy answered while still keeping the girl in his sights.

Teddy, probably a year older than any of the three, pulled out a five-cent piece, half of what he'd just earned, and tossed it to the boys. "How about you leave the young lady alone?" The three wrestled for the coin as they moved away.

"Friends of yours?" the girl asked.

"Maybe," he said. "I'm Teddy."

"Lavinia."

"Where are you headed?"

"Jackson's on Carpasian Road," she replied.

"You should be all right from here," Teddy said.

"Maybe I won't."

Teddy grinned. "I'd walk with you, miss, but I've just come from the stables."

"It's Lavinia, and I don't mind," said the girl. "Just keep your distance." Her eyes sparkled as she spoke.

They talked until they got to the door.

"Teddy." Lavinia tossed him a piece of bread. "That's for the nickel. I get off after supper and might need a walk home."

Teddy grinned the whole way back to Water Street.

When he reached the dock, a dark-haired girl a year or so his senior accosted him. Her hair was braided yet looked matted and fly-away all the same time. A scowl crossed her dirty brow before she threw a punch at his face. Teddy grabbed her fist before she could land the blow.

"What's that for, Rosie?"

"The bread, that's what."

"You mean this bread?" Teddy took the loaf from beneath his coat, pulled it in half, and tossed it to her. Rosie grabbed the portion and sank her teeth into the end, tearing off a bite. He did the same with his half. He eyed her while they chewed. She was pretty enough, if he were to notice such a thing. After swallowing, he said, "I told you I'd bring something back."

"Boys said you stopped them from taking the basket from the girl. They had their money spent and bellies full before they got back. Didn't bring me anything, either."

"They're a selfish bunch, Rosie," Teddy said. "You know that."

She looked skyward and then glanced around the docks. "Rain's coming. Where are you staying tonight?"

"I left the hayloft open at the barns. I'm heading back there later. You?"

"Don't know yet. The girls on the dock say I'm old enough to join them. Maybe tonight's the night."

"Don't do that. Come with me. I've a dry place tonight."

Rosie had shown up on the streets early spring the year before. At first she was mercilessly bullied by all of them. Although he pitied her, Teddy couldn't show it. That would make him weak in the eyes of the others. He'd worked too hard to gain importance in the street hierarchy, and he couldn't risk losing his place. The weak didn't survive. He didn't expect her to make it through the summer, but somehow, she had.

He remembered the day the man tried to haul her into his carriage. Rosie kicked and screamed and struggled to get clear, but he held her fast. Two police officers ran to the scene, and Teddy overheard the man say he was her father. She was cursing him and calling him names. One of the policemen struck her arm with his stick to release her hold on the carriage. She yelped with pain but would not let go.

That was when Teddy really gained an admiration for her. She spat at the man and accused him of being too friendly for a real father. Many of the storekeepers and shoppers were gathering around. Teddy noticed a cart of vegetables left unattended on the sidewalk. He stood behind it and pushed with all his might. The cart overturned, and turnip, potatoes, and cabbage rolled out into the street. The vendor shouted at him, and he fell in amongst the vegetables, feigning being hurt. The constables came to see what the commotion was about, and Rosie bit the arm of the man who had grabbed her and fled down the street.

One of the constables helped him stand up, and he limped away from the ruckus while the farmer got the stand righted with the help of some of the others. Teddy moved through the crowd and quickly left the area with the policemen not far behind. He saw the carriage speed out of the downtown area as the rider whipped the horses.

Rosie caught up with him the next day and thanked him.

He told her to go home, that the street was no place for her. She responded that it was better than home and left it at that.

That was almost a year ago. She'd sometimes disappear for days and return with black eyes or covered in bruises, but she didn't complain. The boys who Teddy moved around with tended to look out for her, and she them.

Rosie nodded, and they made their way to the stables Teddy had left earlier. It had already started to rain by the time the hands went for the evening. They waited patiently at the base of a big old apple tree, out of sight of the barn. Teddy pulled out some carrots he'd taken from the street vendor and shared them with her. They munched on the last of the bread. Neither of them spoke as they listened to the sound of the horses and the voices of the men on the other side of the fence.

When the way was clear, Teddy ducked low and ran along the edge of the whitewashed pickets. He'd hidden a ladder there. He threw it over the fence and motioned for Rosie, who followed his lead, and before long they were pulling the ladder up through the hay shaft on the loft of the stable. He carefully closed the wooden door behind him. It creaked if he didn't lift it while shutting it.

She sat cross-legged on the hay as he put the ladder to the side. Dust was flying everywhere in the grey light from the window at the other side of the loft. He searched around under the edge of the hay and pulled out a blanket that was used to cover the horses on cold nights. He threw it to Rosie.

"That will keep you warm." More dust flew, stirred by the force of the blanket hitting the planks near her.

"What about you?"

"I'll be all right. I have to leave for a bit, but I'll be back." Teddy hoped he would meet the young lady he'd walked to work earlier that morning. "You're safe here."

The horses stomped below as Rosie moved back toward the bundle of hay and shook out the blanket. It settled on the dry straw near the back of the loft. She patted it down so that it wouldn't be too lumpy.

"I've had worse places to sleep," she said.

"I've got to go," Teddy said. He pushed out the ladder and fixed the hatch, then hid it once more before racing off to Carpasian Road to walk Lavinia home.

The rain and drizzle had soaked his ragged coat, and he shivered slightly when Lavinia came down the step. She grinned at him when he moved out into view from the other side of the road.

"I see you didn't forget about me," Lavinia said.

A warmth that started in his belly and flowed through him was something that he hadn't experienced before. Teddy grinned at her, and she linked her arm in through his. "How could I forget a lady such as yourself?"

Conversation was easy, and before he knew it, they had arrived at her house. She boldly and quickly kissed his cheek and ran toward the door.

"Good night, Teddy."

"Good night, Lavinia." He wanted to ask her when he could see her again, but his tongue was the full of his mouth.

Lavinia called out from the porch. "I could use an escort the same time tomorrow evening." She closed the door and was gone before he could answer.

Teddy whistled the whole way back to the barn. He could hear the soft sounds of Rosie's breathing when he got inside. It was hard to be quiet in the darkness.

*T*HE *LIARS*

He found another blanket near the trough below. Wrapping it around himself, he settled into the hay. Despite the wet clothes, the night seemed a whole lot warmer as he closed his eyes.

Rosie dropped her blanket on him, and he woke abruptly. The greyness of dawn highlighted her form as he sat up. Neither made a sound as they crept from the barn just before the door creaked in the house and footfalls hit the step. A rooster crowed and a dog barked somewhere in the distance.

They scurried past the apple tree when Rosie turned to Teddy. "Late night?"

"Something like that."

"Heading down to the docks?"

"Nope, I'm going to wait around and head back to the barn to look for a few hours work."

"I'll see you around?"

"Sure," Teddy said. He knew Rosie was headed to the convent on Queen's Road. The nuns set out breakfast for her if she was there early enough before they left for the day. She wasn't always successful. If the sisters were off tending to the sick at night, they wouldn't be there. But Rosie got a meal there two or three times a week because of her persistence.

There was no work for Teddy that day, so he headed to the docks to see if he could pick up something to make a few cents. He hated having to scavenge behind the diners when he could get two-day-old bread for a penny and a couple of slices of meat from the butcher for a few more.

It wasn't much, but it got him through the week. He shared when he could, but that wasn't often. Each of them had their own territory for foraging, and some days were better than others. They usually met just before supper in the woods near Victoria Park. They had built a little shelter there out of crates and boards they found, mostly in the alleys. It was cold and damp on rainy nights and didn't offer much protection from the elements, but it did the job when there was nowhere else.

Last year, one of the boys found a piece of canvas which they used on the roof. That was Bobby, he believed. Bobby had been gone since just before the winter. Nobody knew what happened to him. He was probably dead. They had no way of knowing. That's the way things were. You grew up on the street, or you didn't. What happened if you were lucky enough to grow up was a mystery. Teddy was one of the oldest boys on the street now since Bobby was gone. Therefore, he had a higher rank, so to speak. He hadn't gotten to the position without proving himself, nor did anyone. Teddy hated to lose his human side when things were desperate, but he had to do what it took, and he knew how to do that. He didn't have to like it, but he did it anyway. Survival was survival, and it wasn't always easy, but it was easier to do every time something had to be done.

Every evening that Lavinia worked, Teddy walked her home. They spent more and more time together. She saw the good in him. "Teddy, money is not related to goodness. Believe me, I know from working with the Jacksons." She continually told him that he was worthy and that he could make something of himself if given the chance. He tried harder to earn a few coins instead of stealing, but sometimes, when he was hungry and penniless, he did things that he didn't tell Lavinia about. She often snuck him food from the Jacksons when he didn't have any money.

Rosie gave him a wide berth once he started seeing Lavinia. "You think you're too good for the likes of me," she said.

"What are you talking about, Rosie?"

"I thought you had eyes for me, Teddy." Rosie lowered her eyes, and she played with her hands when she spoke. When she was like this, she reminded him of the Rosie he knew the year before and not the hardened Rosie she'd become.

"Only to help you, Rosie. Only to help you."

"So, you *do* think yourself too good for the likes of me?" Teddy saw the hardness return to her eyes.

"That's not what I said. What's gotten into you?"

"Not a thing," said Rosie. "I thought we'd get off the streets together, that's all."

"I don't have a way off the streets," he said.

"I do." She wrung her hands again and looked at him beneath hooded eyes.

"How?"

"Laura and Geraldine want me to hang out with them," Rosie told him. "They said I could make some money."

"That's a hard life, Rosie."

"I've seen harder."

"I don't know," Teddy countered. "There sure have been a lot of Geraldines and Lauras since I came here."

"I got nothing else. I'm tired and hungry more often than anything."

"What about the convent?"

Rosie laughed. "There's no God going to take me in. Besides, my father would have to sign for me. He won't do that."

With that, she threw her arms around Teddy and tried to kiss him. Startled, he pushed her away. "What are you doing, Rosie?"

"Too good to take what I'm offering," she spat at him. "Someday, Teddy White, you'll regret throwing me aside. You mark my words." Before he could say anything, she turned and ran toward the harbour. He didn't see her after that and gave her little thought as time passed.

11

Then there was John MacDonald. John was about Teddy White's age, maybe a year younger. Probably fifteen when they first met. Some of the boys had stolen his money and left John beaten and bloodied in an alley near Duckworth Street. Teddy heard his moans and cries for help. He found John and helped him up. John, his light hair matted with blood, staggered on his feet. Teddy put one arm around the young man's waist and laid John's arm over his own shoulder. John told him that home was a mile away, on Empire Avenue.

Mr. MacDonald was either watching for his son or must have heard the commotion as they neared the step. He rushed outside as they approached.

"What happened, Johnny?" asked the tall man whose dark hair was flecked with grey. He looked from his son to Teddy. "Did you do this to him?"

Teddy was about to push John away and run when John said, "No, Father, he helped me."

"Well, come in, then. My name is Alexander." He smiled and guided the two through the door.

The Liars

Teddy helped John to a chair. Mr. MacDonald said, "You must stay for supper."

Teddy gave a half-hearted protest, but they both insisted, and he was hungry. Lavinia had the day off and was doing chores for her mother, so he had no plans with her that evening. As Mr. MacDonald looked him up and down, Teddy blurted out, "It was probably my friends who did this."

"Were you there?"

"No, sir, I was not." Teddy almost said that if he were he might have joined in.

"Then we can't blame you, now, can we?" The man smiled. John was unaccustomed to kindness from strangers. "I believe I've seen you down on the docks carrying sacks of flour to the warehouse."

"Yes, sir, I work when I can."

John's father nodded. His mouth opened as if he were about to say something else, but he remained silent and tended to his son.

At the table, Teddy quickly grabbed for two pieces of bread. He looked from father to son, and neither pointed out that there was enough. Teddy relaxed and decided to enjoy the meal. It was a strange feeling not to have to fend off the boys trying to grab his food. He stirred awkwardly in the chair, not used to the routine of a civilized meal.

He learned a lot about John and his father that evening. Alexander MacDonald had been widowed when John was born. There were just the two of them. Mr. MacDonald worked at the docks six days a week, loading and unloading ships. They lived a comfortable life in a small house. They ate more than once a day, they were warm, and they had beds to sleep in at night.

Mr. MacDonald asked Teddy questions about his family, and Teddy was truthful. His own circumstance angered him, and he excused himself to leave.

"Begging your pardon, young man," Mr. MacDonald said. "You could use a place to stay tonight. We don't have much, but I'm guessing it's more than you have."

"I'll be just fine, sir. I don't want your goodwill."

"Look, lad, no need to get affronted. I wouldn't want my John on the street if somebody had room for him, that's all."

"How do you know I won't rob you in the night?" Teddy asked blatantly.

"Because you brought my boy home. Anyone who'd bring home my boy can't be a bad fellow."

Teddy, unused to kind-heartedness, felt torn. He certainly could use a soft bed under a warm roof, but he had his pride. He turned to leave.

"Thanks for helping me, Ted." John got up from the table and extended his hand. "We really would like you to stay."

Teddy hesitated. His knitted brow and habitual scowl gradually relaxed. Slowly, he nodded acceptance and shook John's hand in a warm, reassuring grip. The genuineness in John's smile was unmistakable. That was the beginning of a brotherly bond, and Teddy stayed on with the MacDonalds.

As his new stability sank in, Teddy began to make long-term plans for himself and his sweetheart. He wanted to marry Lavinia, but he needed a job. Lavinia continued to work with the Jacksons to contribute to their dream. It was simple—they wanted to be together.

THE LIARS

John's father got the two boys a job on a schooner heading for Halifax, and so began their life at sea. Each trip home, they had stories for the senior MacDonald, and Teddy would see Lavinia as often as possible.

"Oh, Teddy, I'm so glad you're back. I've missed you so." Lavinia, her black hair shining in the glow of the porch light, rushed into his arms. Teddy held her close.

"I've missed you, too," he said. "Let's get out of here." She finished buttoning her brown woollen coat, and they held hands as they turned onto the street to stroll toward Victoria Park.

The door latch clicked, and Margaret Jackson called, "Lavinia, you be back in this house by eight. I need you to draw a bath for me and help me prepare for bed."

"Yes, miss," shouted Lavinia. She tensed beside Teddy.

"What's wrong?" he asked quietly.

The door closed before she spoke. "That Margaret, she's such a spoiled girl. She has me working constantly. Lavinia do this, Lavinia do that. It's getting to be more than I can bear. Then there's Mr. Jackson. He's tried to corner me in the kitchen a few times. I've been able to fend him off, though."

Teddy's anger boiled. "What?" He turned to go back to the house.

Lavinia grabbed his arm and stopped him. "Teddy, I can take care of myself. Before too long we'll be married and I'll be out of there. Please, I need this job. We need this job."

Teddy, calmed by her pleading, took her arm once again, and they walked toward the park. That night, he decided it was time to get Lavinia out of that house.

He asked Mr. MacDonald to watch out for a better berth. John was interested, too. On his next trip, Lavinia gave him a small black and white photo of herself. She'd paid Margaret's photographer five cents to take her picture.

"I'm afraid you'll forget me, Teddy. You are gone so much," Lavinia said.

"Don't be silly, Vinie. How can I forget you? I can't wait to return to you. I'll treasure this picture and look at it every night before I go to sleep." Teddy held her and spun her around. "Soon, Vinie, soon. Before the end of the summer, I promise."

He missed her more and more each trip. They had so many plans and were so excited about their future together. Teddy told John all his hopes and dreams. John had none of his own but followed Teddy like a water dog pup on the dock. Berth to berth, they were inseparable, but on the land it was Teddy and Lavinia. John helped him save money and helped him find a house near John's father's that he could call home. He just needed one last trip to make it possible. Lavinia was more and more anxious to leave the Jacksons. She didn't talk much about it, but Teddy sensed the change in her each time he came home.

12

"Well, John, we're home."

"Yes, Ted. It's good to be back. Lavinia will be so happy to see you."

"It'll soon be time for you to settle down, too, John. Any girl would be happy to have you."

"I'm not ready for that yet, Ted. That'll come in time," John said, dismissing the remark. "I can't wait to see the look on Lavinia's face when you tell her you're buying a house."

"I know. It seems strange that a homeless boy could end up the richest man in the world," Teddy said. "I couldn't have done it without you and your father." Ted reached his hand out for John's and shook it firmly. John clapped him on the back.

"Hey, Whitey, heard you're going to marry some maid," McPherson shouted from the bowsprit. "Is that true? You can't even get a real woman for yourself." The rest of the crew roared with laughter.

"The five of you are just jealous," Teddy shouted back.

"Maybe I'll find the maid and teach her a thing or two," McPherson hollered.

Teddy dropped the crate he was carrying and turned to McPherson. "You touch her, and you'll die. That goes for any of you. You hear me?"

"Ted, come on," John said. "Get back to work, and we'll be out of here before dark. They're not worth the bother."

"You're right, John. Somehow you're always right, my friend. How my life has changed since the day we met." Teddy chuckled and ignored the taunts from the bow. Eventually, the men quieted down.

They had almost finished unloading the boat when John's father rushed toward them where they stood near the crates on the wharf.

"John, Ted, I was afraid I'd miss you," said Mr. MacDonald. "I told the harbourmaster to let me know when you arrived. He said he almost forgot."

"What's wrong, Father?" John asked. Mr. MacDonald's face was flushed, and his eyes flitted between the two young men.

"You must come home with me now. I have a wagon waiting for us." John and Ted followed the older man. He didn't speak until they were home and inside.

"I've some sad news for you, Ted." Mr. MacDonald hung his head and reached for Teddy's hand. "Your Lavinia is dead."

Teddy reeled and gasped for breath. "*Dead?*"

"Yes, son, she's dead."

John came up behind him and helped him to a chair. Teddy put his head in his palms for a few moments before he stood up again. "But how? What happened?"

"I'm not sure, really. There are two stories going around."

Mr. MacDonald told them both that Lavinia had been whipped by Mr. Jackson, supposedly for stealing liquor and money from him. But one of the other maids said that Margaret wanted Lavinia whipped because she was being disrespectful and wasn't paying enough attention to her needs. The maid also said that she'd heard noises from the kitchen and that Lavinia had run out. Jackson had come out a little while later, and his face was red on one side, as if he'd been slapped.

"I don't understand. How would that have killed her?" Teddy voice was calm, but he was infuriated and ready to strangle the whole Jackson household.

"Jackson tied her outside near the stables and whipped her. She was out there all night, and the staff were under threat of arrest if they tried to help her or even speak of it. One of the maids returned the next evening with Lavinia's mother. Jackson threatened her as well, but the woman refused to leave without Lavinia. Apparently, it was quite the scene. By this time, Lavinia's back was raw from the beating. Her wounds had become infected and she died two days later. Lavinia's mother has left town for nobody knows where, and the three brothers had unexpectedly come into a fishing enterprise of their own."

Mr. MacDonald crossed to Teddy and put his arms around him. Teddy's stance was stiff and straight. "I'm sorry, son. She's gone." Teddy felt awkward. He didn't return the embrace.

"What of the police?" he asked. "Surely this cannot be allowed or to go unpunished."

"Horas Jackson has not been arrested. He claims he was defending his property."

"But that can't be! Lavinia would never steal. When we were first together, she told me she'd leave me if she found out

I was stealing." Teddy sat on the chair and rested his head in his palms. "I can't believe this."

"Son, I know you're angry and upset." Alexander MacDonald clasped Teddy's shoulder and squeezed it. "Please don't get yourself in trouble."

"You're damn right I'm angry," Teddy shouted, standing once more. He paced the room.

"I'll look out for him, Father," John said. He put an arm around Teddy's shoulder and led him to the table.

Teddy ate his supper without knowing what was in front of him. The evening went by in a blur. John's father mixed him a few stiff drinks of rum and put him to bed afterward. He awoke sometime during the night and stared at the ceiling until dawn. His Vinie was gone—he couldn't believe it! He tossed and turned before he finally dozed again. The crackling fire and a pan scraping on the stove awoke him. Mr. MacDonald was making breakfast.

"Shouldn't you be at work?" Teddy asked him.

"I should be here with my sons," was the man's simple reply. The three had breakfast before visiting Belvedere Cemetery to see Lavinia's grave. Teddy brought daisies he'd picked from a nearby meadow. He sat with Vinie while John waited near the fence.

"There was always one more trip, John. Always one more," Teddy said after they left the graveyard. "I should have gotten her out of there earlier."

"Don't blame yourself for this, Ted."

"How can I not?"

"I liked Lavinia. She was good for you" John said. "Don't dishonour her memory by doing something stupid."

"I loved her, John. I couldn't tell her that. I wasn't ready. Now I'm ready, but she's gone."

"I spoke to my father last night," John said. "He told me that the whole town is angry about this. No one is buying anything from Jackson's stores. The town is demanding justice."

"Lavinia won't get justice. The town will forget, but I won't forget."

"Father also said that there are a bunch of homeless boys hanging around outside the three stores," John said. "People are afraid to go in. The police have tried to drive them away, but they keep going back."

Those boys hadn't forgotten Teddy's kindness to them each time he was ashore. He spent the next week in a daze, and then it was time for them to sail again. McPherson clapped him on the back when he got aboard. The crew all steered clear of Teddy that trip, but not John. John was his rock. He let him talk about Lavinia and his plans. He told Teddy that he'd help pick out a stone for her when they arrived back home again.

Back in St. John's for the second time in two months, Mr. MacDonald told Teddy that Horas Jackson was to be tried for Lavinia's death. Teddy continued to visit her grave and left wildflowers for her each time. "You'll have your justice, Vinie."

However, the following trip, he learned that the courts had determined that Lavinia Walker had died from venereal disease and that Horas Jackson was cleared of all charges. His Vinie was disgraced. Teddy also learned that Jackson and his family were returning to England. They'd sold all their property and were leaving on the morning tide.

"I'm going out for air."

"I'll go with you, Teddy," John said.

"This time, I'd like to go alone."

"Ted, I know you. You are planning to do something stupid."

"John, I'd like to go alone."

"That means 'yes.' I'm going with you."

"I must insist, John," Teddy said. "But I swear on Lavinia's life and death that I won't go to Jackson's place."

"Ted, I'm worried."

"There is nothing to worry about. I'm just going for a walk to clear my head and think about all this."

Teddy made his way to the docks. He met McPherson, who introduced him to a cousin who was crewing on Jackson's ship, the *Loue*. Teddy could think of no better way to spend the bulk of the money he'd saved for his life with Lavinia. A deal was struck—the *Loue* would not see England.

On his next trip ashore, John's father gave Teddy the news that the *Loue* had been wrecked off the Isle of Man. No lives were lost, but Jackson's fortune was gone, and it was unlikely that it would ever be recovered.

McPherson sent him a message the next day that the schooner belonging to the Walkers had mysteriously sunk in Petty Harbour the week before. Lavinia's brothers had a complete loss.

Teddy visited Lavinia's grave for the last time. He laid wildflowers near her new stone and whispered, "That's the best I can do, Vinie. Please forgive me."

Several months later, Mr. MacDonald brought home news.

"The *Walrus* is looking for two crewmen. The captain told me this morning. He heard about my sons and wanted to know if both of you were interested."

Teddy reddened at the mention of being a son. Pride rose from his belly and warmed him. John looked at him and smiled. Teddy grinned, lowering his head. Belonging was a powerful thing.

"What do you think, Ted? Want to try the Labrador?"

"When do we leave?"

"Day after next," Mr. MacDonald said.

Two days later, they boarded the *Walrus*. McPherson greeted them. "Friends of the captain," he said. "I told him about you boys." John and Teddy shook his hand. "Hope you brought your mittens, fellows. It gets mighty cold on the Labrador."

They set out on the evening tide, bound north. They had to pick up salmon, trout, fish oil, and salt cod along the coast before heading to Montreal to exchange for provisions to bring back to Labrador. The Labrador Coast was dotted not only with small settlements but migratory fishing enterprises the residents called "green fishermen," who inhabited the area from early spring till late fall. The *Walrus* was to replenish the outports while the fishing was active and return to St. John's, depending on the weather, in late November. The Hudson's Bay Company paid well, and John and Teddy had come into a prosperous berth. They would be away for the rest of the summer.

Teddy didn't mind. In fact, he wouldn't miss St. John's. He was glad to have John with him. They enjoyed each other's company. The young men talked for hours in the evening and played cards with the rest of the crew. They worked hard, side by side. John and Teddy's was an easy friendship.

A few weeks later, things went terribly wrong when McPherson turned on them all.

13

Teddy dragged John out of the waves and up onto the rocky shore. John coughed, vomiting blood and salt water. Teddy pushed himself upright and scanned for a hiding place. He saw a stand of trees in the distance. "John, can you walk?"

John shook his head from side to side. His breathing was ragged. "Ted, save yourself."

"John, I can get you to those woods and head back to the boat for something to close the wound."

"Ted, listen to me. We both know you can't. I'm not going to make it. You have to tell my father what happened."

"Don't be saying such nonsense. You just have to hang on." Teddy put both arms under John's shoulders and struggled to drag him higher on the beach. His arm buckled under the pain of his own wound. "What the hell were you doing, anyway?"

John groaned and coughed again. This time it was only blood that spewed from his mouth. He motioned for Teddy to stop. John was trying to say something.

Teddy leaned closer just as two shots rang out in the distance. He looked out over the rise of the beach to see the captain and another of the crew fall. Three had already been murdered on the boat, and it would have been five if John hadn't stepped in front of the bullet from McPherson. Teddy had grabbed John and pulled him over the side into the sea as the second bullet creased his own right arm.

John had been wary of McPherson these last few days and had told Teddy so. The man kept watch most of the time, offering to take everyone's shift. He was pacing a lot during the day and scanning the horizon. However, when the rowboat approached with three men aboard, Teddy should have known something was up. McPherson was anxious to get them on the ship and asked them where they'd been instead of asking what happened. Teddy recognized McPherson's cousin. Moments later, the shooting started.

Now, McPherson stood over two dead men with an axe. Their heads rolled down the beach toward the water. Teddy threw up, lurching forward just in time to miss John.

He ducked low when McPherson and the others scanned the area in their direction. "John, we're in trouble. I have to get you out of here." His heart was pounding and his ears ringing. "John, please try."

John wheezed, obviously struggling. Teddy lifted him by his shoulders to help him catch his breath. "Ted, please listen to me. Save yourself," John whispered. "There is no place in this world for me. I love you, Ted. Promise me you'll seek out my father. Tell him I love him."

"Stop talking, John. Save your strength."

"Promise me." John gasped for breath and reached for Teddy's hand.

"I promise," Teddy told him.

John coughed again, and his head fell toward Teddy's chest.

Teddy closed John's eyes and cradled his friend for just a moment before laying him back on the rocks. He held his own face with his bloodied palms and rocked back and forth. Teddy sighed before he summoned the nerve to look once more at the body of his best friend. The men's voices carried on the breeze—they were coming.

The scrappiness he had learned as a boy on the streets of St. John's kicked in. Teddy tore a piece of his shirt and tied it around the wound on his arm. "Damn you, John, for getting in the way. It should be me lying there." He kept low and moved back on the beach. At first he was going to attempt to reach the woods, but he realized that was where they would look. Instead, he hid behind a shelf of waist-high rocks, out of sight of the boat, close to the water's edge.

McPherson and the others came over the rise and ran to John's body. "That's MacDonald." Teddy cringed and felt the bile rise in his throat when McPherson brought the axe down on John's skull and left it there.

"McPherson, what'd you do that for?" his cousin asked.

"I told you, nobody can know I'm alive. That leaves White," he said. "Spread out and scour that woods. He can't have gone far. Looks like he dragged MacDonald here, but I know I hit him."

"Who put you in charge? Captain Baker's not going to like this."

"We won't tell him, now, will we, Simmons?" McPherson said. "He wants a ship, and a ship he'll get."

McPherson grabbed another man's arm. "Dixon, you

come with me. We have to get their belongings off the *Walrus*.
Make it look like it was them that camped here."

McPherson and Dixon headed back toward the rowboats
as Simmons and two other men passed within earshot of Teddy
on their way to the woods.

"Thought them two was supposed to be easy to get rid of,"
the tall man said.

"That's what McPherson said. It looks like this compli-
cation might cost us another night here," Simmons replied.
"Damn the shoals. Captain shouldn't have listened to McPherson wanting to take over the *Walrus* so far north. We'd still
have the *Vagabond* if we hadn't run aground."

"Now McPherson can forget the captain's job," the tall
man said.

"The new *Vagabond* will be mighty fine and sturdy," Simmons said as he glanced over his shoulder toward the *Walrus*.
"Wasn't McPherson's fault we ran aground. Damn winds, that's
all. Now stop your prate and let's find that . . ."

Teddy lost the rest of the conversation as the men headed
away from him toward the woods. He had to find a better hiding place before they returned. The three men had their backs
to him when he rose to search for a more secluded spot, one
that would shelter him from the wind but also keep him out of
sight of the others.

He froze in place, then silently retched when McPherson
kicked the heads of the captain and his crewmate into the
ocean. McPherson and Dixon got aboard the smaller boat
and rowed out to the *Walrus*. Teddy scrambled to a hiding
place a little higher on the beach that would give him a van-
tage point. A small outcrop of rocks and sod connecting the
cliff and the landwash would serve that purpose. With the

tide coming in, the men probably wouldn't venture around the bend to find him.

Teddy's arm throbbed as he squeezed into the cavern. He was cold and wet and knew his chances of coming out of this alive were minimal at best. What would he do if he did survive? McPherson and the crew would hunt him down wherever he went.

He was contemplating his predicament when the men returned. "Any sign of him?" a voice called from the other side of the beach. Teddy knew the man, McPherson's cousin.

"No, none," Simmons shouted.

"Come help bring the supplies to the camp. The winds are too high to take the *Walrus* out of here tonight."

The men grumbled as they trudged across the rise. They went to the rowboat and unloaded trunks, two of which Teddy recognized. One was his, and one was John's—a crate of food, and a cask of rum. Now two different men were coming from somewhere beyond the point. Teddy would have to be careful. He was outnumbered.

14

Teddy was cold and hungry, something he hadn't been since befriending John. He left his hiding spot just at dusk. There had been no movement on the beach where the two rowboats were tied, but loud voices were coming from a sheltered cove not far from his position. He saw the flames from the campfire as he crawled through some low spruce and tall beach grass near the crew.

Two canvas tents had been set up and seemed to have been there a few days. They looked like they had been made from sails. So, the three men's story had been partly true when they said they had run aground, and their boat had been wrecked. The name on the rowboat was the *Vagabond*. They must have been her crew and cronies of McPherson. Every time Teddy thought of McPherson, he raged inside.

The men were drinking and well into the cask by the looks of things. He crept closer as the sky darkened to see if he could make out any of their conversations. The men bragged about being glad they'd lucked out on McPherson. Teddy surmised from their talk that the *Walrus* had been the first ship they'd seen in days since the wreck. The *Vagabond* had broken apart on the reefs in a heavy gale. They planned on renaming the *Walrus* and leaving people to assume she'd sunk or met with some unfortunate fate. The captain had approved of McPherson's efforts, saying it showed a sign of good faith among his crew. They planned to do a brief search for Teddy after dawn, then leave on the morning tide if the winds blew out. McPherson was convinced Teddy was dead.

"It should be easy to find a dead man," one man said.

"I fired two shots," McPherson exclaimed. "One hit Mac-Donald, and the other White. White grabbed MacDonald, and they both fell overboard. I'll find his body in the morning and leave him with the rest."

The crew all drank to that. Teddy had heard enough. He backed away from the camp and waited within view. One by one the men went to relieve themselves or fell asleep where they sat.

Teddy watched for his chance. When McPherson moved away to the trees, Teddy circled around and struck him hard with a stick he'd found near his hiding spot. McPherson didn't know what hit him and fell over in the brush. Teddy whacked him again for good measure—each sickly thud was for John. He quickly looked toward the camp in case somebody heard the noise and came looking, but everyone was either drunk or asleep or distracted.

Grabbing McPherson's legs, Teddy pulled him away from the encampment toward the beach. His strength was propped by his anger and hatred for this man who'd betrayed him in the worst way. He quickly removed McPherson's pants and shirt and exchanged them with his own. Then he returned to where John lay and retrieved the axe from where it rested after McPherson's blow. He went back across the beach, carefully watching so that nobody else had come in search of the man. Teddy rolled McPherson onto his back and swung the axe. He carried the head, all the while heaving and retching, and using the butt of the axe, he dug a hole and buried it in a shallow grave in the sand near where he'd been hiding.

He crossed to the ocean and dipped the axe and washed his hands. Then he moved up the beach, back to John, and knelt beside him. The light of the quarter moon outlined the body of his only friend. Teddy bowed his head into his cold, wet palms and wept.

In the end, John had wanted Teddy to save himself. He got up, took the axe, scaled the rocks, and crept back into the crack beneath the outcrop. The morning was a long time coming.

"McPherson, where are you, man?"

"McPherson!"

He could see the men on the other side of the beach circling the dead bodies. One of them crouched beside McPherson's and checked the pockets of his shirt and pants. He got up, and the gathering talked amongst themselves before they began shouting McPherson's name again.

They headed for the rowboats. They made two trips to the *Walrus* before four men returned to the shore, two in each boat. One man—the cousin, Teddy believed—came over to the spot where John had been murdered. He shouted McPherson's name a few more times before turning back again and shrugging toward the others.

The four pulled the rowboat from the *Walrus* up on the beach and turned it over. One of the men grabbed a large rock and struck a hole in the bottom. The four then jumped into the other rowboat and went back to the *Walrus*.

Men moved around the deck. Teddy pulled himself back into the hole so he wouldn't be seen from the ship. A couple of men watched the shore while two others went to work piling the bodies of his former shipmates at the stern. Teddy guessed they'd all be tossed overboard when the *Walrus* was miles away.

He waited until the ship was out of sight before venturing out of hiding. Cautiously, he moved toward the campsite, fearing somebody might have remained behind. Seeing nobody, he hunted for scraps of food. The crate they'd carried ashore had a few tins of beans. Using a sharp rock, he beat the top off of one and wolfed down the contents. The fire had long gone cold, and he dared not try to start it again. He took the can with him and went back to find another spot on the bluff to stay out of sight. Things would be as they left them if they came back. The weather was cold, and very little warmth came from the sun. Fear, sadness, and despair paralyzed him. The cold drove him from the den in the rocks when darkness swaddled the land. He crept to the camp to take shelter under the tent and went back to the bluff early the next day.

Memories and instincts awakened in him, remnants of his life on the streets. He had fought then to stay alive when all seemed bleak and would do it again.

15

On the third day, Teddy rummaged through the trunks. His hand fell on the picture he kept of Lavinia. First Vinie and now John. He wouldn't be able to take John with him when he left, so he would leave his Vinie behind with his friend. He found a crevice in a nearby rock wall and pushed her picture there, then took the items from John's trunk and stuffed them in around the photo. John had kept a journal of their ports of call, some things he had collected for his father, and various papers describing their cargo.

Teddy folded the last letter John had finished but hadn't been able to post. He shoved it in his shirt pocket. There was also an envelope of cash in a small, hard-covered journal at the bottom of the trunk. There was nothing of consequence in his own trunk aside from Lavinia's picture.

He thought for a while about how much John would be missed. Mr. MacDonald would cry for his son. Nobody would care about Teddy White. The only ones looking for Teddy White would be a bunch of murderers from the *Walrus*. Teddy mulled it over in his head for most of the day. McPherson had identified John, but nobody had identified him. By evening, he decided Teddy White would die here, too. He'd leave the life of Teddy White here on the Labrador with the body of John MacDonald and the picture of Lavinia Walker. In honour of his only friend, he'd carry John with him wherever he went.

He ate the last tin of beans and used a sharp rock to carve off some of the canvas from the sails of the *Vagabond*. Then he stuffed as much as he needed into the hole in the rowboat. He righted the boat back over into the water and allowed the wood to swell around the patch to seal it. He'd test it in the morning.

Saying goodbye to John was the hardest thing he ever did. Saying goodbye to Lavinia wasn't easy, but she was already gone when he'd gotten home. He didn't see her or touch her after he'd kissed her on the pier. That was a fond memory, but John's final moments had been horrific.

"John, I don't know how to do this," Teddy said. "I have to leave you like this in case they come back. I'll make sure you're found and buried properly. That much I'll promise you." He squeezed John's cold, lifeless hand and closed his eyes. "You didn't deserve this. You saved me, John. I hope I've made it right."

A single tear escaped, and he brushed his face with the back of his hand. Teddy squeezed his eyes shut and massaged his brow and cheeks before quickly standing. He looked out over the water. It was calm enough for him to row north in hopes of reaching a settlement on the mainland. So, with prevailing light winds and tides, a strong back for the oar, and an arm that had healed enough for the job, he landed in the small village of Indian Harbour.

"You look tired and hungry," the leather-faced man in town said to him. "Where'd you come from, son?"

"George's Island, I believe, sir. McPherson's the name." He deliberately used the dead man's name to throw off the crew from the *Vagabond* should they ever come looking for him.

THE LIARS

Teddy told the gathering men that he was the only survivor from the boat, the *Walrus*, which had been wrecked on George's Island. He said that all hands had drowned. They gave him provisions and landed him in Rigolet the next day. From there he headed inland, intent on living a solitary life.

Meanwhile, news of the wreck spread along the coast. Fishermen from the nearby village of Black Tickle were shocked and bewildered to find the headless men. They knew something horrible had happened and that the men from the *Walrus* had met a fate worse than drowning. They were laid to rest in a proper grave. News from the site did not reach the Island of Newfoundland until the next spring, where it was reported in the *Twillingate Star*.

The new John MacDonald made friends with the indigenous peoples of Labrador and learned from them how to survive. After all, he told himself, he had lived. It wasn't the first time he'd started from nothing with a leaden heart. He bought and bartered for dogs and began to bring supplies between the missionary communities on the northeast coast. He remained outside the bounds of humanity wherever possible, until the day his path crossed that of the black-haired woman who reminded him of Lavinia. Her desperation matched his own as he'd fled George's Island. Maybe it was the loneliness of his life that drew him to her. He wasn't sure. But he answered her plea just the same. It was time for John MacDonald to walk amongst the living once again.

16

Present day, 1895

The wagon stopped in front of the Whitbourne Hotel.

"Thanks, Richard," Danol said. He grabbed the canvas bag from the rear and helped Erith down from the seat. "Are you staying the night?"

"No, I'll make my way back home. The missus will be expecting me," Richard said, his red hair almost haloed in the glow of the evening sun.

"I'm glad you and Meg could make it to the church," Erith said.

"It was a fine wedding, Miss Erith." Richard paused and looked at her intently. "Don't go fretting about anything at home."

Erith nodded at Richard Dalton. He and his wife, Meg, were Mary Ro's dear friends. She took his hand. "Thanks, Richard. I'm not worried about home." She squeezed his hand once more and then linked into Danol's arm. Her husband escorted her inside.

Erith's stomach clenched once more. Her head was full of worry for what tonight and tomorrow would bring. She tightened her grip on Danol as they climbed the steps to the reception area.

Danol registered them as Mr. and Mrs. Cooper. With the room key in hand, they made their way upstairs.

Cream-coloured wallpaper festooned with tiny yellow and purple flowers with matching pinstripes brightened the room. A shiny oil lamp with a smoky chimney adorned the small dresser near the lone window. Thick yellow curtains hung from ceiling to floor. The ceiling, not much higher than Danol, had glistening white oil paint over planked boards. The chamber pot and washstand were in a tiny room behind the door.

Danol plopped the canvas bag on the bed. Erith stopped and eyed the blues, greens, yellows, and reds in the patchwork quilt and the fluffy white pillows resting against a gold-coloured headboard. She remained quiet. She was afraid that if she spoke she might cry.

"You must be tired, Erith. Do you want some supper?" Danol asked and came around the bed to her.

"I couldn't eat if I tried," Erith said absently.

Danol put his arms around her and stroked her hair. He kissed her tenderly, but she remained tense. He held her away from him. "Erith, honey, I know this has been a long day. Why don't you get ready for bed? Tomorrow will be difficult for you."

"I'm worried about tonight, too, Danol," she ventured shyly.

"Tonight?"

She burst out crying. "I'm so sorry. I know tonight is our wedding night."

He pulled her to him and embraced her once more. "Oh, my darling, I hope you are not worried about tonight because of me."

"Things are supposed to happen, you know . . ." She pushed away again to look into his eyes, blushed, and then buried her head in his chest.

"You silly woman. Or, should I say, you silly wife?" Danol said playfully. His lips moved against her hair.

"But Danol, Mary Ro said . . ."

"Don't mind Mary." Danol smiled and lifted Erith's chin so she could meet his eyes once more. He bent and lightly kissed her lips. "What kind of man would I be if I didn't look out for my wife?" He paused and kissed her again. "I still can't believe you're my wife, Erith. God, I'm a lucky man."

"That's just it, Danol. I'm your wife. I want to *be* your wife."

"We have the rest of our lives for you to be my wife," Danol said. He embraced her once more. "Tonight I want to hold you and comfort you so you can sleep. Tomorrow will be a big day for both of us."

"But Danol, what kind of wife is that?"

"That, my dear Erith, is the kind of wife I want. When the time is right," he said gently, "we'll have our wedding night. I don't want you to feel like it has to be tonight—or any night, for that matter."

Tension released in Erith's spine and jaw, she reached for his hands. "Oh, Danol. I love you."

"I hope so," he said with a grin. He picked her up and twirled her around. "Tomorrow you'll see Beatrice, and I'll be by your side. No matter what has happened, Erith, I will always be by your side."

Erith blushed when she entered the room a short time later with her flannel gown tied tightly at the neck and her bare toes showing. The tension had returned, and the strain showed on her face. She eased herself beneath the patchwork covers. By habit, she reached to fix the hair away from her face, then patted the short tresses instead.

Danol closed the curtains and blew out the lamp. Clothes dropped to the floor. The springs squeaked, and the mattress dipped as he sat on the edge of the bed. When he stretched out, gravity drew Erith toward him. Before she could react, he was tucking her into the crook of his arm. She continued to roll until their bodies touched and her hand rested on his chest.

He inhaled sharply, and the muscles flexed where her fingers grazed his skin.

"Good night, my love," he whispered as he tucked the quilt around her.

"Good night, Danol," she said as she nestled closer to him. His arm tightened around her, and she relaxed into his embrace. The even rise and fall of his chest and the surprising comfort lulled her into a deep sleep. She dreamt of Beatrice and what tomorrow would bring.

Danol shook her. She stretched, and her hand lingered on the warm imprint where he had lain. Her cheeks reddened. "Good morning, Mrs. Cooper. It's time to get up if you want some breakfast before the train is due."

Her husband was sitting, shirtless, on the side of the bed. He quickly leaned in and kissed her. "I hope I get to do this every morning," Danol said as he stroked her hair. "I can't believe *that*, either," he said playfully as he caressed her short mane again before turning back to the dresser to grab his shirt.

Danol gave her some privacy. The sunlight streaming in around the curtain brightened the room and shone across his back as he stretched forward. When he sat back down on the bed, Erith reached and gently stroked the red puckered scar left from the gunshot wound that had struck just below his ribs. He stopped what he was doing and rested his arms on his legs as she gently explored, first one and then the other one, a little bit lower and closer to his spine. She bolted out from under the covers and threw her arms around his neck, almost pushing him off the bed. He chuckled as he tried to hold his position.

She kissed him behind the ear and hugged him tighter. "I almost lost you then and hadn't told you that I loved you." Before Danol could face her, Erith pushed back to the other side of the bed and scrambled to the little room to change. When she returned, he was dressed and waiting for her with a smile on his face.

"How about that breakfast, Mrs. Cooper?" He bent his arm, and she circled hers in through.

"That sounds just about right, Mr. Cooper." She lowered her eyes and smiled shyly at him. He pulled her arm closer to his side and patted her hand, then kissed the top of her head before they left the room.

They met the train a short time later. Despite her easy conversation with Danol, tension crept in once more. He held her hand and squeezed it when he felt the change in her. She sighed heavily and put her head on his arm.

Without Danol by her side, Erith wasn't sure if she could step down from the train when they reached St. John's. With ease, he took her waist and swung her from the platform to the ground. With cautious hope that she would be able to get through the rest of the day, she let Danol guide her. He gathered her to him as they walked the half-mile to the solicitor's office on Duckworth Street. There they would determine what they had to do next.

17

Holyrood

"Caddy, the mail is in," Mrs. Carroll said. "Looks like there's lots there to be sorting."

"Yes, Mrs. Carroll, I'll finish up with Mr. MacDonald and be right there," the young flaxen-haired girl said. "Will that be all, Mr. MacDonald?"

"I almost forgot the tea, Caddy," John said.

"I'll get that," Mrs. Carroll said. "You go on over and start the mail."

Caddy Healey smiled at Mr. MacDonald. He came in quite often of late, she noticed. He seemed to be better off now than when she started working at the store and post office a few years before. But that was none of her business, as Mrs. Carroll continued to remind her.

"Of course, Mrs. Carroll." Caddy nodded to John while Mrs. Carroll waited for her to come out from behind the shop counter before she moved in to tend on her customer. The Carrolls were good to have hired her so young. She suspected it was to help her mother out after her father had died just three years ago, when she was twelve. She continuously tried to prove her worth both here and home in a conscious effort to help her mother and her five younger siblings stay out of the poorhouse.

Mr. MacDonald had given her mother vegetables in the last few years to help the family get through the winter. Caddy liked him. He was a nice man.

Caddy delved into the bag of mail and began to sort the packages and the envelopes. She was lucky that her parents had insisted she stay in school and not go out into service to some of the rich folks, where the need to read and write was not a requirement of employment. The fact that she could do both had made it easy to get a job at the store. The hours were long, but the work wasn't that hard, and she enjoyed the people.

"There you go, Mr. MacDonald. On your account?" Mrs. Carroll asked.

"No, I'll settle up with you now." The register clanged, and moments later, the bell over the door rang as Mr. MacDonald left. Beatrice had been playing outside with Caddy's sister, Penny. Caddy glanced through the large store window as Mr. MacDonald offered them both a sucker and said something to her sister, who instantly smiled and took three more from him. He reached for Beatrice's hand, and they both waved at Penny. Beatrice skipped along beside her father on their way toward home.

Penny peered through the window at Caddy. She shook her head at the girl and nodded toward their house across the road. Penny acknowledged she understood, beamed as she held up the suckers, and turned to go home.

Caddy smiled to herself and hummed as she took out the brown-paper-wrapped parcels and sorted through the envelopes. She paused on one envelope and held it in the air. "Mrs. Carroll, I got another one here for Nancy Martin."

"Put it in the bag for return," Mrs. Carroll said.

"Yes, but this one is marked 'Urgent.'"

Mrs. Carroll came around the postal counter and grabbed the letter from Caddy. She inspected it, holding it to the light of the window, and then tapped it several times on the metal edge of the ink box.

"There is nothing we can do," Mrs. Carroll said. She tapped the flat side of the letter gently on her chin. "It's an offence to open, and we don't know who this Nancy Martin is."

"But it's urgent," Caddy said. "What if—"

"Stop that 'what if,' young lady. We have to send it back, just like we've done with the dozen others we've received over the years."

"But—" Caddy continued.

"No buts, Caddy." Mrs. Carroll opened the ink box and found the roller marked "Returned Unopened," pushed it through the sponge on the blue ink pad, and then spread it across the front of the letter. She threw the envelope into the outgoing mailbag for the next day. "No more about it, Caddy. You hear me?"

"Yes, Mrs. Carroll. I hear you." Caddy put her head down and continued with the sorting. Several people came for their mail and to post letters and packages. She left the returned envelope on the top of the pile. The next day, before closing the bag, she stuffed the letter into the pocket of her dress when Mrs. Carroll was serving the counter on the other side of the room.

Caddy brought the mailbag to the train platform, as she had done three times a week since she started working at Carroll's Dry Goods. She patted her pocket. "I'll find you, Nancy Martin."

That night, she placed the letter between the mattress and spring of the bed she shared with her two sisters. She tumbled the notion of finding Nancy Martin around in her head until she fell asleep.

18

"What's on your mind, Caddy, my dear?"

"Nothing, Ma."

"You're awful quiet this morning, and you forgot to set the table before the young ones got up."

"I was getting to it," Caddy said. She shuffled to the sideboard and took out the sugar dish. Seeing it was nearly empty, she filled it from the tin container in the pantry before returning to the kitchen. Her mother was rooting at the fire with the poker and motioned for Caddy to hand her another few sticks. She was moving toward the door when her mother said, "I already brought in the milk." Caddy changed her route and went back to the pantry for bread and the knife. She sat on the edge of the long bench behind the old wooden table and began the job of slicing the loaves.

She had ten slices on the faded yellow oilcloth when her mother touched her wrist. "We're not feeding the place this morning, Caddy," she said. "What's gotten into you, child?"

"Just puzzling, that's all," Caddy said.

"Quit your puzzling or I'll have to be baking again today," her mother said. She grinned at Caddy and took the knife.

THE LIARS

The woman sat on the chair across from her. "What's wrong, Caddy? Is it your monthly come early?"

"No, Ma." Then Caddy told her mother about the letter. She left out the part about leaving it upstairs under the mattress.

"Mrs. Carroll is right, it's not your business, Caddy."

"But Ma, it was urgent," Caddy argued. "What if it was life and death?"

"Caddy, you and your imagination. It's going to get you in trouble sometime." Her mother chuckled. "What could be so life and death around these parts?"

"I don't know, Ma. But I'd like to find this Nancy in case she was in trouble."

"Well, I can't help you there, child. Now, let's get the toast on the damper before the others come down the stairs."

"Yes, Ma." They both went about the morning breakfast routine before Caddy left for the store.

Two days later, Caddy still hadn't figured out the mystery of Nancy Martin. Her mother sat her down again and asked her what was wrong.

"I told you, Ma, nothing's wrong."

"Is it this Mary what's-her-name business again?"

"Martin, Ma. Nancy Martin."

"So, it is the same thing. What are you worrying about it for?"

"I can't help it, Ma. She could be needed for something."

"Now, Caddy, mind that imagination of yours."

"I'm sorry, Ma." Caddy went about sweeping the floor, her last chore before going to work. Her mother took her arm and sat her at the table once again.

"I know when you get something in that head of yours you won't stop until it's figured out," Caddy's mother said gently. "So, figure it out."

"I've been trying. But there's nobody named Nancy here."

"Well, how long have the letters been coming?"

"About three years, Ma."

"Well, who's new here since around that time?" Her mother counted the people who had moved to Holyrood. There were four families and five schoolteachers. "Some of the schoolteachers are gone. Maybe it was one of them?"

Over the next two weeks, Caddy waited for an opportunity to bring up Nancy Martin to each of the people her mother had counted out. The first few didn't prove fruitful. James Millmore, a short, stocky fisherman, and his wife, Mary, equally proportionate to her husband, were the last two on the list. She was sure that Mary Millmore had to be Nancy, although she couldn't fathom why. Caddy couldn't wait to deliver the letter to Mrs. Millmore. She brought it to the store every day. She almost gave up on seeing Mary Millmore at the store after the others turned out to be wrong. Growing impatient, she was tempted to go to their house on her next day off and deliver it, but the thought of losing her job kept her from going.

Keeping the letter was an unlawful act, maybe unforgivable, and it might mean she would have to go before the magistrate. Then again, maybe the magistrate would open the letter and reveal what was in there. Caddy had been tempted to look but drew the line at going to jail. Mrs. Carroll had warned her many times that peeping in others' mail would have dire consequences. She was only allowed to read letters to somebody if they asked. Caddy often read the newspaper out loud when an article was of particular interest and groups gathered after supper to hear her.

*T*HE *LIARS*

Most recently, folks had been coming to the store to hear about the man who'd escaped from authorities during a jailbreak at the penitentiary in St. John's. He was captured again, without incident, in Labrador, only to escape once more in Harbour Main. A sudden windstorm had kept the boat from docking in Harbour Grace, where he was due for court. Many constables from the Newfoundland Constabulary had passed through on the train and had set up stations in towns from Holyrood to Harbour Grace in an attempt to capture the criminal. It was really quite sensational, and Caddy put a lot of effort into emphasizing the words to bolster the imaginations of those gathered.

That evening, Saturday, would draw a bigger crowd. Caddy hoped to see Mr. and Mrs. Millmore. She planned to mention the name Nancy Martin and hoped Mrs. Millmore would ask about the letter.

The store was full when Mr. and Mrs. Millmore entered. Caddy had already read the paper, and the place was alive with chatter about the escaped criminal.

"Out for a stroll?" somebody asked the Millmores.

"It's a grand evening for it," Mary Millmore replied.

They exchanged pleasantries amongst the crowd before Caddy called her aside.

"Some lovely drinking glasses over here, Mrs. Millmore," Caddy said as she took the larger lady's arm and guided her away from the milieu. Halfway down the aisle between the two rows of dry goods, Caddy stopped in front of a selection of glasses.

Mrs. Millmore reached for one glass. "Very fine, indeed," she said as she inspected the glass.

"Mrs. Millmore, I wanted to talk to you about something."

"Yes, dear," Mrs. Millmore said as she replaced the glass and took another. She didn't look at Caddy.

Mr. Millmore called out to her. "How much longer, Mary?"

"We just got here," she called back to her husband.

"I'll have that drink, then," he said. "Caddy, will you get it?"

"Just a moment," Caddy said.

"I don't have all night," he said.

"Just a moment," Mrs. Millmore said, and she waved her hand as if to dismiss him. "What is it, Caddy? Anything wrong with your mother?"

"No, no. Nothing like that?"

"What is it, then?"

"Are you Nancy Martin?" Caddy blurted out under her breath.

"Am I who?"

"Nancy Martin," Caddy repeated.

"Nancy Martin?" Mrs. Millmore's brows furrowed. "Why would you ask such a question? I was christened Mary Agnes Josephine Chaulk."

Caddy's shoulders sank.

"Are you all right, girl?" Mrs. Millmore asked. She took Caddy by the elbow and looked her in the eye. Tears were welling there. "What's this about?"

Caddy quickly explained the situation, leaving out the fact that she had the letter with her. Mr. Millmore grumbled loudly near the counter. "I better go," Caddy said finally.

The girl scurried back to the counter and grabbed a bottle of rum from a shelf beneath and a small glass from behind her. She poured a sizable drink and laid it before Mr. Millmore. Caddy filled a few more glasses and exchanged them for coin or a mark on a monthly bill. The women all gathered near the window, chatting, while the men finished their drinks. Mrs. Millmore joined the women.

19

By the time she got home that evening, Caddy was ready to give up on finding Nancy Martin. She had a headache from puzzling over it—she was getting nowhere. When Monday came, she sneaked the letter into the mailbag and sent it back where it came from. That was the last she'd think of Nancy Martin.

Wednesday, her day off, she was bringing in the clothes from the line when Penny came home crying. Caddy grabbed the last bedsheet and threw it over her shoulder, jammed the pins in the pocket of her apron, and entered the house a few steps behind her younger sister.

"Quit that bawling, you hear me?" her mother said.

"I can't help it," Penny sniffled. She rubbed her eyes with the back of her hand to try and stop the tears. "Beatrice is my best friend, and she's going away."

"Where's she going?" Caddy asked as she folded the clothes on the daybed.

"Somewhere far away. To North Harbour, she said, but we don't know where that is," Penny cried. "I'm going to miss my friend."

"Who's she going there with?" Caddy asked offhandedly as she continued with her chore. Her mother had grown tired of the conversation and went upstairs.

"Beatrice said it was with the man who talks funny and his wife."

"You mean he stutters?"

"No, he's not from around here," Penny said.

Caddy remembered well the tall man who had bought things for the MacDonalds last year. He talked differently than most. Somebody mentioned he was from Boston.

"I know the one you mean," Caddy said. "He's living in St. Mary's Bay."

"Is that far?" Penny asked.

"Far enough. Why is she going there?"

"Beatrice doesn't know. Her mother told her not to ask questions. They're leaving tomorrow." Penny started to howl once more and ran upstairs.

Caddy started to mull that around in her head till her mother reprimanded her for taking too much time at the clothes. She fetched the black iron frying pan for the fish and forgot about Penny's woes as she prepared supper.

Two days later, Mrs. Millmore came to the store in search of Caddy. "I dropped in to see your mother, and she mentioned you were working today."

"I work every day except for Wednesdays and Sundays," Caddy said as she wiped the rag across the counter. "I spilled pickle there. Mind your sleeve." Mrs. Millmore moved back to give the girl room to finish cleaning the reddish brine off the wooden rack. "Mrs. Carroll will be here soon if you want to see her."

"No, Caddy. I was looking for you."

Caddy stopped. "For me?"

"Yes, I was thinking about your question."

"I gave up on that," Caddy said.

"Oh, that's too bad."

Caddy laid the cloth in the pan of warm water and wiped her apron over the top of the counter to dry it off. "Too bad? Why?"

"Well, I remembered something. But if you don't want to hear it, well then . . ."

Caddy bolted from behind the counter and stood face to face with Mrs. Millmore. The woman smiled at Caddy's excitement.

"What is it?" Caddy asked.

"You know I was the schoolteacher here before I married John." Caddy nodded and leaned in to make sure she caught every word. "Young Beatrice had just started school. Your Penny, too."

"Yes," Caddy said. "But what's that got to do with Nancy Martin?"

"I'm not quite sure if it has anything to do with it, but it was strange just the same."

"What?" Caddy asked. Her hands clenched and her face reddened.

"I shouldn't be spreading rumours," Mrs. Millmore said. She looked toward the floor and lowered her voice.

"Cross my heart, I won't tell anyone, Mrs. Millmore," Caddy said. "I won't go starting stories. I just want to deliver her mail." She didn't tell Mrs. Millmore that she had already sent it back.

"You're sure, Caddy? You won't go telling anyone?"

"I'm sure!" Caddy held her breath. She was afraid she

would miss something. "You were saying . . . Beatrice and Penny had started school . . . and . . ."

"Well, that's just it, it might not be the same thing."

"What?"

"Mrs. MacDonald. Alice," Mrs. Millmore said. "She asked me to write a note for her and an address on an envelope."

"What has that got to do with Nancy Martin?"

"The note said something like: 'I've settled in Holyrood, Conception Bay. Don't worry about me.'"

"What's so unusual about that?"

"She asked me to sign it 'Nancy,'" Mrs. Millmore said. "And the address on the envelope was somewhere in Labrador. I can't quite recall where."

"Was it Nain?" Caddy asked.

"I can't really say. Could very well be."

"So, Mrs. MacDonald, Alice, is Nancy Martin?" Caddy could barely contain herself.

"I'm not saying that, Caddy. I'll deny saying anything if this gets out," Mrs. Millmore said. "I shouldn't have said anything. I should have left the woman to her privacy."

"I won't say. I promise."

The bell over the door jingled, and Mrs. Carroll walked in. "Why, Mary, strange to see you around today."

"Caddy was showing me glasses the other night, and I decided to come back and get them." Mrs. Millmore squeezed Caddy's arm and followed Mrs. Carroll to the glasses.

"I'll ring her in, Caddy," Mrs. Carroll said. "You go get the mail."

"No mail today," Caddy replied.

"That's right. I should have known when there was no one around."

*T*HE *LIARS*

Mrs. Carroll helped Mrs. Millmore and told Caddy to put the glasses on her bill, and the two women left the store together.

"I'll be back around suppertime so you can go home," Mrs. Carroll called over her shoulder.

"See you then," Caddy said.

Caddy grinned to herself. She had done it! She'd solved the mystery. Now she had to figure out how she could talk to Mrs. MacDonald. Did her husband know? Why did she change her name? Why was she here? All the questions jammed in her brain at the same time. How would she get through the rest of the day without bursting? Would she have time to go to the MacDonalds? What would she say about the letter?

Then she began to second-guess herself. What kind of wasp's nest might she be poking? Would Alice welcome being found out? Maybe Mrs. Millmore was right and she should mind her own business, too. With so many thoughts going through her head, she was going to drive herself out of her mind.

She contemplated what she would do. Most afternoons were quiet. When it wasn't mail day, it was worse. Mrs. Carroll was saying she should close the store till after supper on these kinds of days. Nevertheless, she was working and had to stay. Caddy boiled water on the little pot-bellied stove in the corner. It was a good day to wipe down the shelves to keep herself busy. She was kneeling by the canned food when she heard the bell tinkle again. She grabbed the rack for balance and stood, straightening her apron before looking up.

A tall, dark-haired man entered the store. He seemed to fill the whole room. He looked like he hadn't seen a razor's edge in quite some time, and his clothes were ragged and dirty.

Caddy's knees started to knock. She walked behind the counter, wanting to put something between them. "Can I help you, sir?" She hoped he hadn't heard the slight quiver in her voice.

For a big man, he was very light on his feet. He put his two hands on the edge of the counter. "I'm looking for Nancy Martin."

Caddy's mouth dropped open. She stared at him, wide-eyed. Her legs trembled, and heat rushed to her cheeks.

"Nan-an-cy Mar-ar-tin?" she stammered. She pushed her chin slightly forward. "I don't know a Nancy Martin." False courage helped her finish the sentence. She straightened her back and took a step away from the counter to be farther from him.

"You lie!" he roared. Before she could move, he sprung over the counter and struck her across the face.

20

"Caddy," Mrs. Carroll said. "Caddy, where did you go?" Mrs. Carroll felt the chill in the air. "You let the fire go out." She pulled the damper off the stove and poked the few embers in the ashes at the base. She tut-tutted loudly at the inconvenience. "I'll have to get Val to come over and light that in again. Caddy, where are you?"

Mrs. Carroll threw a few small dry sticks in the stove and laid the damper just shy of the hole to give the flame some draft. "Caddy, you better answer me," she said as she walked toward the counter. "I don't suppose she's gone home and never locked the store," she mumbled to herself. "Caddy? Caddy! I don't know what's gotten into that child lately."

She noticed the pan of water by the shelf and picked it up. The water was barely warm. She brought it to the counter, muttering under her breath about the young ones having no cares for other people's property.

"Caddy," Mrs. Carroll called out once more.

"I'll have to go across the road and see where she has gone, I suppose," she said under her breath. The bell tinkled as she stepped out into the evening air. "Wish I'd brought my shawl."

As she crossed the gravelled laneway between the store and Caddy's house, Mrs. Healey came to the door before she made it inside the gate.

"Caddy's not coming home?" Mrs. Healey asked.

"I thought she was here, Madge," Mrs. Carroll said. "She's not in the store, and the fire's gone out."

Mrs. Healey pulled back inside the door and shouted for Penny to see if Caddy was in her room. Her frown and shake of her head sent Mrs. Carroll back to the store.

"Caddy! Caddy!" she shouted. "Where are you?"

The bell jingled, and Mrs. Healey came in with Penny right behind her. "Penny, be a dear and go fetch Mr. Carroll for me," Mrs. Carroll said. Penny glanced from side to side and then to her mother. Her mother nodded, and Penny took off as fast as her legs could carry her.

"I haven't seen her all day," Caddy's mother said.

"I was here earlier when Mary Millmore was here. I told her I'd be back so she could go to supper."

"I was expecting her." The two women gathered near the counter. The door opened, and Mr. Carroll and Penny rushed in.

"What's happened?" Mr. Carroll asked.

"I don't know. Caddy wasn't here when I got here, and she's not home."

"She can't be gone far. Did you check around? Maybe she fell asleep out back." He pushed open the door to the storeroom, peered around, and then shook his head. "She could have fallen and hit her head or something," Mr. Carroll said.

"Really, Val?"

"Well, it could have happened," Mr. Carroll said, shrugging.

Penny skirted up and down the aisles and behind the mail counter. She shrugged her shoulders and made a motion that she couldn't find her.

"Where could she be?" Mrs. Carroll mused. Then she moved behind the counter. "Strange, the cash is open." The woman reached to push in the cash drawer but noticed there was no money in there. She moved in to investigate further, and as she did, her shoe slid on something sticky. She lightly kicked something soft. Holding the counter to keep from falling, she glanced down. She screamed, then covered her mouth and looked to Caddy's mother.

Penny tried to come around, but Mrs. Carroll stopped her. She looked at Mrs. Healey and shook her head. Caddy's mother grabbed Penny's shoulders to keep her back.

Val Carroll grabbed his wife about the waist and moved her out of the way. The sight before him was gruesome and bloody. "Get the child to go for the doctor," he said to Caddy's mother.

Penny latched onto her. Mrs. Healey stooped before her and wiped the hair from her face. "Do this for Caddy," she said, her voice trembling. Penny nodded, and her mother kissed the top of her head before she bolted through the door.

"Don't come over here," Mrs. Carroll warned the woman.

"I have to. She's my first-born." Caddy's mother walked toward them as Mr. Carroll picked up the limp and bloodied body of her daughter. He laid her on the counter after Mrs. Carroll pushed books and ledgers out of the way.

"Is she . . . ?"

"I don't know," said Mr. Carroll. "She's awful cold."

Caddy's mother turned toward the door. "I'll get her a blanket," she said calmly. She turned and left.

Moments later, she came back with two patchwork quilts and handed them to Mr. Carroll. "Keep her warm." He took them and nodded at her. He tenderly wrapped Caddy while they waited for the doctor.

"Val, see to the fire," Mrs. Carroll said. He nodded and left while she stayed by the counter.

Val fiddled with the fire and the wood before he got a flame going. "A blast of heat will do us all good," he said. He went into the back room and brought two chairs for the women before relieving his wife at Caddy's side.

Mrs. Healey pulled a set of white beads from her pocket and began the decades of the rosary while she rocked back and forth in the chair. Mrs. Carroll sat silently beside her and reached for her hand to give some sort of comfort. She didn't look up when the horse and cart came barrelling toward the store and the doctor and Penny jumped out. Penny ran to her mother, knelt at her feet, rested her head on her lap, and watched the doctor tend to Caddy.

The doctor whispered something to Val Carroll, and he nodded toward the back room. He gently picked up Caddy, and they crossed to the door. The sound of its closing was deafening. There was scraping of wood on wood in the other room before things got quiet. Penny started to cry.

People began to gather at the store. Mrs. Carroll whispered that something had happened. Women came and milled around Caddy's mother while the men lingered outside. Somebody called on the two constables who were staying at Veitch's.

*T*HE LIARS

When they arrived, Mrs. Carroll tilted her head toward the back room. They knocked on the door and went inside.

Penny cried when Mrs. Millmore brought her home with the other children. "I'll go with them, Madge. You stay here as long as you want," she had said. Mrs. Healey didn't raise her head. She continued to pray the rosary quietly.

Val Carroll stuck his head out and asked for water and cloths. Two women went to work at the old iron stove and brought hot water and cloths to the door for the doctor. They removed the bloodied rags inside a porcelain pail so that Caddy's mother wouldn't see.

Men brought in chairs from nearby homes. Several women sat in a circle around Mrs. Healey and began reciting the rosary, heads bowed as they prayed.

The doctor, a short, small man with thinning grey hair, came from the room, followed by the constables. Mrs. Carroll went in with her husband to stay by Caddy.

The silence was only broken by the scrape of the chairs on the old wooden floor as Dr. Lane made his way toward Mrs. Healey. She looked up as he approached.

"I won't lie to you, Madge. It doesn't look good," he said solemnly. His clothes were covered in Caddy's blood.

"Where there's life, there's hope," Mrs. Healey said defiantly.

"I know, Madge. I'm so sorry."

She lowered her head. The crowd waited as she slowly put the rosary beads back in her pocket. "I want her brought home. If she's to die, it will be where my James died," she said. "Can we bring her home to the daybed in the kitchen?"

"Yes, of course." The doctor made a motion for the constables and the menfolk to grant her request. Mrs. Healey gasped aloud when they brought Caddy's still form from the room on a small, narrow bench. She was partially covered by a bloodied quilt. Her face was swollen, battered, and broken beyond recognition.

"Are you sure 'tis Caddy?" Madge asked. Mrs. Carroll came from the room with Caddy's shoes and some red-stained clothing. She nodded, and Mrs. Healey let out a wail. She laid her hand on Caddy's foot before they moved on. With great care, the men navigated the front step, and a parade of people followed them across the road to Mrs. Healey's.

Two of the women fussed over the cushions and quilts—fetched by Penny and Mrs. Millmore—to make a comfortable spot for her on the daybed before the doctor guided the transfer.

Caddy didn't move. Her still form was reminiscent of death. Penny started to scream, and Mrs. Millmore tucked her into her embrace for comfort and to quieten her. The townsfolk went to work to relieve the pressures of living. Somebody brought wood, others carried water, someone tended to a pot on the stove, and another made tea—everything a ritual of caring for the suffering that existed for as long as the town came into being.

Mrs. Healey took a chair by Caddy's head, and Mary Millmore put a cup of tea in her hand. "Caddy belongs home here with me," she said. "If James were alive, she'd be home."

"Don't blame yourself for this, Madge. She loved working in the store," Mary said. Everyone there nodded in agreement.

"She was good as a concert, reading out the newspaper to us," a neighbour mentioned.

"Yes, she'd read my mail for me whenever I asked," a fellow said.

"She loved the mail," Mrs. Healey said. "Even tried to find some Mary what-do-you-call-her."

"You mean Nancy Martin," Mary Millmore said.

"Yes, that's right. She even asked me if I knew her," Betsy Fewer said.

"Me too," said Mary.

"Who did you say?" one of the constables asked. "I'm Constable Jeffries, by the way." He held out his hand to Mary Millmore.

"Nancy Martin."

"Yes, Nancy Martin," Mrs. Healey said. "I kept getting it mixed up. Poor Caddy was always puzzling over something."

"What about this Nancy Martin?" Constable Jeffries asked.

"I'm not quite sure," Mary said. "She said she had a letter for her. Mrs. Carroll might know more."

"Ah, yes. Nancy Martin," Mrs. Carroll said. She went on to explain the letters.

"You're sure it was Nancy Martin," Jeffries said.

"Positive. I even stamped the last one to be returned myself."

"Yes, that was the one Caddy was puzzling over. She said it was marked 'Urgent,' and we all know Caddy and her imagination," Mrs. Healey said. Then she wailed loudly and gently laid her hand on Caddy's hair. "My poor girl."

"Why?" Mrs. Carroll asked. "Is that important?"

"Very important," Jeffries said.

"Why?" asked Mrs. Millmore.

"The man who escaped, Ezra Shawe, was looking for Nancy Martin. He left her sister in a bad way on the Labrador. Don't know if she'll recover."

"He knew Nancy Martin?" Mrs. Millmore asked.

"She was the reason he was in jail. He murdered her husband and her mother-in-law. He is said to have killed his first wife as well." A collective gasp went through the room.

"That still doesn't help you," Mrs. Carroll said. "We returned all those letters. There is no Nancy Martin here."

"Well . . ." said Mary. She went on to explain the conversation she'd had with Caddy about Alice MacDonald.

"Assuming Ezra Shawe got that information out of Caddy, Alice MacDonald is in a whole heap of danger," said Constable Jeffries. "Where does she live?"

One of the men stepped forward. "I can show you. We'll go with you." He made a motion to the dozen or so men who were around the kitchen area.

"But they're gone," Penny said from the bottom of the stairs. With everyone preparing to leave, only Mrs. Millmore heard her. She crossed the room to Penny.

"What did you say?"

"They're gone."

"Hold on, everyone," Mrs. Millmore cried out.

Constable Jeffries had been about to step outside. "What is it?"

"Penny says they're gone." They urged Penny to come forth into the room and explain what she knew.

"Did Caddy know this?" Jeffries asked.

Penny nodded. "I told her a few days ago. They went to meet the man who speaks funny and go to North Harbour."

Constable Jeffries looked around the room to see if anyone knew who this was. "North Harbour, you say. The man who speaks funny, does he suffer some ailment?"

"No," said Penny. "He's not from here. He came from somewhere far away from here, where there are lots of people."

"Like St. John's? That has lots of people," Jeffries said.

"No. Beatrice said it was bigger than that. I don't know how she'd know because she had never been to St. John's, but she said the man with the funny voice told her. He bought her a nice dress last year."

"She must mean the Cooper man," Mrs. Carroll said. "He was a friend of the MacDonalds. Had an odd first name. He bought supplies at the store for them. Although he has only been here a couple of times."

"Cooper. Must be Danol Cooper. I know of him. Had some dealings with him," Jeffries said.

"A criminal?" Mrs. Carroll asked.

"No, the opposite," Jeffries said. "We've tried to recruit him several times. Used to be a policeman in Boston."

"That's the faraway land!" Penny said at once. "Boston! Me and Beatrice used to make up stories about it."

"I'll need to telegraph St. John's and call the constables back. It looks like our criminal might be headed to North Harbour." Jeffries strode across the room to Mrs. Healey. He took both her hands in his. "We'll get the man who did this to your daughter."

With that, he marched out and took several men with him. They were making plans together as they left the yard, heading for the telegraph office.

It would prove to be a long night.

21

St. John's

Erith truly felt that her encounter with Beatrice was as two people. The inside person whose tingling limbs and churning stomach had her shifting, almost imperceptibly, from foot to foot to hold herself back as she bore the crushing weight of an unfulfilled brokenness. That one was unable to breathe.

Then there was the outside person, whose voice didn't quiver, who said the appropriate things—hopefully, anyway—and who smiled at the right time. The same one who bent and grinned at the beautiful child staring up at her. The one who reached out with steady hand and tenderly cupped the face of her first-born and smoothed her hair while the girl beamed back at her, unknowing.

Both at odds. The inner one, who wanted to grab the girl and hold her tight and cry tears that would shed her soul of anguish without care for what anyone thought of it. The outside one, who was trying to do what she thought was best for them while scouring away the suffocating inner self.

"Pleased to meet you, ma'am," the girl said, her voice as melodious and bubbly as Erith had imagined it would be. Beatrice's first words to her passed her lips to the ear of a stranger, a stranger who had birthed her and rocked her for the first few months of her life.

Erith pulled her arm back and kept it by her side for fear she would overwhelm Beatrice—or possibly herself. Danol's fingers gently squeezed her upper arm, perhaps to keep her upright.

"Pleased to meet you, too," she replied, her voice no more than a croak. She coughed to clear her throat.

"And you, Mr. Danol," Beatrice said. She held out her tiny hand to Danol. He shook it.

"My, how tall you've gotten since I saw you last," Danol said as he grasped her hand.

"You still talk funny," she giggled. Her parents gasped collectively.

"Beatrice, what did we say about that?" Alice admonished her.

"But he does, Mommy," Beatrice said.

"That, I do," said Danol. He winked at her.

The inner Erith fought to keep despair from gaining ground as she watched the scene unfold before her. The outer Erith acted as if everything was normal. Alice kept an eye on her after the introductions were made. Erith couldn't be civil and ask how their trip was or where they were staying or if they wanted lunch. She had difficulty holding on to her inner self, who wanted to scream out that Beatrice was her daughter and should be with her.

Alice's protective stance, then her softening expression as she gazed at Erith's child, indicated that Beatrice would not be with her real mother. Or, conceivably, Erith thought, she was with her real mother now, as Annie, George, and Tommy were with her, and she had no place in Beatrice's life.

"John, good to see you again," Danol said as he reached out to grasp John MacDonald's hand. "This is my wife, Erith. Erith, John, Alice, and you've just met Beatrice."

Erith nodded to the two adults, and as much as she tried, she couldn't keep her eyes off of Beatrice.

William Horwood, Erith's solicitor, cleared his throat. "If the ladies would like to wait outside with Loretta, we can attend to business in here."

"Danol, do you mind if I stay?" Erith asked.

"Of course not," he replied.

John MacDonald whispered something to Alice, and she took Beatrice outside the office. Horwood followed her to the door. "Loretta, make some tea and coffee and bring it in when you're ready. Get something for Beatrice and her mother as well."

The young woman with the brown curly hair who had greeted them when they came in took Alice and Beatrice into another room. "Yes, sir. I'll get that right away." Horwood closed the door and showed them to a large, dark wooden table that matched the walls. He pulled out a brown leather chair for Erith and showed John and Danol to a seat. Danol took the chair next to his wife and reached for her hand. He squeezed it once more and then covered it with his other hand. John sat across from them, and Horwood took the chair on the end.

Erith's heart pounded. She looked at Danol to see if he could hear it. He smiled reassuringly and patted her hand once more. She didn't know what to do with her other hand, so she laid it on top of his.

"So, what's this all about?" Danol asked.

"I have not been apprised of the situation as of yet," Horwood said. "The MacDonalds came here two days ago and asked me to contact you about Beatrice. They wouldn't say why. Is that not so, Mr. MacDonald?"

"It's John, please. Yes, that's right. We didn't want to say why. We, I mean Alice, is in a tough predicament." He told them about Ezra. When he mentioned that Ezra had killed Alice's husband and she had fled, Erith gasped.

"I wouldn't expect you to understand, Mrs. Cooper. But Alice is terrified that he will find her and put Beatrice in danger."

Erith only caught part of the conversation after that. Alice MacDonald was doing what any mother would do for her child. Whatever doubts might have been lingering because of her own needs were banished at that moment.

"So, to sum this up, Ezra Shawe was sentenced to be hanged for murder, was commuted to life at the St. John's Penitentiary, escaped after four years, turned up in Labrador months later, was captured again, escaped in Harbour Main, and is on the loose, probably looking for Alice," Danol said. "Could he have found out where Alice was from family in Labrador?"

"We haven't been in contact with anyone," John said.

"Seems too much of a coincidence that he'd escape in Harbour Main, so close to where you were living," Danol said.

"I know, but Alice swears her sister didn't know where she was. That's the only family Alice has."

"So, what is your plan?" Danol asked.

"We wanted to leave Beatrice with her mother," John said. "Alice figures if anything happens to her, Beatrice would be safe then."

"Alice is Beatrice's mother," Erith said.

"Thank you for that, ma'am," John said. "But Alice has nobody she'd trust more than you to do right by Beatrice."

"You want us to take Beatrice, and then what?" asked Danol.

"Alice and I will go back home and wait. Ezra will either be caught or will find us."

"He's already murdered how many people?" Erith asked.

"Three that we know of," John said.

"Then why don't you come with us?" she said. Danol looked at her. "We have your house and my house. We have room."

Danol looked at John. "Do you mind if I speak to my wife in private?"

"I'll go check and see where Loretta has gone for that tea," Horwood said. "Mr. MacDonald, John, would you like to accompany me?" John nodded, and they both left the room, closing the door.

"Erith, what are you saying?"

"Danol, I can't let that woman, the mother of my child, I might add, sit in fear while she waits for some man to come and kill her."

"I understand that part, Erith, but this would have been your chance to get to know Beatrice without any interference from the MacDonalds."

"I've seen the way that Alice looks at Beatrice," Erith said. "Though it pains me to say this, Beatrice belongs with her. I can't interfere with that. It wouldn't be right. I made a decision about this last year, and I won't go back on that now."

Danol put his arms around her. "You, my dear, do the most unexpected things. Did I tell you yet today that I love you?" He kissed her. "Looks like we'll have to make some more room on the *Angel*."

"That's not a problem, is it, Danol?"

"Of course not, my love." He quickly guided her to the chair. "I'll go get the others."

"Danol, I think I'll go with Alice and Beatrice while you work this out with the men."

"You're sure?"

Erith nodded. He held her hand and walked her out of the room. She passed the two men and went to find Alice. They were seated at a small table in a kitchen off the waiting area. Beatrice was munching on a cookie while Alice was fussing with her teacup. Erith noticed it was still full.

"Mind if I join you?"

"Not at all." Alice moved to the chair closest to Beatrice, allowing Erith to take the chair she had just vacated. Erith took the pot from the table and poured a tea before sitting down. Beatrice commented on her dress and her hat.

"Maybe we can get you one before we leave," Erith said.

"Oh, can I, Mommy?" Beatrice asked.

"We'll see," said Alice.

"That usually means no," Beatrice said with a pout.

Erith laughed. "Now that I think of it, it usually means no when *I* say it, too."

Alice let out a sigh. Erith looked at her and grinned. She gave Erith a half-hearted smile. Loretta came in to see if there was anything she could get for them.

"Loretta, can you show Beatrice around your desk? If it's all right with her mother," Erith said.

Alice nodded, and Loretta asked Beatrice to go with her. The little girl skipped out of the room behind her.

Before Alice could say anything, Erith said, "I know this must be difficult for you. I assure you, I know Beatrice belongs with you. It's not that I don't want her. . . . I wish more than anything I could have kept her all those years ago." She folded her hands around the teacup for warmth and gazed at the swirling liquid inside. "It was not meant to be. I couldn't keep her because of things that were out of my control. I don't want that to happen to you."

Alice shifted in her chair. She was about to speak, but Erith went on. "John explained what's happening. Danol and I would like you and John to come with us to North Harbour and stay there until the threat is over. We have lots of room, and you'll be safe there."

"Why would you want to do this for us?" asked Alice.

"Let's just say that I know what it's like to feel trapped and to choose someone you love over yourself. That's what mothers do. You don't have to choose in this case. There is another way."

Alice silently wept into her hands. Erith went around the table and squeezed her shoulders. "Now, why don't we go to buy that hat? I have a little girl a year older than Beatrice who would love to have a hat, too."

"We owe you so much," Alice said hesitantly. "We can never repay you."

"You do it every single day," Erith said. "Besides, I have another reason." Erith removed her hat to show Alice her short hair. She explained what she had done and why, and it later occurred to her that Annie might ask questions. It would be easier if they were playing hats for a few days.

"What about if I braided Beatrice's hair? I do that sometimes, and she likes it."

"Yes, and I could do that with Annie," Erith said. She smiled and put her hat back on. "We'll pick up a few things for you and John as well. No need to go back to Holyrood. We can leave from the docks tomorrow." Erith explained that the *Angel Endeavours* and crew had been dispatched to pick them up.

22

Alice told Beatrice that her parents were going with her to North Harbour, and the little girl was very excited. John came out moments later, and Erith told him that things had already been settled, if he agreed.

"Are you sure, John?" Alice asked him.

"It's for the best," he replied.

"Can I get a hat?" Beatrice asked.

"Yes," both Erith and Alice said at the same time.

"Maybe your mom will get one, too, and I'll get one for my little Annie," Erith said.

"Is it safe for us to go out?" Alice asked as an aside to John.

"I'll go with you," Danol said. "John, are you coming?"

"No," John said abruptly. "No, I have things to attend to in the room we rented."

"The *Angel* should be in," said Danol. "We can stay on the boat tonight."

"We'd rather stay at the boarding house," John said.

"Please, Daddy, can we stay with the angels," Beatrice asked.

Alice searched John's face. "Mind your father, Beatrice," she said.

"I'll go," Danol said. "Maybe I'll buy a hat, too."

"Boys don't wear hats," Beatrice said.

They ate lunch at a small restaurant on Duckworth Street not far from their solicitor's office. Erith felt much better about the whole situation with Beatrice. The little girl was well-behaved and was quite jolly. She seemed to have had a happy life up to this point. Erith was very grateful for that.

At Ayre and Sons Department Store, Danol left them so he could run a few errands. He told Erith to take her time and that he'd be back before they finished. Erith felt a new freedom in the city she hadn't known before. She realized that *before* meant before Danol. He had changed her life in so many ways.

At first, Alice protested that she was spending too much, but Erith was insistent on the dresses, undergarments, hats, footwear, and so much more. Beatrice was having a wonderful time, but Erith made sure that she was not stealing the little girl's favour from her mother. Beatrice helped her pick out items for Annie, and when Danol returned, he selected some things they thought George and Tommy would like.

The bill was totalled, and Erith added the items to her account. She signed and asked them to send the invoice to her solicitors.

"Your husband doesn't mind you spent all that money?" Alice asked after Danol left to arrange for the packages to be delivered to the ship. He had confirmed to her that the *Angel Endeavours* was docked and being loaded while they shopped.

"This is the money that I inherited from my father," Erith said. "But if it were Danol's, I don't think he would mind at all."

"I'm sorry. That was not my place to speak," Alice said. "This is all new to me."

"It's okay," Erith said. "I didn't always have money. I came into my father's fortune a few years ago. Before that, I worked three jobs in order to adopt the children from the orphanage."

Alice tried to hold back a gasp. Erith laughed. "I'll tell you all about me on our trip around the coast."

"How long have you and Danol been married?"

"Well, since it's now afternoon, just over a day."

Alice gasped again. "You mean you came for Beatrice on your *wedding day*?"

"It sounds a bit selfish to get married before coming here, but everyone was waiting," Erith said.

"I'm sorry. That didn't come out right," Alice said. "I can't believe that you would come. That's still not right. I don't know what I'm trying to say. . . . You're not what I expected you to be."

"What did you expect?"

"I don't know that, either. It's hard to say. I guess I was so worried about Beatrice, and maybe never seeing her again, that I didn't expect you to be . . . nice. That's not fair of me, I know." Alice lowered her gaze. "I've said too much."

"Not at all. To be honest, I was hoping that I'd hate you and that I could take Beatrice home with me. But then I heard that you were willing to sacrifice yourself for the good of your daughter, and I realized I was trying to right a wrong that neither you nor Beatrice were a part of. All I wanted for Beatrice when she was taken from me was that she be loved. I can see she is." Erith held out her hand to Alice. "I can't hate a person who loves my child. I should say, who loves *her* child."

Alice slowly took her hand, and Erith squeezed it. She reminded Erith of herself before Danol. She pondered on Alice and John's relationship for just a moment. It was not her affair to worry about, as long as they were good to Beatrice. That part was obvious. They both loved her little girl.

"Mommy," Beatrice said. She ran and hugged Alice. Danol's eyes met his wife's, and she smiled at him.

"You two have returned," Erith said. "What have you been up to?"

"It's a secret," Beatrice said.

"Can you tell me?" Alice asked.

"No, then it won't be a secret," Beatrice laughed. "Right, Danol?"

"That's right," he said and winked at Alice. "I heard you were the best to keep secrets. That's why I told you."

Beatrice grinned and ran to Danol and hugged him. He tossed her hair, and she laughed and ran back to Alice. "It's time to go see Daddy," she said.

They walked back to the boarding house on Gower Street. On the way, Beatrice asked a multitude of questions about the boat, North Harbour, and the children. John met them at the door, and the child ran to him. He scooped her up and hugged her.

"Can we please go with the angels, Daddy?"

"I've been thinking that maybe it's a good idea," said John. "If it's all right with your mother."

Alice stared at John for a moment before she nodded.

Beatrice grabbed him around the neck and hugged him fiercely. "Thank you, Daddy," she said.

"I thought you were shopping," said John. "I don't see any packages."

"Danol sent them all to the boat. I got a pink hat."

"A pink hat for a beautiful young lady," John said.

"Do you need a ride?" asked Danol. "I can send somebody for you."

John looked at him. "We have a small trunk," he said.

"Can we walk and send somebody for the trunk?" Alice asked.

John didn't answer right away. "Yes, we can do that," he said at length.

Danol nodded. "We'll have supper on the boat. I told the cook we might have a few extras. Everything is ready for you."

Alice smiled. "That's awful kind of you."

"Nonsense, we're going that way. There's always room for more."

Beatrice held her parents' hands as she skipped along the street between them. Danol and Erith hung back and strolled arm in arm. "How are you doing, Erith?" Danol asked his wife as he patted her hand.

"Surprisingly, I think I'll be all right," she said. "Right now I feel like the luckiest girl in the city."

"I know I'm the luckiest man around here," Danol said, picking her up and swinging her around.

"Danol Cooper, put me down!" Erith exclaimed as heat rose in her cheeks.

But her husband just grinned and spun her again. Somebody laughed behind them as a man tried to avoid the hem of Erith's flaring skirts. Danol laid her down and muttered an apology to the man. They both giggled, linked arms, and followed the trio along the sidewalk. As they neared the place where she'd been stabbed the year before, Erith drew closer to Danol. He put his arm around her back, and they continued past the spot. She relaxed and eased into his embrace.

As they neared Water Street there were more horses, carts, and foot traffic to contend with. Workers were making their way home for the evening, and some businesses had already closed. The overcast sky put a grey hue on everything it touched. John picked up Beatrice and sped up as he hurried toward the boat at the far pier. Beatrice's hair was flying all around his face, so he kept his head low, while Alice scurried along beside him. They hurried up the gangway and onto the boat, where they were greeted by one of the crewmen who came to the rail, spotted them, and waved. Danol waved back. They weren't too far behind.

"Erith, I have a couple of things to do," Danol said. "I'll take a cart before they've all left for the evening and pick up the trunk on my way. I won't be long. Save me some supper."

With that, he was gone.

"Who's hungry?" Erith asked.

"Me, me," Beatrice said. They all laughed as Erith showed them to the galley.

23

Danol flagged down a buggy driver. "Heading home, Tom?"

"I always have time for you, Mr. Cooper."

"I won't be long."

"Hop aboard," Tom said. "Where to?"

"The Constabulary office," Danol said.

"Not many of them boys around, Mr. Cooper. You can tell by the thieving on the docks of late."

"Where are they gone?"

Tom flicked the reins on the horses. "Chasing some feller who escaped prison, I hear."

"Yes, I heard about that, too." They chatted about the weather for the rest of the ride. When they got to the headquarters building, Danol gave Tom the address for the trunk and asked him to pick it up and come back for him.

Inside the building, the place was almost empty. One lone constable sat at the desk near the entrance.

"Can I help you, sir?"

"Cooper, Danol Cooper," he said as he stretched out his hand to the young man.

"I've heard of you. How can I help you, Mr. Cooper?"

"I was looking for Jeffries. Is he around?"

"No, sir. He and a dozen more were dispatched to the Holyrood and Harbour Grace area. He left yesterday."

"When will he be back?"

"Who knows? Orders were not to come back without that murderer. Folks are spooked, and with good reason."

"Why is that?"

"He escaped a few months ago. The missionaries caught him on the Labrador. He beat this woman something shocking, they say. Never heard if she made it or not."

"Why was he after the woman?" asked Danol.

"Seems it wasn't her he was after. It was her sister. The woman's husband came home and kept him from killing her. At least at the time. Like I said, that could have changed," the young constable said. "He just gave up right there and then. Quiet as a lamb, they said. He was in jail for killing the man's brother. A week later, they were bringing him to Twillingate for court, but there were high winds, so the boat veered for Harbour Grace. The storm was blowing something fierce, so they took shelter in Harbour Main for the night. In the morning, the prisoner was gone."

"Tell Jeffries I have the sister, Alice MacDonald, and her family on my boat, the *Angel Endeavours*. I'm heading to North Harbour."

"You must be mistaken. I don't believe that's her name, sir." The constable looked through some papers. He read a few lines. "Her name's Nancy Martin."

The constable showed Danol the notice. "Nancy Martin. I see," Danol said. "Well, whatever that paper says, she says she's the one the prisoner is looking for. Can I leave a note for Jeffries?"

"Sure, but I don't know when he'll be back."

"That's fine, I'm in no big hurry."

The constable handed Danol some paper and a pencil. Danol scribbled a note and took an envelope from the basket on the front of the desk. He put Jeffries's name on it, sealed it, and handed it back to the officer, who took it and turned to a wooden wall unit behind him. He scanned the names at the top of each section until he found the right one, and he stuck the note inside.

Danol thanked the young man and left. Tom was waiting when he went outside. When they arrived at the wharf, he paid the man, told him to be careful, and hefted the trunk. At the top of the gangway, he handed it off and instructed his crewman where it should be stored.

24

Danol had one more thing to take care of before heading to the galley. He made it just before the meal was done.

He pulled in on the bench beside Erith, and the cook brought a plate of fish. He reached for two slices of bread from the middle of the table and joined the conversation. When Beatrice began to yawn, Danol got his newest crewman, Peter's son, Eddy Nolan, to show them where they'd sleep. Beatrice hugged them before John and Alice bid them a good night and took her to their cabin.

"You were gone a long time just to get a trunk," Erith said once they were alone.

"I stopped to see what Jeffries knew about this Ezra fellow, but he's out in Conception Bay somewhere," Danol said.

"Are you on watch tonight?"

"No, I'm all yours tonight. You've had a long day. You must be tired."

"I'd like to go up on deck for a while," Erith said. "Just to sit and enjoy the night air."

"Do you mind if I join you?" he asked teasingly.

"If I said no, would it matter?" Erith smiled playfully.

"Depends how long I'd have to get you to say yes." He winked.

"Makes me almost want to say no to find out." Erith laughed. He reached for her and she made a swat at him, feigning outrage. They fell into an easy conversation. She collected the dishes while he finished off his plate before he followed her up on deck. A light drizzle had started.

"Where are the packages, Danol? There's something I need."

"They're in the medical room. Tell me which one, and I'll get it for you."

"There are a lot," Erith said. "I'd like to get it myself."

"If you're sure. The room is on the way, but wait for me there."

Danol checked on the men while Erith went below. He caught up with her just as she was coming out of the medical room. "Got it," she whispered.

"It's only us back here," he said softly.

"I've never been in the main cabin before. You'll have to show me the way."

Danol took her hand and led her along the narrow hallway. The boat gently rocked beneath them. At the cabin door he told her to close her eyes. He opened the door and guided her in. Her chin lifted slightly as she caught a hint of something in the air.

"Okay, open your eyes."

He watched her face as her lids fluttered. Then her mouth dropped, and she stared wide-eyed at the scene before her. Danol smiled.

"Is this what took you so long?"

"Partly, yes. Do you like it?"

"I love it," Erith said. "Where did you get so many candles?"

"I must confess, all of this, or most of this, was Mary Ro's wedding gift to us," Danol said as he motioned around the room. "The candles, the pillows, the bedding . . . it was all her idea. She even placed them. She said I wouldn't understand." As he gazed upon her face, milky and shimmering in the glow of the candles, a visceral, raw, and primal emotion lay siege to him, almost taking his breath. A burning hot sensation gathered in the pit of his stomach and blazed through him. He tenderly touched her face with the tips of his fingers. Danol almost pulled back, so overcome was he by something foreign yet intoxicating and beguiling.

"But I think I do."

Danol stared, taking in every inch of his bride. "I hope you know how much I love you, Erith Cooper." He sighed. "I plan to tell you every day."

"I'm counting on that, more than you know," Erith said as she pressed tightly to him and buried her head in his chest. She trembled, and he tightened his embrace. He had to remind himself to breathe.

"The flowers were my idea. That was the secret Beatrice mentioned today. She helped me pick them out." Danol grabbed the floral bouquet from the table and handed them to Erith. She drew deeply on the scent of them.

"That's the nice smell that was in the air. They are beautiful, Danol."

"Nothing compared to you." He caressed her upturned lips with his thumb. Then he kissed her.

"I have one more room to show you," he said as he gently

pried his lips off hers. "As much as I'd like to have you in my arms all night, I believe that women have needs they must attend to. Mary kept beating that into my head for weeks leading up to the wedding."

Erith laughed. "She told me the same thing. Poor Mary and Peter. It didn't seem fair to leave everything to them."

"Mary's in her glee," Danol said. "She's probably bossing people around right now."

"Oh, Danol, if she ever heard you . . ."

"I know. I will always have a healthy fear of Mary Ro," he said. They both laughed. He wasn't kidding. But truth be told, Mary was the reason he had asked Erith to marry him. She was a good friend. He had been too stubborn to come to that conclusion on his own. Without Mary, Danol figured, he'd be alone for the rest of his life. He wouldn't be spellbound by whatever had taken over him right now. Right at this moment, he was glad he was kind of afraid of her. He grinned to himself and nuzzled the top of Erith's head.

"Danol, it might sound odd, but I feel so good about Beatrice. We had a lovely day. She is such a sweet child. Whatever the MacDonalds are mixed up in, they love her, and she loves them."

"She is indeed a beautiful child. There is no doubt that they love her." He wanted to say more but decided to wait for a better time. He guessed that Erith's intuition was aligned with his about the MacDonalds.

"Now, about that room," she said.

"Yes, the room."

He guided her around the table and chairs that were situated near the entrance to the cabin. A few steps farther on, he pushed on what could have been mistaken for a part of the wall but instead was the door to a small room fitted with a wash basin, a toilet, and running water from a barrel overhead. Danol had modernized it all on his last trip to Boston. An elegant table and matching wrought iron chair were nestled between two large oak closets. A small lamp cast a glow on the mirror with combs spread out on a fancy tray beneath it. The floor had a small, woven, multicoloured rug. Draped over the chair was the heavy flannel nightdress Erith had worn on their wedding night. A pair of slippers were pushed in beneath it. Candles burned on either side of the wash basin, and a jug of hot water scented by some sort of oil that smelled like wild roses sat in the corner.

"This is the best I could do," Danol said. "There was supposed to be a tub, for a steaming hot bath, but with the need to leave so quickly, it was overlooked."

"It's all beautiful, Danol." Erith pecked his lips, grabbed the package she'd fetched from the medicine room, and closed the door.

25

Danol put the fragrant lilies in a vase of water on the table and blew out some of the candles from the window ledge above the head of the large bed. He hoped the room wasn't threatening to her. Erith didn't need that after the day she'd had. He blew out the candles on the table and turned out the wicks of the lanterns in the corners of the room, leaving two candles burning on either side of the headboard so his bride could see where she was going. Pulling back the white lacy coverlet, another of Mary Ro's doings, he lay back on the pillows and waited for Erith to come out.

He must have dozed off, because he was startled when the latch clicked on the door. Erith was backlit by a lantern, and for a moment he thought she was shrouded in a fog. He was confused and shook his head. Then he noticed the flannel nightdress he had strung over the back of the chair was still there. His eyes fixed on her again.

A gasp escaped him, and he shot up from the bed. He stumbled for his boots, which he now realized were poorly placed, and kicked them to the side. "My God, you're a vision," he mouthed as he made his way toward Erith. The sky must have cleared, because the bluish splendour of the luminescent moon spilled through the windows above them and cloaked her in what could only be described as a halo. Flickering candlelight cascaded over her like a waterfall. It stroked the satin that barely covered her. She reached for him.

"If this is a dream, I'd better not wake up," he whispered. "Not now. Not ever."

Danol groaned when their fingers met and intertwined. What was happening to him? She moved closer, and it felt like her body seared him where they touched. His legs melted beneath him. He staggered backward, trying to stay upright.

Erith was moving with him, moving for him. The flames from the candles danced across her features, reflecting both fear and wonder in her wide-eyed naivety as she offered something sacred. The backs of his legs met the edge of the mattress.

"I'm tired of being afraid, Danol. I want to know the look that Mary and Peter share. I want to be your wife." Erith gently pushed him. She had total power over him. He reached for her as he fell back onto the bed. She was like a white-hot flame as candlelight shimmered across her on her way to him.

Her features softened in the moonlight. She was vulnerable—yet she was powerful. "Show me, Danol." Her breath was hot and soft on his ear. Her lips moved on the skin along his jawline. "Show me."

Danol was lost. The kind of lost he hadn't felt before. The kind that there was no finding his way back from. The kind that he didn't want to find his way back from. The kind of lost that, he suspected, only came with loving Erith Cooper. He wouldn't be the same again.

When he awoke, she was stirring against him. He opened

his eyes, and she was smiling shyly. Her cheeks reddened, and he reached out to tenderly stroke her face.

"What a beautiful vision to wake up to," he said. "Please tell me that I wasn't dreaming."

Erith leaned over and kissed him. Emboldened, she kissed him between each word. "It . . . was . . . not . . . a . . . dream . . ." Breathlessly, she moved her lips from his forehead to his eyes, his nose, his mouth. "I was wondering the same thing."

He grabbed her and rolled her on top of him. "Well, thank the heavens for that. I wouldn't be able to bear it." Danol grinned up at his beautiful wife. "By the way, it's a new day. I love you, Erith Cooper."

They showed up for breakfast long after the boat had left St. John's.

26

North Harbour, St. Mary's Bay

"The day Danol told me Beatrice was alive was everything that I had hoped for and made me very happy," Erith said. "If he had told me she died, I would have been sad and mourned her once more. If I had acted on the hope that I'd get her back without regard to anything else, I would have been thinking about myself."

Alice nodded. "But sometimes hope is all you have," she said. "It's what gets you through hard times."

"It certainly does," said Erith. "But sometimes it keeps you in hard times without you realizing it."

"So, does that mean that you had no hope of seeing Beatrice again?"

"Not at all, Alice. I look at hope as a privilege that requires great care in its use. If I had been lost in hope with constant thoughts of Beatrice, then I would have missed being part of the life of the three little children whom I love so much. I would have missed Danol. I would have made my children sad, Beatrice sad, and both of you sad, because that hope would have been about me."

"You must think me a fool," Alice said.

"Of course I don't," said Erith. "I am grateful every day that you saved Beatrice. I understand the fear. I thought about Beatrice every day from the day my stepmother gave her away. But I had to be careful that the thoughts didn't fill me and leave room for nothing else."

"Even with everything that is happening, you are not wary about her being with us?"

"Even with everything that is happening." Erith squeezed Alice's shoulder. "You can't hope for things to be different in the past because of how things have turned out. Hoping and wishing and worrying are all tangled up together. They can rob you more than you know."

"So, you're saying stop sitting here and fretting," Alice said. Erith nodded and smiled. Alice smiled, too. "How about I put some bread in rise for you today?"

"I would like that. The kids have been asking for sweetbread. Does Beatrice like sweetbread?"

"Very much so."

Together they got everything needed for the chore laid out on the table in the kitchen. "I'll leave you to it, Alice."

The girls ran in, donning their hats. "Mr. Danol and Daddy are taking George and Tommy over to the yellow house. They said we could go if we asked," Beatrice said hopefully.

Alice looked at Erith, but Erith didn't acknowledge the question in her eyes. "You go have fun," Alice said. "Stay out from underfoot, you hear? Do what your daddy tells you."

"Yes, Momma," Beatrice said.

Annie, her pigtails in disarray beneath her hat, skipped over toward Erith and hugged her leg. "I'm going with Danol. He said to tell you."

Erith bent and kissed her cheek before straightening her hat. "You do as Danol says."

"I will. Can I call him my new daddy now? Or maybe just Daddy."

"Why don't you ask Danol that question?" Erith said with a grin. Although she would like to be there to see Danol's reaction, she wouldn't discourage the child from doing it just because she wasn't present.

"Maybe later, over supper," Annie said absently. "Bye, Momma!" Annie and Beatrice held hands as they skipped and giggled their way out of the kitchen.

"Did you want to go?" asked Alice.

"No, I have things to pack away up here," Erith said as she nodded toward the stairs. "What about you?"

"I have bread to put in rise," Alice said with a smile.

At the front door, Erith waved at her family as they left the dock. Danol's smile was brilliant as he waved back. The two boys—George just turned fourteen, and Tommy eleven—had gathered around him, asking for directions on how they could help. He was a very patient man.

Erith and Danol had decided that Danol would move into the house with her while he finished everything he wanted to do with his own place. She wasn't allowed to go anywhere beyond the first floor, not even in Danol's room. She smiled, and her cheeks reddened, remembering what he told her they could do by the fire. Danol had big plans for the house, so he had told her. He wouldn't even let Mary Ro help him.

Erith watched them go. It was a beautiful day on the water. All the fishermen were out. By the look of the clotheslines on the other side of the harbour, the women were busy as well.

She turned and went inside and poked her head in the kitchen. "I'll be upstairs. If you need anything, just shout."

"I will," said Alice. "Where do you leave the bread to rise?"

"Over on the woodbox," Erith said. "Just enough heat there."

Erith went upstairs and began moving some of her things from the drawer to make room for Danol's clothes. She packed some towels for Alice and John to take with them to Danol's house. He had already set it up for John, Alice, and Beatrice. Mrs. Whalen had offered some bedding and got things ready for them. It was only their second day, but things seemed to be working out.

The curtain stirred on the open window. Erith listened to see if somebody had come for the mail, but there was no sound. Sitting on the edge of the bed, she pulled out another drawer. She'd bought too much the last time she was in St. John's. Lost in thought, she pulled the drawers in and out and moved things from one to the other. At this rate there would be no room for Danol's things. She needed another trunk.

Erith felt a waft of air on her neck. With short hair, this was something still new to her. She turned to see the sheer white lace curtain flowing out from the sill. "That's odd," she said. "There must be a door open. Hello? Is there somebody down there?" She listened. "Alice?"

She shuffled around the end of the bed toward the window. Maybe the wind had changed direction. Erith pulled back the curtains and grabbed the sill of the windowpane to close it. Movement from the backyard drew her attention, and she froze.

A tall, dark-haired man had his hand clamped on Alice's mouth and was dragging her along with him. They were almost out of sight behind the shed when Alice's eyes, wide with terror, met her own. Erith gasped. She bolted from the room, down the stairs, and into the shop. She scanned the walls for the guns. Seeing none, she combed the storeroom. Marie, the young girl who helped around the shop, must have stowed them away. Erith grabbed the tarp in the corner of the room and pulled it back. "Where are they, Marie?" she said. "Where would you have put them?" She began to panic when she couldn't find them. Turning to search the shop again, she almost collapsed in relief when she saw three rifles leaning against the corner behind the door.

She grabbed two and put them on the mail counter. The ammunition was always stored under the scales behind her. Thankfully, the boxes were still there. Erith put a bullet in each gun, grabbed one of them, and ran out on the step. Danol and John were pulling in the dory on the far side of the harbour. The children had already gone up the beach toward the house.

Erith fired a shot into the air and planned to wait for the sound to reach them. She forgot about the kick and fell back against the door frame before losing her footing and toppling over the step. Leaving the gun in the grass near the corner of the house, she clambered to the top of the stoop once again.

Danol and John stopped and looked toward her. She frantically waved her arms and saw them scramble aboard the dory before she went in to grab the other gun. Taking a fistful of the colourful glass candy from the jar on the counter, she stuffed them in her pocket. Her heart was pounding as she dashed through the back door in hopes of catching up with Alice and her captor. Maybe waving the gun would stop him.

The wind carried a coughing sound from the slide path heading into the woods. Erith dropped two candy and ran up the path toward the sound. The hill was steep, and her chest was heaving, but she forced herself to keep going. Alice was in trouble.

She reached a clearing where Tommy and George had cut wood the winter before. Pausing for a moment to get her breath, she wiped the sweat from her eyes. Erith felt ill at ease as she looked around the tangled area. A glimpse of blue caught her eye.

Immediately, she crouched low. She edged toward whatever it was that she'd seen. Perhaps George or Tommy had left a cap or something and this would delay her. But then she saw Alice lying behind a pile of blasty boughs.

Erith stumbled toward her. Tangled sticks and knotty stumps tripped her along the difficult terrain. She had almost reached Alice when the boughs rose up before her, and a giant of a man grabbed the gun from her hand. Erith screamed and lost her footing as a tree root caught her toes. The man made a swing at her but missed. She toppled backwards into more dried limbs, which knocked the wind out of her. She scrambled to get up, but the boughs had her wedged and she couldn't get her hands under her.

Ezra grabbed an unresponsive Alice and slung her over his shoulder. She moaned. Erith could see the bloodied cut above her eye and the red stains on her dress. Ezra stepped over the tangle of branches as if they were flowers in the meadow. Erith had not seen anyone so tall and muscled in all her days. She was struggling to get free when Ezra pitched Alice to the side, onto another pile of dead limbs, and raised the gun.

Erith's ears were pounding as Ezra fired the shot. He dropped the gun and crouched in waiting as both Danol and

John tackled him at the same time. They rolled together, and Ezra went backward onto the ground. John flew one way and Danol the other. Like a bear, Ezra rose up before John while Danol recovered. Danol scrambled to stand and ran at him, hitting Ezra in the midsection with his shoulder. At the same time, John had gotten himself close enough to swing a punch that struck the giant under the jaw. Ezra stumbled and fell near Erith, and both John and Danol leaped on him.

Erith's heart raced as she twisted, stretched, and wriggled, trying to get free of the boughs. Finally, she was able to get loose. Grunts and groans and the sound of fists hitting flesh filled the air as she stood. She saw the rifle in the bushes to her right and clambered across the brambles to get it, all the while praying she wouldn't fall again. She turned in time to see Ezra elbow John in the jaw and send him flying. He landed on his back with a hollow thud, unmoving, a few yards away. Ezra rolled and trapped Danol beneath him, grasping his throat with his huge hands. Danol clawed at the man's fingers and arms but to no avail.

Erith was petrified. She found a strength she didn't know she had and sprinted toward them, hurling herself over the boughs and limbs that had tripped her before. With all her might, she swung the butt of the gun down on the back of Ezra's head. He flinched and loosened his hold on Danol. Before she could take another swing, Alice brought a stick down on his skull from the other side.

They both pummelled Ezra, again and again, until he collapsed on top of Danol. Danol sucked in a breath and pushed the large man off of him. Erith helped him to his feet, and he grabbed her and hugged her fiercely. He put his hands to each side of her face and looked her up and down.

"My God, what were you thinking?" Danol said. He pulled her to him once more and squeezed her tight.

"I wasn't," said Erith.

Alice tripped on a stick as she staggered to check on John. He opened his eyes and managed to ease her fall on top of him. Alice cried and hugged him.

Danol held Erith away from him. "I need your apron," he said. She pulled the muddied and bloodied cloth over her head and gave it to him. He used it to tie Ezra's hands behind his back. "I need strips of your dress to bind him."

"Here, use this," Alice said as she pulled off her own apron and threw it toward him. John stood to help, and Danol secured Ezra's ankles.

Erith gasped and blanched as she put her hand to her mouth. She slowly reached for Danol's chest. "You've been shot," she said as she touched the bloodied material of his shirt.

"My blood," John said weakly. Alice screamed.

27

"Danol, Erith, where are you?"

"Is that Mary Ro?" Erith asked.

"Here in the cut-out," Danol shouted back. "Sounds like her."

"Mary, up here," Erith shouted. She looked at Alice. "Mary Ro's a doctor. She'll fix John."

John couldn't keep his legs under him any longer. Danol helped him to the ground.

Moments later, Doctors Mary and Peter Nolan, accompanied by six constables, rushed into the clearing. Mary's eyes were wild when she saw the blood on Danol's shirt.

"Did you get yourself shot again?" She felt along his rib cage.

Danol grimaced. "It's not my blood," he said. "At least not from a gunshot." He hugged Mary, and she put her arms around him.

"He's going to be the death of me," Mary said to Erith. She pushed away from him and went to Ezra as Peter tended to John.

"I see we arrived in time to save you," Constable Jeffries said as he shook Danol's hand.

"How? No, why are you here?" Danol asked him.

"It's a long story," Jeffries said. "I'll tell you when we get out of the woods."

"We have to get this man to the house," Peter said, looking up. "He needs attention right away."

Alice reached out and touched John as Peter and three of the constables picked him up. Danol helped her up and then let her go to assist John. Erith comforted Alice as they rushed toward the house. Mary caught up with them before they reached the back fence.

"Whichever of you gave him the cracks on the head, you didn't kill him," she said. "But you stopped him."

"It'll be me if he dies," Erith said in a low tone. "I allow the gun was harder than the stick."

"He attacked you. There's no question about that. He left a young girl in Holyrood in a bad way, so the constables said."

"Do you know who?" Alice asked Mary.

"No. The constables said it happened at the post office."

Alice began to bawl. "This is all my fault!"

"This is the fault of that man back there," Mary told her sternly. "You're safe now."

John moaned, and Alice walked beside the men carrying him.

"Where did you come from?" Erith asked Mary.

"We were coming to meet the children on the other side. At the top of the hill we heard the shot and knew something was wrong. We met the constables on the wharf in front of the house and followed Danol and John to the ridge."

Mary put her arm around Erith as they walked out. "You did good, Erith."

At the house, Peter said to Erith, "Kitchen table. Will that be a problem?"

Erith shook her head. "It's fine," she said. Peter and Mary had saved Danol's life on that table a few years before. Erith remembered the horrible circumstances that had brought Danol close to death's door. At the time, she had blamed herself. She had to choose between him and the boys, and deep down she had known that he wouldn't want it to be a choice. That was when she knew she loved him.

Danol found her after he'd seen to John. He always came to find her. His warm embrace and soothing words would see her through anything. "You need to change your clothes," he said. "Maybe find something for Alice." He signalled to where Alice stood facing the kitchen door, covered in dirt and John's blood.

"I will. You should change, too," Erith said as she looked her husband over.

"I'll go first, then I'll speak to Jeffries." He quickly kissed her and took the stairs two at a time while she went to talk to Alice.

"He'll have the best care," Erith said. "You can stay here as long as you want."

Alice hugged her. "Why are you so kind to me?"

"I've been at that door, Alice. I was alone. I want you to know that you are not alone."

Danol came down the stairs and brushed past them on his way out to the shop, where the constables had gathered. He gently squeezed Erith's arm as he went.

"Now, let's go get you out of those things before John sees you," Erith said. Alice smiled half-heartedly and reluctantly turned to follow her upstairs. "Waiting there won't make it go any faster."

"I know, but what if something happens?"

"We'll be right there."

28

"The bullet is out," Mary Ro said when she came to speak to Alice and Erith. "He's going to be sore for a week or two, but he should make a full recovery."

Alice sucked in a deep breath and reached for Erith, who helped her to a chair. "Can I see him?" she asked.

"Not yet," Mary said. "We still have a bit of cleaning up to do." She looked at Erith. "Where's Danol? We need help to move him. Or even one of the constables would be fine."

"I made a place in the storeroom for him," Erith said before Mary could ask. "Danol's outside with the children. I'll get him. The constables have all gone."

"I'd better get back. Peter is finishing up."

Mary eased back through the kitchen door, and Erith left in search of Danol.

Alice rested her back on the wall and wrung her hands around one another in an attempt to ease her mind. She had brought so much trouble to these people. It seemed like no matter where she went or how hard she tried, if it wasn't one thing, it was another calamity following her. Someone, somewhere, was keeping track of her sins, and there were many. As soon as she'd let herself think that things were going to work out, something else was thrown at her.

In her past life, when she was Nancy Martin, her father had put her and Irene on the Labrador floater boats when she'd been barely fourteen, and Irene fifteen. She remembered him coming into the house and shouting to their mother, "Belle, come here! It's written here."

Alice's mother was upstairs and had just put baby Michael in the cot. They had nine girls before he got his first son, and Irene was the eldest.

"What are you wailing about, Cyril?"

He handed her the *Twillingate Star*. "Look here, Belle, the girls can go on the boats now." He slapped the newspaper on the table and pulled out the chair for her to sit. "All these hungry mouths. It's time. Old Albert Pearce, the collector at the custom house, posted that there would be privacy for the women on the floaters or the owners would pay a hundred-dollar fine."

"You must be mistaken, Cyril. Not unlike you to get things mixed up."

"Read it for yourself, woman. It's right there!"

"How would you know? You can't read," said Belle.

"Carl told me, that's how," Cyril said. "Carl said he allowed that because I had so many girls I'd be interested in this fact."

"Did he, now? And did you tell Carl to mind his own business?"

"Now, Belle. Don't go getting on like that. He was just saying, that's all."

*T*HE LIARS

"I hope he don't go sending that good-for-nothing crowd that he's rearing up here after my girls. Maybe he thought they'd make some money and be a good catch for Simon or Archie."

"Well, Archie is sweet on Nancy," Cyril added. "She could do worse."

"Worse than Archie? Near impossible around here," Belle said as she turned the paper over to read.

The headline read, "Notice to Schooner Holders."

"*Sailing vessels carrying females engaged as servants in the fishery or as passengers between Newfoundland and Labrador shall be provided with such separate cabin or apartments as will afford at least fifty cubic feet for each of such females, and the owners of such vessels shall provide for such females sufficient accommodation for sanitary purposes.*"

Mrs. Martin drummed her fingers on the table. Nancy was putting bread in rise, and Irene was washing clothes. "You girls hearty enough to cook for seven or eight men?"

"Suppose they are, Belle. They cook here," their father said.

"Yes, Cyril, but cooking for a bunch of hungry men is a lot different."

Nancy spoke first. She had no intention of staying in Ragged Head and marrying Archie Barnes. That's what her father would have her do. Archie Barnes, of all people! She could see herself doing everything that her mother did and everything her father did because Archie was as lazy as a cut ram. Just like his father. Carl had worn out three women and was on his fourth. The other three were glad to be dead, she reckoned.

"I can do it, Momma," she said.

"It's a rough life, girl. Nothing to be taken without some thought."

"I can do it, too," Irene said. She looked at Nancy and winked. Both girls had had more than one talk by the light of the lamp about getting out of Ragged Head. Neither knew how to do it, aside from running away, and they were just shy of plans to do that. They'd have been out in service a few years before but for the fact that there were lots of girls in Ragged Head, and her mother had a crowd of small young ones and needed help herself.

Neither one wanted to sound too eager to go. "Whatever you say, Momma," they both said in unison.

"We could use the money, Belle. There are lots of floaters out of Twillingate. They wouldn't even need to go ashore in Labrador. The boats go up north and come back. The girls are handy at the cooking and at the fish."

"I'm not saying yes, but . . . what would I do here with you two gone?"

"Lucy can make bread as good as any," Nancy said.

"She can do the washing, too," Irene put in.

"See what you can find out, Cyril. Maybe nobody's looking."

"They're looking, all right. Pearce at the custom house said he knows of five who are in desperate need. All the men will be at the fish. Nothing left for them only to hire women."

Belle looked from Nancy to Irene. "I'm not saying yes just yet."

29

The next day, she did. Nancy was looking forward to a great adventure with Irene. Trouble was the cabin turned out to be a bunk behind a curtain. The hours were long. She had to gut the fish when she wasn't cooking or cleaning dishes. Although she didn't see her sister for the few weeks they were gone, she later learned that Irene had it worse. To add to her misery, she was seasick.

But after the first trip, staying home and making bread wasn't as agreeable as she thought it would be. Irene moved to a larger schooner, where she fared much better. That one landed in Nain, where she met Paul. Irene was smitten. During the last trip of the fall, Irene stayed in Labrador, married Paul, and moved to Zoar.

Nancy followed her the next spring after spending a winter being chased by Archie Barnes and listening to her father's tirades about Labrador. Their father had been livid over Irene's choices and refused to let Nancy go the next spring. He had insisted she accept Archie's offer of marriage. He told her she wouldn't get one better.

Nancy got aboard the first schooner heading north and didn't look back. She stayed with Irene, and that led to her relationship with Paul's brother.

Nancy, now Alice, drew in a long breath. *Look how that had turned out for Philip.* Thanks to Ezra, she'd lost a husband. She took a big gulp of air to suppress a sob. Maybe she'd lost Irene, too. The constables said they didn't know. Although she hadn't seen her sister in years, Alice considered Irene the only family she had besides Beatrice and John.

She didn't know when John had become family. She didn't believe she had loved Philip. Not like Irene had loved Paul. She had to marry him or she'd have nowhere to go. Nancy liked spending time with him, and he was good company in the beginning. In many ways they grew up together over the two years they were married. Although she was sad that he had died—and because of *how* he had died—she chose not to dwell on their life together. She took care of what needed to be taken care of when she left Zoar all those years ago.

Alice wasn't quite sure how or why John MacDonald had followed her. He was kind enough. He'd saved her from the bear. She thought he would leave her in Hopedale, but they spent the night there in the woods in an abandoned hut on the outskirts of the town. The boat had tried to reach the settlement but failed to break through the heavy sea ice. They would have to go on to Makkovik where the boat was located—another day by sled.

She overheard the merchant tell John that there had been a lot of thievery and unsavoury characters on the coast and that he hadn't seen it as bad as he had in the last two years.

He said it was getting such that he couldn't trust anyone. John asked a few questions, bought some provisions, and had been quiet the rest of the night.

When they arrived at the store in Makkovik, she recalled, John refused to take her money for the ticket.

"I have money," John said.

"Yes, but it's not mine," Nancy replied.

"You will need it more than I will." That led her to believe that he wasn't going—not that she even thought he would. They entered the store and overheard a crowd talking.

"That's right, Ike, isn't it?" asked one man.

"Yes, Norm. Hard to say who is good and who is up to no good," Ike responded.

"You take Lindy, now. If he had sold his fish to that first bunch that came along, I'd say he'd be wiped out last year."

"Good thing we got word that there were fellows taking off with the fish and not providing any supplies," Ike went on.

"Imagine that," another man cut in. "Hard to trust those merchants to do right by us, but now that the pirates are around, it's hard to trust anyone. You heard me, they're nothing but a bunch of pirates."

"You're right, Will. Look at what happened there on George's Island. That had to be pirates, or unsavoury characters, at best," Norm said, nodding.

"Something shocking, that was," Ike said. "Terrible."

"They says there was a fellow got clear," Norm said. "Did you hear that?"

"Word came down that fall from Indian Harbour, I believe it was."

"I believe you're right, Ike."

"Don't say we'll ever know, I allow."

"I suppose you're right."

"Can I help you, sir?" the storekeeper asked as he twisted to see over the men who stood between them.

The others moved aside to let John through, mumbling their apologies.

"He could be one of the pirates, right there," Ike said in jest.

John stiffened. He stopped, turned to Ike, and stared at him.

"That's enough, boys," the storekeeper said. "They didn't mean any harm, mister."

"No, sir," said Ike. "Just flapping our gums, that's all."

John nodded and walked to the counter.

"Seen you around a few winters ago, I believe," the storekeeper said. "You're usually farther north." John didn't respond but just stared at the man. When he realized John wasn't going to answer, he looked past him toward Nancy. "How can I help you?"

"Do you sell tickets for the boat?"

"Yes. Do you want one for you and one for the missus?"

John turned back toward Nancy. He paused for a few moments before taking money from his coat. He nodded and asked the price.

"I have dogs and a sled that I won't be needing. Can I get a fair price?"

They bartered back and forth before settling on a price that was agreeable to them both.

John left the store and offered Nancy a ticket on the way out. They walked to the dock in silence and boarded the boat shortly after noon. She didn't ask why he was going, and he didn't offer. A few days later, after some anxious moments for her trying not to be seen in Twillingate, they ended up in Gambo. There was only one room available at the hotel. The clerk signed them in as Mr. and Mrs. MacDonald.

They had known each other for almost eight days, and most of those had been spent in silence. She had become Alice to him and to everyone from then on. The next morning, they left Gambo to head to St. John's. The boat made a stop in Conception Bay, and John seemed like he was desperate to get off the ocean and onto land. They caught the train in Harbour Grace to go to St. John's. She hadn't seen a train, but she had heard talk of the railway in Twillingate and Ragged Head a few summers before.

The events of that day had changed their lives and led them here, and somewhere along the way, Alice had come to love John MacDonald. However, he hadn't known her secrets, and she was sure she didn't know his. They had Beatrice, and that seemed to be enough.

She remembered it well. When they arrived in Whitbourne, they were told the train was going to be delayed and that they could get off. Her mind was tossed.

There were so many people milling around at the station and on the streets. Alice didn't know that the ruckus and the crowds were there for a special occasion and that the scene before her wasn't a normal day for the train. There were bands and speeches because the town was renaming the stop from Harbour Grace Junction to Whitbourne. This meant nothing to her, and standing there in all the commotion with the excited crowd on the wooden platform, she had, for a brief moment, forgotten her troubles. That was when the priest came up to her.

"Are you travelling to St. John's?" he asked. His voice was high-pitched. The fidgeting and his knitted brow told her he was troubled. A baby was crying loudly in the basket he was carrying.

Alice didn't know how to address him, so she merely said, "Yes."

"Could I trouble you to mind the baby while we travel. I'll pay you. The lady who was supposed to come with me hasn't shown. All this noise is bothering the baby." The priest was pushing the basket toward her.

"Maybe she is here in the crowd," Alice stammered.

"I don't think so. She was supposed to be here yesterday. All the hotels are booked for this." He motioned to the crowd. "I don't think she's here."

Alice moved to take a peek at the baby. "Do you have diapers for her? She's probably wet and hungry."

"I don't know," said the priest. "The other lady would have looked after that for me."

"Did you feed her?"

"I suppose she was fed when I got her," he said. "How often would she eat?"

"When did you get her?" Alice asked. John came to see what was going on.

"Early this morning."

"And you haven't done anything with her since?"

"No. Should I have?" asked the priest.

"Let me take her," Alice said.

The priest laid the basket on the wooden walkway and pulled money from his coat. "Here, get what she needs at the store," he said. "I don't normally do this, as you can tell."

Alice picked up the baby first. Her blanket was wet right through.

"Oh, you poor little thing," she said as she laid the baby on her shoulder. The infant squealed louder. Alice jockeyed her up and down and made cooing noises. She took a wad of money from the priest, who looked like he would have given her anything to take the baby. With John at her heels, she entered the store. The baby couldn't be consoled. She went to hand the bundle to John, but he refused to take her.

"I need diapers and milk and bottles," Alice said, pushing money toward him. He looked from the money to the baby and back again. Reluctantly, he took the baby from her and awkwardly held her away from him.

"I might hurt her."

"You will if you hold her like that," Alice said. "Here, put her in the crook of your arm instead of in your palms. The baby will feel the comfort."

"Are you sure?" John asked as Alice fixed the baby on his arm.

"I'm sure." She paused for a moment before finishing. "I'm second-eldest of ten."

Alice raced off to the counter in search of supplies. The storekeeper, a lady twice Alice's age, told her to take the baby in the supply room to change her. "It will be quieter for everyone if you're in there," she said with a grin. "I'll get some warm water for the milk."

Before long, Alice found out the baby definitely was a girl and that she was soaked through her clothing. One of the blankets had words on it. She hid that one from the storekeeper when she brought the milk. Alice sat on a sack of oats and watched the child gulp down the warm liquid. She coughed a few times when she drank too fast, and Alice burped her. She picked up a few more dry blankets to swaddle the child before she returned to the platform. The train whistle blew, and the priest rushed toward her.

"I beg your pardon," he said. "I need to know if you can watch the child on the train before I can get on."

Alice wasn't quite sure why he would ask, but she looked at John. He nodded, and she agreed.

The priest reached for John's hand. "Thank you, mister," he said.

"MacDonald. John MacDonald." John shook the man's hand.

"Well, Mr. and Mrs. MacDonald. You have saved me a great deal of trouble."

Alice held the baby in her arms while on the train. The child kept her mind occupied, and for once she didn't have to think of Philip or Ezra. She just had to think of this little one.

"What's her name?" Alice asked.

"I didn't know it was even a girl at first," the priest replied. "The mother didn't want the child."

Alice thought she felt John stiffen beside her, but she couldn't be sure.

"What's on this blanket?" Alice untangled one of the wet layers that had been closest to the child and held it up to him. John took it from her and spread it out. He carefully held it between fingers and thumbs so he would have the least amount of contact with the wet material.

The priest inspected it from the seat facing them. "This is Beatrice, she was loved," he said. "Hmm, so her name is Beatrice."

"Beatrice," Alice said. "What a beautiful name for such a little angel." She rocked the child and cooed to her, whispering her name over and over again. John just looked on.

The priest didn't engage in conversation until they were getting closer to Holyrood. "Are you in a hurry to get to St. John's?"

"Not really," said John.

"I'm wondering if you would consider staying in Holyrood for the night." He looked anxiously from one to the other. "I will put you up at Veitch's Hostel and get your train tickets for tomorrow. I'd be extremely grateful."

He reached in his jacket pocket and pulled out a small blue velvet bag. Once he opened the bag, he offered John money to cover expenses for the bed and meals for the night. He took some extra bills and handed them to Alice. "You can get the child whatever she needs with that," he said.

The priest began to pull on his collar and fan himself as the train slowed to a stop in Holyrood. The light streaming through the window showed a sheen of sweat glistening on his forehead. He stood up and staggered before he grabbed hold of the rail on the back of his seat.

When Alice rose to follow the priest, John collected the basket from the rack above them. Alice noticed the holy man had left the blue bag behind and pointed it out to John. He picked it up and followed the priest, who had already stepped down on the platform. John turned, she guessed, to see if she needed help with the baby. Suddenly, a commotion outside drew their attention, and moments later, they looked down upon the struggling priest, Alice saw John slip the blue sack into his pocket.

Somebody called for a doctor. Another directed the surrounding crowd to move him to the hotel. John helped, and Alice followed.

The train left, and they waited. The unlikely duo had grown by one in a matter of a day. People referred to them as Mr. and Mrs. MacDonald. The priest succumbed to his illness and was sent to St. John's on the train the next morning. There was a car for his body, accompanied by some pastoral members of the church who had shown up to escort him.

They waited two more days before realizing that nobody else was coming for the baby. By this time Alice had grown so attached to Beatrice, she knew she wouldn't give her up. Looking after the baby helped her forget her troubles. The Veitches told them about a farm, and it was settled. John paid a summer's rent with the money from the blue bag.

As quickly and as easily as that, they were man and wife and daughter to the outside world. Alice figured John would tire of it, but he grew to love Beatrice as much as she did. Neither one had asked anything of the other. Though they'd shared a room on occasion for appearances, they hadn't shared a bed. John hadn't asked, and she hadn't offered. She'd been tempted on cold, snowy nights in the winter, when she was particularly lonesome and yearned for the warmth of a man, but she didn't want to lose what she had. She was afraid that if she tried to change things, they might change too much and she'd lose Beatrice.

Alice didn't know anything about Ezra, nor what happened to him, and she didn't want to. She wanted to hide from her whole complicated past and not think about what she'd lost and given up.

Her one attempt to let Irene know where she was had led to the downfall of her peculiar family situation and the fragile roots they had planted, as well as the possible death of her sister. It was conceivable that she would lose everyone that she cared about, all because of her selfish act.

Erith joined her a short time later, drawing Alice out of her reverie. Several men from the harbour who had gathered outside came to move John. Once he was made comfortable on the bed that Erith had fixed up in the storeroom, Alice took Beatrice to see him. Danol had kept the child busy with the other children while the doctors were working on their patient.

Beatrice cried in Alice's arms as she gazed upon the man whom she knew as her father. Alice had been shocked when Erith told her what had happened when Erith was barely sixteen. She had been assaulted and became pregnant as a result. In spite of the circumstances, though she fell in love with her new baby. But in the end, Beatrice had been taken from Erith by her stepmother and given away!

Alice told John about the situation, and somehow he seemed relieved. They both had taken a liking to Danol and Erith and shared a whole new outlook on them now.

Who was she to cast judgment? Alice had to but look at her own life and all the mistakes she had made. Her doubt made her wonder if she should give Beatrice back to her mother. Maybe it was the right thing to do. But sitting here with the little girl snuggled in her arms, crying for the man who had been more of a father to her than most would have been, Alice didn't care what she thought was the right thing to do—she simply loved the child. She hoped that would be enough.

30

John grew stronger every day. He enjoyed Alice's company. Beatrice, tired of keeping watch, chose to play with her new friend, Annie. The two little girls ran in and out several times each day. John worried about what would happen now that things had been settled for Alice.

Danol Cooper brought news that Ezra was back in the jail, where he would finish out his sentence under close watch until the time he would be hanged.

"I wonder how things would have turned out if Beatrice hadn't come home from school that day and mentioned the prisoner being on the loose?"

"I don't even want to think about that, John. I always thought he was free," Alice said. "I hid for years without need. He was already in jail."

"You're free now, Alice," John said. "Ezra can't hurt you. What will you do?"

"I don't know. What will *we* do? Will we go back to Holyrood?"

"Is that what you want?"

"What do you mean?"

"You're free, Alice. You're free." He watched her expression change from confusion to realization.

"I'm free. Do you want me to be free?" she asked hesitantly. "We have Beatrice. What are you asking?"

"I'm not asking anything, Alice. I don't have the right."

"I don't know what that means," Alice said.

"I've done things, Alice."

"I've done things, too, John. I don't want to know. That's not my right."

John wanted to tell her that he wasn't a good person. He wanted to tell her everything, but he couldn't. If he told her, he'd lose her. He was sure of that. He could continue to live as they were living. Having some of her was better than having none of her at all. But he wanted it to be her choice.

"We can go back to Holyrood, if that's what you want," he said slowly.

"I like it here, John." Alice paused and stared at him. "I like people, you know. I forgot that I liked people," she said. "But we can't stay here. It's too complicated with Beatrice. She has friends in Holyrood. Maybe we could, too."

"That would be nice, Alice." She could make friends in Holyrood, but he'd remain on the outskirts of the town—and of life. Things would be different now that Alice could get to living again. He could bear that if she was happy.

Maybe he could take some small steps that he'd been putting off. He still carried a letter he hadn't delivered. Maybe Alexander MacDonald was dead. Perhaps it was too late. But he owed it to the rightful owner of his name to try. He wasn't risking anything that had to do with Alice. The only threat he carried was to himself. Maybe, like Alice's situation, this would work out, too.

He was up and about a few days later. The doctor dropped by every couple of days. Alice made sure he followed her orders. A lady doctor. Who would have guessed? John liked her just fine, and she seemed to know what she was doing.

He sensed a change in Alice. She was more relaxed, and their conversations were comfortable. They told the Coopers of their plan to return to Holyrood. Beatrice was sad to leave her new friends, but Alice agreed, after talking to Erith, that she could come back and visit them later in the summer.

31

St. John's

It was Teddy White and not John MacDonald who stood quietly on the steps of the small single-storeyed house on Empire Avenue. The surroundings were as familiar as if he'd never left the place that had once been home to him. Upon further inspection, he noticed the house needed a coat of paint and the fence needed repair. He raised his hand to knock, then quickly lowered his arm. He stood for another moment taking in the surroundings. The bees buzzed, and the soft rustle and movement of the flowers meant something was approaching. A loud mewl alerted him before the old orange tomcat pitched near his boots.

The shuffle of feet from inside the door sent him back to the bottom of the steps. He looked up when the door opened.

"There you are, boy! I thought you'd never come home. Mustn't have caught any mice . . ." The old man's voice trailed off when he saw Teddy. "Can I help you, sir?"

Instant memories of this man and his son, John, flooded through Teddy's head. It took the wind out of him as if he'd been punched in the gut. He didn't speak. He couldn't. Why had he come here?

"Mister, are you lost?" Mr. MacDonald asked. The old man stared at him. His brows furrowed. "Do I know you? Is that you, Ted?" He paused a moment and sized him up. "Well, merciful God, it *is* Ted!"

Mr. MacDonald came down the step toward Teddy. Tears brimmed in Teddy's eyes. The old man grabbed him and put his frail arms around him, tenderly clapping him on the back. "Come in, son. Tell me where you've been all these years. I thought you were both dead."

Teddy believed his tongue had swollen or maybe his jaw was clenched too tight, because he couldn't get a word out. Memories of time spent with the man who had become more of a father to him than any he'd known tumbled around in his head. Mr. MacDonald took his hand for him to follow. Teddy helped him navigate the step. He could feel the tension subside as he allowed warm memories about this place and this man to permeate his senses.

"Mr. MacDonald, I wanted to talk to you about John. I'm sorry, sir. I have bad news."

The old man looked at him intently. "Bad news is better than no news, Ted. I've been stagnating in the hope that I'd see my sons again, and here you are."

Teddy halted. His voice cracked when he spoke. "I couldn't bring him home to you this time." The old man stiffened as he led his adopted son inside.

"You came home to me," said Mr. MacDonald. Tears glinted in the old man's eyes.

Teddy stayed for hours and purged his soul of everything that had happened. Talking was a pulley that lifted the weight from his chest. He could breathe again.

He spoke about Alice and Beatrice. They hugged, and

T*HE LIARS*

Teddy promised to return again soon. Mr. MacDonald invited him to move back home with his family.

"I won't live forever, Ted. I'd like to spend some happy times before I go. I hope you can consider it, for the sake of this weary old man."

"I'll talk to Alice," Teddy said. "Would you consider a life away from the city?"

The old man looked at him. "I'll ponder on that."

Teddy whistled a tune as he left the house.

32

The night was unusually dark as Teddy, now living the life of John MacDonald, made his way from Empire Avenue toward the docks and the *Angel Endeavours*. The slivered moon hung behind rolling clouds, creating ghostly shadows in the ebony of the evening. Faint sounds of laughter and murmured words from the lighted windows echoed in the still air. This was familiar to him and brought back memories of his years on the street as a boy.

Being with Mr. MacDonald filled his head with thoughts of his friend John. He smiled to himself. John was his best friend, probably his only friend. He thought about his days with Lavinia. She hadn't crossed his mind in years. His solitary existence had changed with Alice and, soon after, with Beatrice.

Now that the Ezra affair was settled and he'd finally spoken to John's father, things could quieten down. Maybe he could take Cooper up on his job offer and move to St. Mary's Bay. He was here with them on this trip to try it out. Although he'd been young and hardy when he first took to the boat, he now realized how much he missed the sea life. Perhaps even real life. He missed being around people. Maybe that could change now. Maybe he was hiding for nothing.

When he reached the cobblestoned streets, he made up his mind that he'd talk to Alice. Although she spoke of returning to Holyrood, maybe she would welcome a change. Funny how he didn't think of a life without Alice. They had both needed something from each other that was no longer important. He didn't want to lose her and Beatrice.

Lost in thought, he was surprised by the footsteps that came quickly behind him. Before he could turn around, someone pulled a sack over his head, and at least two people grabbed him by the arms to hold him fast.

"Hello, Whitey. It's been a long time." He felt a chill course through him. He refused to fight; he'd take whatever was coming. They could have killed him in the street, so he figured he'd take his chances on them wanting something from him.

One time, he wouldn't have been taken. He'd fight to come out on top. That's what had kept him alive. A lot of things had changed since the old days on these same streets. Not fighting now might be what kept him alive.

They led Teddy from the street. He tripped several times but was buoyed up by those on either side. They manhandled him going through narrow paths, probably between houses or buildings. By their grip, he could tell they were at least his height, and their movements suggested they were strong and hefty. They walked half a mile before stopping, a door creaked, and he was pushed forward. Within moments he was dropped in a corner on what felt like straw. Barn smells wafted around him. The whinny of horses confirmed his location.

He didn't try to remove the sack. He was here for a reason, and he'd hear it out. There were whispers and rustling of boots in straw and scuffs across the wood before the same voice said, "Got nothing to say, hey, Whitey?"

"What do you want?" he asked steadily.

"Right to the point. That's what I always liked about you." The horses stomped in their pounds near him. The wood quivered beneath him. Somebody grabbed him and stood him up.

"Are you scared, Whitey?"

"What do you want?" he repeated.

"Maybe you should be scared for that wife and the little girl of yours."

Teddy felt the heat rise inside him. His jaw tensed, but he forced himself not to show any reaction. He was tempted to throw off the mask and start swinging. "Don't know what you're talking about," he said calmly. It was dark in the barn. He saw the movements of at least three men, maybe four, passing back and forth in the shadows between him and some distant lantern. None were recognizable in the blackness, and he couldn't place the voice.

"I knew you didn't perish on the Labrador."

"You mean I wasn't murdered on the Labrador," Teddy said. One of the figures punched him in the midsection, which caused him to double over. He coughed, staggered, and stood again.

"That was for my cousin."

"How is McPherson, anyway?" Teddy asked. He managed to clench the muscles in his stomach before he got the next punch. He righted himself again. "What do you want? I'm sure you're not here to talk about old times." He braced for the next hit, but it didn't come.

There was a hushed conversation, and then a different voice said, "Heard you're in league with this Cooper fellow."

"What of it?" It was no good denying it. They knew a lot about him.

"We have plans for his boat."

"What kind of plans?"

"Let's just say that the captain wants to expand his fleet." Snickers from the others caused the horses to stir. They snorted and stomped as they moved restlessly about in the pound.

"What's that to do with me?"

"A couple of the crew have had a bit of an accident, leaving Cooper short-handed. You and our boy, Willy McPherson, are going to step in." A clap on the back must have been for Willy.

"And if I don't?"

"Well, Whitey, let's just say that wife and girl of yours won't be in mourning for too long before they join you."

"What's in it for me?" Teddy asked.

"Maybe a cut of the loot we pull from the hold."

"And what do I do after that?"

"Maybe we let you live." He took another punch to the gut.

"Maybe I want a place on the boat," Teddy said.

"Now we're talking," Willy McPherson said. "Once a gutter rat, always a gutter rat."

"Got to look out for myself," said Teddy. "Nobody else's going to do it."

"Told you," Willy said.

"How do we know he won't turn on us as he did with your cousin?"

"I didn't turn on McPherson," Teddy argued. "He never let us in on the plan and fired first. Took us along because he thought us to be green. But where did that get him? A place on the beach beside the crew."

"I *knew* you killed him," Will said. He struck Teddy again and kicked him once he went down.

"Enough," the other man said. He pulled Willy away. "Is what he's saying right, Willy?"

Willy waited a moment before speaking. "Whitey's telling the truth. Jimmy started shooting before I knew what was happening. Shot the two brothers first. That didn't give you the right to kill him, Whitey."

Teddy braced for the next kick. He rolled into the corner and pulled himself up to a sitting position. "I got the scar to prove it," he said. "It was him or me then." He wanted to change the conversation. McPherson's cousin was out for blood. "How'd you find me?"

"Got friends everywhere, Whitey. Fellow saw you a few months ago. Have a bone to pick with Cooper. Imagine our surprise when you showed up together."

"I can't stand the man," said Teddy. "Mite uppity for my liking. The wife had dealings with his missus, not me. I'm enjoying not scraping for leftovers, that's all."

"Told you," Willy said. "Paid for a couple of jobs that he wouldn't want anyone finding out about, either."

They questioned Teddy some more before devising a plan.

"The wife will be getting off in the morning with the girl," he said. "Your word that no harm will come to them. I'll hunt you down if anything happens. McPherson, you'll be first." He received another fist to the jaw and then a kick to the gut. He coughed a few times before he could catch his breath. "Beat me all you like. They get off and are not harmed, or kill me now and there's no deal."

There was a hushed conversation that he couldn't make out. "You cross the captain and you'll regret it."

"I won't cross anyone but Cooper," Teddy replied.

"Wait a considerable length of time before untying that sack. Remember, we'll be watching."

Teddy sat in the corner for a while and rubbed his midsection. He untied the sack and threw it over the stall. The horse sidled and stomped its displeasure.

Once a good-for-nothing, always a good-for-nothing. He didn't know why he thought he deserved anything better than the gutter. Tonight would be the last he'd see of Alice and Beatrice. No matter how this turned out, he couldn't risk their lives. Alice had just got done with running, and he wouldn't ask nor expect her to do it again. He rose from the dirt, got his bearings, and realized it was the Jacksons' stables, where his beloved Lavinia had perished at the hands of her accuser. He bowed his head, turned, and walked back to the ship. Teddy could no longer deny his past. His fate was sealed. One time, that wouldn't have bothered him.

33

Danol was glad he had left Erith home on this trip. She didn't want him to go, and the truth was he wanted to stay home, too. If she were here, he'd be too distracted. He was responsible to return John, Alice, and Beatrice to St. John's, where they were getting the train back to Holyrood. They were going to take some time at their home to decide whether they would move or stay put.

Danol offered John a job if he wanted one. From what he saw of him working on the boat between North Harbour and St. John's, Danol thought John would make a good crewman for either of his vessels—the *Angel Endeavours*, if they moved closer to him and Erith, or the new boat he had bought for shipping iron ore from Bell Island, if they chose to stay in Holyrood. Either way, Danol was sure things would work out.

"Uncle Danol," Eddy Nolan said, "somebody's here to see you."

"Who is it?"

"A constable," Eddy replied.

"A constable?"

Eddy nodded. Alice poked her head out the door of the cabin as they passed. "Have you seen John?" she asked. "It's getting late, and he said he wouldn't be gone long."

"No, but I'm going up on deck now. If I see him, I'll tell him you are looking for him."

"No, that's all right. Can't help but worry, been doing it for years."

Danol smiled. "Your worrying days are over, Alice."

"Old habits," she said. "Old habits."

Danol left her and went up into the night air. "Ah, Jeffries," he said. "Good to see you. What brings you around here to-night?" Danol held out his hand to welcome the man aboard.

"Just following up on the note you left me," Jeffries said. He took some papers from his pocket and handed them to Danol. "There are a lot of newspaper clippings there, too. It's all I could find."

Danol reached for the envelope and looked at the name on it. "Oh, yes. I forgot I asked you about that."

"Some interesting items in there," Jeffries offered.

Shouts from the wharf interrupted them. "Cooper, Cooper!"

Danol and Jeffries ran to the side rail of the boat. "What the devil," Danol said as he eyed the scene below. "What the hell happened?" he shouted.

His men were coming up the gangway, bedraggled, blood-ied, and bruised. They all started talking over each other. "One at a time. Hearn, what happened?" Danol asked. He did a head count. "Where's Walsh and Power?"

"We were coming out of the bar, heading back to the boat, when we were jumped by a bunch of men," Hearn said.

"Did you have words with them inside?" Danol asked. "Maybe somebody had too much to drink."

"No, sir," Hearn replied. "We only had the one. We knew we were sailing in the morning."

"Well, where's Power and Walsh?"

"We carried them to the Riverview Hospital," Dalton said. "Power's got a broken leg, and Walsh got a busted arm. They'll be there for a week or more."

Danol couldn't believe what he was hearing. "So, out of nowhere, and for no reason, these men started a fight."

"Swear it's true, Captain," Hearn said.

"There were a few robberies when we were chasing that prisoner," Jeffries said. "But this seems even bolder than that."

"Was MacDonald with you?" Danol asked.

"No, sir, he went out before supper," Dalton said.

"Suppose nothing has happened to him," Danol said to Jeffries.

Moments later, John MacDonald came aboard. When he came into the light of the lanterns, Hearn asked, "What happened to you?"

John looked them up and down and said, "I should be asking *you* that."

They explained the fight and told him about Walsh and Power's condition.

"I ran into an old friend," John said. "He was looking for work down here. He'll be back again in the morning. I left him a while ago, and on the way back I was set upon by these three young men." John rubbed his belly. "I'm not as young as I used to be."

"Check in with Alice," Danol said. "She's worried."

John nodded. "I will." He walked away with the other men but then turned and came back to Danol. "Sounds like you're down by two men. I'll stay on tomorrow, and my buddy, he'll be down around in the morning. I'll ask him to come to see you."

"Is he a good fellow, John?"

"Knew him long ago, Danol," John replied. "He was a good hand."

"I'll take your word for it."

John gave him a long, steady look. He nodded. "Better go see Alice and tell her about tomorrow," he said before disappearing down below.

"Got time for a drink, Jeffries?" Danol asked the constable.

"Thought you'd never ask. I'd like to go over what's in there." Jeffries pointed at the envelope Danol had poked inside his jacket.

"Let's forget about that," Danol said.

"Better not."

Danol eyed him and nodded. "Let's go below."

34

The next morning, Danol watched John say goodbye to Alice and Beatrice. Not for the first time that morning, he thought of Erith. He would be glad when this was done and he could get home to her.

John's friend, McPherson, showed up and seemed able-bodied enough. John introduced him to Danol. Before they could untie, the harbourmaster shouted for his attention. He pointed at several loaded wagons on the wharf. Danol signed the slip of paper and waved to the drivers to bring the carts. He shouted orders for the crew to load the large crates.

"What is it, Captain?" Hearn asked as they gathered and waited for the carts to bring the freight alongside.

"Seems there was a fire sometime yesterday at Pennell's Dry Goods Store in Trepassey," Danol said. "They're in desperate need of supplies."

"Looks like they're supplying the whole coast," Dalton said.

"Get to it, men," Danol said. "That's our business right there."

THE LIARS

The crates were heavy, and it took four men to load each one. They grumbled as they worked. More than one black eye, and undoubtedly stiff muscles, were among the lot this morning. Jeffries said he'd get word to Walsh and Power that the *Angel Endeavours* would be back in a week to take them home. Their ship was the last to leave St. John's harbour that morning, and they would be expected in Trepassey by nightfall. The day was bright and the waters calm with a northerly wind, breezy enough to make good time.

Shortly before they finished the midday meal, Eddy Nolan rushed in. "Ship in distress a couple of miles off the bow," he said. "She's billowing smoke, and looks like men in boats in the water."

Everyone bolted from their seats and rushed to the stairs.

"Eddy, grab my spyglass from the cabin. The one Mary Ro gave me," Danol said.

"Yes, sir," Eddy said as he sped toward the main cabin.

John was the last of the crew to reach the steps. Danol caught up with him and clapped him on the back before he entered the stairwell. John didn't turn around. On deck, Hearn rang the bell to signal the *Angel Endeavours* was en route, and the crew took to the rail as they approached the burning ship.

"Lots of smoke, Captain," Dalton said. "No sign of fire yet."

"Get as close as you can," Danol called back to Hearn, who was now at the wheel.

The first of the lifeboats was near enough for a line. Seven men were aboard, and there looked to be six in the second one.

"Throw the line," Danol ordered. McPherson threw the rope, and one of the men grabbed it. They pulled alongside and climbed onto the ship.

"Glad you came upon us, Captain," the man said.

"Welcome aboard," Danol replied. "When we get the others on, you can tell us what happened."

"Line's out," Dalton shouted. All hands rushed starboard and helped the rest of the men onto the boat.

One of the lot came forward toward Danol. "Let me introduce myself, Mr. Cooper. I'm Captain Thomas Baker," he said. He pulled a pistol from beneath his coat. "We had the pleasure of meeting on the dock in St. John's a few years ago."

"I don't recall," Danol said, eying the well-dressed, dark-haired man. He remembered that day on the wharf as if it were yesterday. He'd been out of his mind after learning that Erith had been raped. He had stormed from the *Angel Endeavours* and grabbed the man who'd accosted her. Peter had kept him from going to jail.

"It must not have been that remarkable," Danol said dryly. There was something off about this man's appearance. Danol had a feeling in the pit of his stomach that this man, though similar, was not Captain Baker.

"You've guessed why I'm here," Captain Baker said. "Men." There was a flurry of activity as the men from the other boat pulled guns and pointed them at Danol's crew. "White, McPherson, check them for weapons."

Danol gasped as John and McPherson began to search his crew. Hearn made a swing at John when he got close. "Enough of that," Danol shouted. He looked at Captain Baker and said, "No need for anyone to get hurt here."

"Is there anyone else on board?" Captain Baker asked him.

"No, sir, they're all here," Danol said.

"What about that kid?" John said.

"What kid?" Captain Baker said.

"Some kid running around this morning," John said. "He's probably hiding somewhere."

"Find him," Captain Baker ordered.

"Another boat heading this way, Captain," one of Baker's crew said.

"How far?"

"Two miles."

"We don't have much time," Captain Baker called out. "White, you find that kid yet?"

"Yes, sir," John said as he walked backward from below deck with his hands stretched out in front of him. "He's right here."

John stepped up on deck and backed toward the bulwark. Eddy came partway up the steps, pointing a pistol towards him. John was at the rail when Danol shouted for Eddy to stop. But Eddy's hand was steady as he pulled the trigger. Shocked, John grabbed his stomach as blood spread across his shirt. He fell back over the side rail, and a spray of water came over the gunwale, wetting the sun-dried deck and mixing with his spilled blood.

Danol ran to the side, grabbed the wooden edge, and stretched out over the rail as far as he could. John's body was floating in the water and drifting away from the *Angel Endeavours*. He turned to Eddy, but the boy had disappeared below.

"That solves that problem," Captain Baker said. "Now for this one. Mr. Cooper, ask your crew to line up on the port side, please. I hope they are good swimmers."

"Let my men go," Danol said slowly.

"Captain, the boat's a mile off and closing," one of Baker's men said.

"Cooper, get your men to the side," Captain Baker growled.

"Men, do what he says," Danol said with a sigh. His crew shuffled together while Baker's men stepped back, guns and attention trained on them. Danol moved closer to where they stood at the stern.

"Now, Captain Baker," Danol said boldly. "I would kindly ask you to get off my vessel."

Baker eyed him and then roared in laughter. His crew followed suit. "Why, Mr. Cooper, what makes you think I would do such a thing?"

"It's Captain Cooper to you," Danol said. "Maybe it's the fourteen police officers who have their guns aimed at you right now—and my ship full of men who are about to board your boat."

Captain Baker looked at his men, who began putting their guns on the deck. He turned around and peered at the black-caped men with the pointed hats who formed two rows, the first row on one knee and the back row standing, rifles pointed at his men. Baker dropped his weapon and put his hands in the air. "How did you know?"

"If you kept better track of your men, you'd know there was one missing," Danol said. "Fields, I believe, is his name. He's in the cells in St. John's, a little worse off than most."

They turned as a ruckus started behind them. Hearn and Dalton had punched two of Baker's men.

"That's for Walsh!" said Hearn.

"That's for Power!" said Dalton.

The police officers made quick work of tying up the pirates. Danol looked at each of them as they shuffled past him. He stopped one of the most ragged of the lot, his clothes too big to fit his frame. Danol gave him an almost imperceptible nod, which was returned. He let them carry on to the hold of the boat with the officers. Captain Baker was indeed dressed as one of the crew.

Danol went in search of Eddy. He was in the galley, the gun still in his hand, and he was trembling. The boy ran to Danol and threw his arms around him. Danol hugged him, pried the gun from his fingers, and laid it on the table. He held him for a few moments then put his hands on the young lad's shoulders and put him at arm's length. "You did good today, son," Danol said. Eddy looked up at him and swiped at a tear in his eye. Danol shook his head and said, "Mary Ro will kill me for this." He pulled him in and hugged him again.

"I'm all right, Danol," Eddy said. "No need to tell Mom."

Danol grinned. "It doesn't work like that with her," he said.

On deck, the crew gathered around Eddy and told him how brave he was. Eddy had helped get all the police officers out of the crates and back to the main cabin and then alerted them of the approaching brigands.

Danol shouted to Captain Dicks on the *Bell Island Explorer*, "Any sign of the body?"

"Not yet," Captain Dicks replied. "We'll keep looking, but we have to be back in St. John's before dark if we're going to tow this one in."

"Understood," Danol shouted back. He scoured the waters around the boat for any signs of John. He paced from one side to the other and ordered his men to search with the glass. Hearn and Dalton took the rowboat out.

A short time later, the bell rang on the *Bell Island Explorer*. "We have the body," Captain Dicks shouted. His men made quick work of the oil barrels that had been set on fire to create the black smoke and illusion of fire on Captain Baker's boat, the *Seafarer*.

The flotilla of three made it into port in St. John's just after the supper hour. Danol tied up first. Alice came to the dock while the police were unloading the pirates. She screamed and cried as she tried to get past him and onto the *Bell Island Explorer*. Danol released her after the constabulary had finished and left the area. Alice ran to the other vessel, and Captain Dicks helped her onto the deck.

Danol gave orders for Hearn and Dalton to go to the Riverview Hospital and check on Power and Walsh. The rest he told to stay on board and be alert. He didn't see much of Alice.

He made arrangements to collect Beatrice from the convent where she was staying with some nuns who were friends of Erith's. Beatrice and Alice would go to North Harbour with them when all the burial arrangements had been made. She thanked Danol for being so kind to her and Beatrice despite all that had happened.

Danol sat in the main cabin and read the papers from Jeffries once more. He left the boat a short time later. On Empire Avenue, he knocked at the door of a small white house. An older man came to the door, and an orange cat squeezed out through before the man had a chance to stop him. Danol was about to reach for the large feline when the old man said to let him go on.

"He likes to hunt," the man said. Danol nodded.

"I'm Danol Cooper, sir. Are you Alexander MacDonald?" Danol held out his hand.

"I am," Mr. MacDonald replied.

"Can I come in?"

Alexander MacDonald moved aside, and Danol followed him to the kitchen. "I was just sitting down for tea," he said. He offered Danol a cup and made a place for him at the table when Danol agreed. They made small talk until both were seated across from each other.

"What can I do for you, Mr. . . . ?"

"Cooper. Danol, please."

"What can I do for you, Danol?"

"I came to talk to you about Ted White."

The old man's hand shook as he placed the cup back on the saucer. It clinked before finding its spot and settling on the porcelain. "What's happened to Ted?"

"When did you see him last?"

"He was here yesterday," the old man said. "Poor boy, he'd been gone for so long and went through something awful. He's like a son to me. He brought me news about my poor John." The old man's voice was shaky. He recounted to Danol what John had said. "He brought me a letter from John, you know.

"I knew Ted couldn't read and didn't have the heart to tell him that I couldn't, either. John always wanted to show me, but I didn't have the interest." The old man looked down at his weathered hands and slowly shook his head from side to side. "Now I wish I did."

"Where is the letter?" Danol asked. "I can read it to you. If you would like me to, of course."

"You would? I'd appreciate that. It's been so long since I saw John." Mr. MacDonald rummaged in a box on a shelf above the warmer on the stove. He brought Danol the letter.

Danol noticed the pages had been folded and refolded and had gone through Mr. MacDonald's hands many times.

He read the contents out loud. The letter recounted the innocence of two young men, of John and Ted's exploits at sea. It painted a picture of the rugged coast of Labrador. John wrote that although Ted had had a hard time dealing with Lavinia's death, he believed Ted would be all right now. He said he felt safe with Ted and that he hoped they would be friends forever. It sounded to Danol like John really admired Ted.

Mr. MacDonald sat at the end of the table with his head just beyond the sun's reach. Dust danced in the rays around his trembling hands as sunlight spilled through the window onto the table. Danol read the last words written from a loving son to his father. By the end of the four pages, Danol was shaken. He'd had no relationship with his own father after the death of his mother. Mr. MacDonald had been a different dad to his child—and obviously to Ted as well.

Silence fell on the room as Mr. MacDonald let the words sink in. His hand moved from the table to the shadow beyond. Danol suspected he was wiping away a tear, though his head was shrouded in the shade beyond the bright surface of the table.

"You still didn't tell me why you're here," Mr. MacDonald said. "Ted's been like a son to me, you know."

"I know," Danol said. He spent some time with the old man and told him what had happened to Ted.

After another night in port, they would set sail for North Harbour with a smaller crew. The freight from the *Angel Endeavours* had been transferred to the *Bell Island Explorer*. Captain Dicks would take care of the business while Danol returned home with Eddy, Alice, and Beatrice.

Before leaving port the next day, Danol went to the cemetery near the St. John's Penitentiary. Ted White was to be buried there. Alice wanted to go, and he wouldn't refuse her. Alexander MacDonald stumbled his way across the field. A well-dressed man came up behind him and helped him to the graveside. He offered his hand to Danol and condolences to Alice.

"You wouldn't know by me now, but I grew up on the streets," the man said. "Ted was on the boats by then. Things would have turned out a lot different for me without his influence. I wanted to pay my respects."

Alice thanked him for coming. Mr. MacDonald shook his hand.

After the priest said a few words over the wooden box and sprinkled some dirt upon it, they turned to leave. Danol noticed two men off in the distance watching from under cover of trees. Alice started to sob and wail and stumbled through the uneven ground. Mr. MacDonald linked his arm through hers on one side while Danol stepped in on the other. The well-dressed man was ahead of them. Danol looked toward the trees. The two fellows turned and disappeared toward downtown.

Danol made sure that Alexander MacDonald was taken care of before heading to the boat with Alice. She went to her cabin to find Beatrice. The *Angel Endeavours* left port soon after. He was tired and missed his family. He couldn't wait to see Erith and the children again.

He rifled through the newspaper articles once more. There was still one thing that was bothering him. Maybe it shouldn't, but it did, and he couldn't settle his mind.

35

The *Bell Island Explorer* steamed into North Harbour three days after Danol arrived home. He told Erith what had happened, and he got Alice and Beatrice settled at his house. Alice didn't want to sleep at the store because of what had happened just a month before, but they spent their days together with Erith and the children.

Danol stood at the end of the wharf waiting for the boat to dock. First to get off was Captain Dicks. Danol shook the captain's hand.

"Thanks for this."

"Happy to do it, Danol," Captain Dicks said. "We have a couple of crates to unload and some mail for here," he said. "The men will get it to the store shortly."

Danol helped the men unload the freight. He went aboard once they were finished and handed out a bonus to each of the men. Some were reluctant to take it. "I know you fellows haven't been in port for a while," he said. "I want to show my appreciation for all you have done."

Danol met with the captain shortly after.

"Who knows?" Danol asked.

"Two of my most trusted," he said. "That's all."

"Here's something for them and for yourself," Danol said as he handed the captain another envelope.

"You pay me well, Danol," Captain Dicks said. He pushed the envelope away. "I don't want this."

"I'm sure Marg would like one of them fancy hats," Danol said. Captain Dicks reluctantly took the envelope. "I won't be around much from now on. I'll be here if you need me."

Captain Dicks looked toward the store. "Can't say as I blame you."

Danol invited them for a meal, but the cook had already put a fish stew in the pot, so Captain Dicks politely declined. He shook Danol's hand, and Danol watched as the boat left the way she came.

Before Danol could get inside the house, he heard a commotion. Once he saw his way clear, he nodded at John MacDonald. "You look pretty good for a dead man." He clapped John on the back. "You had me worried when you didn't turn up right away."

"I was tempted to take my chances for the land and disappear," John said.

"I'm glad you didn't."

"Me, too," Alice said as she embraced John once more. Beatrice was already in his arms and hugging her father fiercely.

"How did you get out so quickly?" Danol asked.

"Your wife," John said. "She was waiting with the pry bar as soon as the men left."

Erith came from the store, wiping her hands in her apron. She looked up at Danol and smiled.

"You have many talents, my dear," he said. "I might have to hire you on."

They gathered in the kitchen, where Erith had prepared a meal for the eight of them. Once the children had finished and left the table, Danol had some questions for John.

"Eddy had the tin of blood ready for me when I went below," he said. "It was only knowing which pocket to put it in so the other crew wouldn't see it. When I hit the water, it spread."

"It was convincing," Danol said. "Almost too convincing. I thought Eddy had really shot you."

"He missed by a good distance," John said. "Good thing the cook was making blood puddings. I'll have to thank him and thank the lad."

John went on to explain that he had swum to the *Bell Island Explorer*, hung on to the rope ladder, out of sight, and waited for Captain Dicks to signal the way was clear. "I lay on the deck, and two men threw a sail over me."

He had stayed still on the deck under the sail until they got to port. Nobody had troubled him, as the captain had ordered. "When Alice came, she did carry on something shocking, crying and calling out my name after she saw me," John said. "I thought she didn't know at that point, even though we had talked about it the night before."

"You would have been proud of her at your graveside, too," Danol said. "I also told Mr. MacDonald what was going on. He showed up for the service."

John looked sad for a moment. "I won't get to see him again," he said.

"Give it some time, John. Maybe there's a way."

"I won't discount your ideas like I did the other night, Danol." John smiled. "Even a pitiful idea is better than no idea, you said. I must admit I never thought this would work." He reflected for a moment, then slowly shook his head from side to side. "I don't deserve this."

"You're a fine man, John MacDonald," Alice said. She reached over and laid her hand on his. He looked up at her and smiled.

"You're too fine a woman for me."

Alice smiled brilliantly. "We're free, John. We're finally free."

"Ted White is dead and buried," Danol said. "Confirmed by a couple of fellows in the graveyard. If they weren't convinced, Alice helped them with that." He told John what had happened. "Mr. MacDonald being there made all the difference."

"I can't believe he came," John said.

"He told me you were his son," Danol said.

John bowed his head once more and remained quiet while Erith and Alice cleared away the dishes. When they were gone, he said, "We never planned any further than this moment."

"You can't go home, John."

"It wasn't home. It was a hideout and a prison. For both of us."

"I wouldn't recommend that you stay here in the harbour, but you can always settle somewhere close," Danol said.

"Alice and I were never married, you know."

"I didn't know that," Danol said. "But that's your business, not mine."

"It's yours when it comes to the child," John replied.

"How so?"

"We put Beatrice in danger because we kept her."

Erith heard the comment as she entered the room. "You kept Beatrice safe and loved because you kept her," she said.

Alice gasped behind her after following Erith from the kitchen. "Does that mean you won't take her?" she asked.

"Make no mistake, Beatrice will always be welcome here. As will you. But why do you think I would take her?" asked Erith.

"As John said, we put her in danger," Alice said. Her hooded eyes barely contained the tears that were waiting to spill.

Erith reached out and embraced Alice. "You love Beatrice. She loves you. I love her, too, but she's not mine to take."

Alice started to cry. "I was so afraid," she sobbed.

"I'm sorry, Alice," Erith said as she tried to console her. "I told you that I hadn't changed my mind."

"But that was before all this happened with John."

"You still love her?"

"Yes, of course. More than anything," Alice said as she wiped at her eyes. John came around the table and gathered her close.

"And you, John? Now that you're a free man?" Erith asked.

"I'd give my life for that little girl," John replied.

"Well, there you go," Erith said.

John reached for Alice's hand. "Can we talk outside, Alice?"

36

They left the house, and Danol watched them walk to the end of the wharf. He scooped up Erith when she returned from the kitchen. "You are one fine woman," he said. Danol hugged her tight, and she nestled into him. He rocked her gently in his embrace.

Erith pushed away from him. "I almost forgot, there's a letter from my solicitor. He's probably inquiring about where to send the payment for the MacDonalds."

Danol followed her to the store. "We'll have to see what they decide," he said. "Did you get a chance to look at the article Jeffries brought?"

Erith nodded while sorting through the mail. "The papers could be wrong," she said. "It did say that, according to Ezra, they had a child together."

"What if they were right?"

"Do you think John knows?"

"I'm not sure," Danol said. "That's hard to say."

She stopped sorting the letters and looked at him. "Maybe she doesn't think there's a way," Erith said. "I know I put Beatrice out of my mind because I couldn't consider anything else. Do you think we could do something about that?"

Danol thought about it for a moment. "Are we meddling in something that is none of our business?" he asked.

Erith nodded. "It is absolutely none of our business. We should burn those papers."

"I know she is terribly worried about her sister. Maybe she would like to visit her."

"Would that be too risky?"

"I doubt that anyone would know where Alice's sister lives. As far as I can tell, nobody has connected the incident with Ezra to John," Danol said. "You didn't see the paper yet, but Ezra's sentence was changed from hanging to life in prison."

Erith gasped. "Why? Poor Alice! What will she think?"

"The judge wasn't sure that the courts here had jurisdiction over the sentencing."

"So, will that mean that he goes free?"

"No, no, nothing like that. He will still be imprisoned for life." Danol leaned on the counter.

"For Alice's sake, maybe getting away to see her sister would be good for her," Erith said. Absently, she pulled a letter out of the pile and tore the seal. "I don't think we should tell her about Ezra. Does it really matter as long as he is out of her life? One less torment for her."

Erith pulled out the sheet and started to read. Danol watched her eyes widen before she dropped the letter. She clasped the counter and breathed deeply. Danol came around to where she stood and put his arm around her waist. "What is it?"

"I don't believe it."

"What? Believe what? Erith, honey, what is it?

She picked up the letter and handed it to him. "I didn't finish it."

Danol took the letter and started to read.

"Out loud," Erith said. "Please." Her voice quivered and cracked.

"My dearest Erith," he began. "I wanted to inform you that I had a visit from a woman who claims to be the daughter of Kathleen Ryan. She said that she wanted to see you, as well as her niece and nephews. She had somebody claiming to be a solicitor with her. However, I haven't heard of the fellow. He said she wants custody of the children. You can expect to see them very soon. I have court proceedings that I cannot change, but I will be along within a few days. I will have the children's papers with me."

Danol folded the letter and laid it on the counter. Erith put her hand over it then crumpled it into a ball. "This is fit for the stove," she said.

"This can't be true. You would have known. Somebody would have said."

"I have to see Mrs. Patsy, Danol," she said.

"I'll go with you."

"No, you stay here. Please."

"Erith, nobody is going to take those children from you. I don't care who they are or claim to be. They're mine, too."

She threw her arms around him. "I know that. I love you for that. But Mrs. Patsy might not tell me what I want to know if you're there."

Danol nodded and fetched her coat. Despite his better judgment, he helped her into her jacket and watched her hurry down the path that followed the shore. John and Alice returned moments later.

"Is everything all right?" Alice asked.

"Erith had something to take care of, that's all," Danol replied.

"We should get out of your way," John said.

"Nonsense," Danol said half-heartedly.

"It's getting late," John said. "We should be going."

Danol nodded. His heart was following the path behind the woman who was going out of sight on a bend in the trail.

Alice left to get Beatrice.

"You're sure there is nothing I can do?" John asked him.

"Sorry, John. I'm distracted. Erith got some news that she has to deal with. That's all."

The children came behind Alice. Beatrice and Annie were pleading to stay together for the night.

"Can I go?" Annie asked.

"Not tonight," Danol replied.

"Please," Annie begged.

Danol picked her up and hugged her. "That's not going to work on me, young lady."

Annie squealed and pecked him on the cheek. "Can Beatrice stay?"

"That's up to her mommy and daddy."

Beatrice looked at her mother and said, "Please, Mommy?"

Alice raised her eyebrows as she looked at Danol. He nodded.

"You be a good girl for the Coopers." Beatrice hooted and squeezed her mother and father and took off with Annie toward the back of the house. "You're sure?" Alice asked when they were gone.

"It's no trouble at all," Danol said. "They love being together."

"Yes, but is it putting you out tonight?"

"Honestly, it's fine."

"We'll be back early tomorrow," John said.

They said their goodbyes, and Danol watched them go in the other direction. Alice linked into John's arm as they made their way toward the crossing. The MacDonalds were getting more use out of his house than he was. Danol looked back in the other direction. His brows furrowed as he waited for his wife to return.

37

"Get a cup of tea for yourself," Mrs. Patsy said. Her bony finger shook as she pointed toward the teacups on the shelf. The old woman hunched on the daybed. Her hump was covered by a yellowed woollen sweater that was buttoned at the neck and draped behind her like a cape. She fixed the sweater about her shoulders. "Bit of a draft today."

Erith fixed the tea and offered the woman a cup. The strong brew was sitting in the teapot on the stove. Erith added hot water from the kettle and stirred in some milk that was clotting on the table. She brought a cup to Mrs. Patsy, who signalled for her to lay it on the table. Erith helped her up, and they both sat facing one another at the corner of the table. The room was warm and welcoming.

"What brings you here, child?" Mrs. Patsy asked.

"I want to know something," Erith said.

"What's that?"

"Please be honest with me, Mrs. Patsy. It's important," Erith said as she patted the old woman's hand.

"What do you want to know?"

"Did Kathleen and my father have a child?" Erith asked.

"A child, goodness gracious, no," the old woman said. "What would make you think something like that?"

"Are you sure?" Erith prodded.

"Of course I'm sure."

Erith heaved a sigh of relief and told Mrs. Patsy about the letter. Mrs. Patsy looked at her wide-eyed and blinked several times.

"You know something," Erith said. "Please, Mrs. Patsy. It's important."

Mrs. Patsy nodded and motioned for Erith to fill up the teacup. "You know why Kathleen came here years ago, don't you?"

"Yes, I believe I do," Erith said. "Her mother died, and Dinn was sent to be reared in Cape Dog with his father's people, and Kathleen was sent here with her mother's people."

Mrs. Patsy nodded. "That's right. Kathleen was only nine or ten when she came here. She went to live with the Whalens. Hester Whalen had a brood of her own almost reared up and she didn't take too kindly to having another mouth to feed. She was hard on Kathleen."

Erith nodded. That reminded her of how her stepmother had treated her. She felt a shiver go up her back.

"When Kathleen was fifteen, a boat came ashore on the point. Some of the men stayed with the Whalens while it was being fixed. One young lad took a liking to Kathleen."

Erith listened attentively. She feared that Kathleen's story would mirror her own. She shuddered at the thought.

"Well, Kathleen took a liking to him, too. He told her he would take her away from here and marry her. The morning the crew was supposed to leave, Kathleen packed her bag and left home without telling anyone and walked to the place where they were moored. It was dark, and when she got there, the boat had gone. She waited until light to be sure. Mr. Whalen found her crying on the beach that morning and beat her the whole way home. It was something awful."

Erith felt a wave of pity come over her for the cruel woman who had raised her. "What has that got to do with a baby?"

"Well, Kathleen wasn't seen for months after that. Then old Hester said that Kathleen was sick and had to go away to the hospital. Folks started talking that Ern Whalen had hurt her when he beat her. It was a bad time here then. Hester and Ern weren't welcomed anywhere. By and by, Hester confessed to her sister that Kathleen was pregnant and that she wasn't going to feed another youngster, especially belonging to a youngster she had already been saddled with."

Erith gasped. Mrs. Patsy patted her hand. "Kathleen returned to the harbour a few months later, and Hester didn't speak of it again. Kathleen became a midwife and stayed unmarried until she met your father. She was tending to your mother when she died."

"I often wondered why Kathleen was so mean to me. Maybe it was all she knew," Erith mused.

"She didn't have it easy, that's for sure. Kathleen was a bitter woman. We all wondered why your father married her."

"I've made peace with what my father did. I don't know if I can ever truly forgive Kathleen," Erith said. "I knew cruelty at her hands, but that made me want to be even kinder to the children, not treat them as I had been treated."

"I know, dear," Mrs. Patsy said. "But not everyone has the same mind. Maybe Kathleen thought that was the way it was supposed to be. Maybe, if your father had lived, he would have shown her how to be a better mother. It's all a mystery."

"That's for sure, Mrs. Patsy."

"I don't like to speak ill of the dead, Erith," Mrs. Patsy went on. "I hope Kathleen has found peace."

Erith felt a wave of sadness wash over her. "Maybe I can hope for that, too. In the meantime, I don't know anything about this woman who could show up any day except for the fact that she could very well be my stepsister."

"Erith, you have a kind heart. Don't forget that not everyone is the same. Trust yourself, but don't be so trusting of others that you believe everyone will behave like you do."

"Thanks, Mrs. Patsy. I appreciate you telling me what you knew." Erith hugged the old woman and helped her back to the daybed. She took the cups and washed them, readied the teapot for the morning, filled the kettle, and threw some wood in the fire, all the while talking about the everyday happenings in the harbour.

"It's getting dark. I'd better get going," Erith said as she reached for her jacket. "Thanks again, Mrs. Patsy."

"Mind yourself, you hear," Mrs. Patsy said. "Mind my words."

"I will. I'll send George and Tommy down tomorrow to fill the woodbox for you."

"They're great boys, Erith."

"They are indeed," Erith said. She closed the door and drew in the storm door so Mrs. Patsy wouldn't have to do it later. Pulling her coat tight around her neck, she began to walk back toward home. She didn't notice Danol waiting at the fence until she closed the gate.

"This is a nice surprise," she said as she reached for his hand.

"I didn't want you to walk home in the dark," her husband said.

Waves lapped on the shore as they strolled in silence toward the house. The moon was bright and the sky cloudless as the blue tinge of twilight brushed across the sky. Despite the worn path, the ground was uneven beneath them, so they watched where they were walking.

When they had almost passed the graveyard, Erith stopped. "Are you going to ask me?"

Danol turned to her and gently smoothed the hair from her face. "It's getting long enough to do this again," he said softly.

"Well?" she asked.

"You can tell me in your own time," he said.

Erith hugged him. "It's true, Danol. Kathleen Ryan had a child when she was fifteen or sixteen. I thought it was my father's, but it was long before they came here."

"Did Mrs. Patsy know anything about the child?"

"No, nothing, really, only the fact that there was one."

"We can't do anything until the woman gets here."

"Danol, I may have a stepsister, and the children a cousin."

They turned and walked toward the house. Danol squeezed her hand. "Erith, you may not like what I'm going to say, but I'm going to say it, anyway."

They stopped again. "If it is something like 'not everyone is good,' then don't bother. Mrs. Patsy already talked to me about that. Don't worry, Danol. I'll be careful."

He breathed a heavy sigh. They both laughed. "Let's get home," he said. "I think Mrs. Patsy might have saved me some anguish."

"I love you," she said.

"I love you, too," he said. He kissed her on the doorstep before going inside.

38

Erith was clearing away the dishes the next morning when Maggie came in. "I was hoping to spend the day with you," she said. "Seems like you've been gone forever."

"Oh, Maggie!" Erith threw her arms around the woman. "Danol told you to come over, didn't he?"

"Of course not," Maggie said, her toothless grin giving her away. "He told me what was going on. I had no idea. I don't believe Dinn would have known, either. Old Hester kept that one pretty close to her chest."

"She may not be here today, Maggie. She may not come at all."

Danol poked his head in. "Why, Maggie, it's good to see you."

"She knows," Maggie said.

Erith laughed at the complete look of innocence that crossed her husband's face. She swiped at him with the dish towel.

Danol came in and hugged her. "I hope you don't mind."

"I'm glad that Maggie is here," she said. She looked at

Maggie. "You're welcome here any time, Maggie. You never need an excuse."

Maggie crossed the room and hugged her. "You're one of my own," she said as tears welled in her eyes.

"Knock that off, Maggie," Erith said. They both laughed. "Hello?"

"Hello," Erith called. "We're in here."

John and Alice came in. "Oh, we're too early," Alice said.

"Just in time to get something to eat," Maggie said. "I'm starved."

"We've eaten already," John said.

"There can't be much food left at the house," Danol said.

"I'm frying some ham," Maggie said. "Do you want some?"

Alice and John looked at each other. They nodded. "Sure."

"I have to make bread," Erith said.

Alice took off her coat. "I'll do that."

"I've eaten," said Erith. "The boys are gone to fill Mrs. Patsy's woodbox, and the girls are upstairs making the beds. Fry some extra, because they'll all be hungry."

"John, I could use your help with the wood," Danol said. John nodded. "There's an old coat in the shed if you want it."

They both left by the back door, and Erith went to the shop. She had some chores to do there and didn't want to leave it all to Marie. She loved the sounds of a full house. The girls joined the women in the kitchen.

George and Tommy came back a little while later. "Mail boat is coming, Mom," Tommy said.

"There's ham frying in the kitchen," Erith said.

The boys whooped in delight as they headed for the back of the house. Erith tried to ease the mounting tension in her belly as she watched the boat through the windowpane. She didn't hear Danol until she felt his arms encircle her from behind. She leaned back into his chest and let the steady beat of his heart quash the feelings that were rising in her. He rested his chin on her shoulder, and they both watched together.

Mr. Johnson carried the mail to the dock, and Tommy and George ran to meet him. George grabbed the sack, and Mr. Johnson said something to them, so they waited. He brought out two more packages, which he gave to Tommy. Both boys turned and skipped in along the wharf.

Erith let out a breath she didn't know she was holding. Danol squeezed her tighter as she glanced out once more. Mr. Johnson was helping two people off the boat. One was a woman with long, dark hair partially hidden under an oversized hat. Her brown coat parted from the waist as she stepped onto the dock, showing a pale yellow dress beneath. The man with her wore a grey suit coat and pants that looked too big for him. He was unshaven and unkempt and seemed not to have enjoyed the boat ride.

The woman linked arms with him as they stood on the wharf. She turned as Mr. Johnson spoke. He pointed toward the shop, and the pair walked up the path.

Erith sucked in her breath and straightened her back. She squeezed Danol's hands at her waist and then walked out of his embrace.

"Remember, you're not alone," he whispered to her. She nodded slightly and strode toward the door. She greeted the two on the step.

The woman held out her hand. "I'm Rose Ryan," she said. "My friends call me Rosie."

"Welcome, Rose," Erith said. "I'm Erith Cooper, and this is my husband, Danol."

Danol shook her hand, and Rose eyed him with a wide grin. "Pleasure indeed," she said. Erith noticed she held Danol's hand a little longer than necessary. Danol backed up and stood so close to Erith that she could feel his warmth.

"This is my solicitor, Mr. Payton," Rose said. "He hails from Halifax."

"Mr. Payton," Erith said and nodded toward him. Danol followed suit. "Please come in. We were just having some tea, if you'd like to join us."

Erith and Danol walked toward the kitchen. She wasn't sure if the others had followed. No matter what happened, she was determined to be civil. The four children were sitting at the table with Maggie, and Alice was at the far end with her hands in the dough. They all stopped when the strangers came in.

Rose saw the children, and her eyes lit up. She smiled as she made her way to the table and rested her hands on George's shoulders. "These must be my dear, dear cousins," she said. George stopped in mid-chew, while the others gaped at the woman.

"Boys, would you mind going outside, please?" Erith asked them. George and Tommy obediently got up from the table and went toward the back door. They met John coming in. He looked at the two strangers, then turned and followed the boys.

Danol stirred behind her, but Erith didn't turn around. "Girls, could you go outside with the boys?" she asked. Beatrice looked at Alice, who made a motion with her head toward the door. Chairs skittered across the floor as the two girls silently left the room.

Alice sprinkled flour on her hands to take the dough off.

"I'll be out of your way in just a moment," she said. "If you don't mind, we'd like to take the children to the other side with us for lunch."

"That would be nice," Erith said. She smiled at Alice and nodded her thanks. Alice quickly finished cleaning her hands and left. Maggie took the pan of dough, covered it with a table-cloth, and laid it on the woodbox. She came back and sat down. Erith held the back of the chair as everyone looked around the room at each other.

"Have a seat," she said.

Rose stared at the back door before Mr. Payton nudged her. "Oh, yes, I believe I will."

Erith fetched the teapot while Maggie set the table with cups, saucers, and utensils. Nobody said a word as they all sat down and she poured the tea.

"So, Rose, tell me about yourself," Erith began.

"Not much to tell, really," the woman replied. "I haven't married. I live alone in a boarding house in St. John's."

There was a long silence before Erith spoke again. "Why are you here, Rose?"

Rose coughed and covered her mouth with a handkerchief before she spoke. "Obviously my mother thought more of you than she did of me," she said. "We're kin, aren't we? I came to claim my relatives and share in some of the Ryan money."

"What do you mean 'claim your relatives'?"

"Why, the children, of course. My uncle does own them, doesn't he? Imagine my surprise when I found out they were young and well-to-do."

"Those children were legally adopted by me," Erith said. "You hold no claim to them."

Mr. Payton spoke. "If you were to gain from the adoption

of the children without proper notification to any living relative, then the adoption can be dissolved."

"How did I gain?" Erith asked him. "Besides, I was unaware of any living relative."

"That doesn't matter in the eyes of the law. Being ignorant of a law doesn't mean you can break it."

"This can't be right," Erith argued. "I'll have my solicitor look into it."

"I already spoke to Mr. Horwood. He is aware of the law."

Rose coughed again. "I plan to take the children to St. John's and buy a house for us to live in," she said. Her pallor went grey, and she gulped for air. She coughed incessantly. Erith got up from the chair and went to her. Suddenly, Rose grabbed for her throat and fell over against Mr. Payton. He moved back, and she slid to the floor. Danol shoved the table back and cleared away the chairs as he rushed to the prone woman.

"I'll get Mary and Peter," he said as he rushed from the room.

Erith knelt by the woman and saw the slight rise and fall of her chest. "What's wrong with her?" she asked Mr. Payton.

"I don't know. She's had a cough for a while now. Maybe the boat ride was too much for her."

"Maggie, get a blanket for her," Erith said to her friend. Maggie hesitated at first, but Erith nodded for her to go.

39

Danol rushed to his house on the point at the other side of the harbour.

"Where's George?"

"I'm here," George said as he came from the kitchen.

"Run to John's Pond and get Mary Ro and Peter. Something's wrong with the woman in our house."

George didn't ask any questions. He just bolted from the house and up over the hill toward the next community. It was about two miles across, and Danol figured that George would get there faster than he could. He had something to attend to here as well.

"John, can I see you outside?"

"Of course," John said. He grabbed his jacket from the post near the door and followed Danol.

Danol waited by the fence, where he'd be out of earshot of the house. He saw Alice looking out as John approached him.

"I know you know that woman. I saw the look you gave her when you came in. I want to know who she is," Danol said.

He tried to hide the impatience he felt, but he was worried for Erith and the children.

"Her name is Rosie Ryan," John said.

"You're sure that's her name?" Danol asked.

"That's who I knew her as. I haven't seen her in fifteen years or more."

"How did you know her?"

"It's not a time that I'm proud of, Danol," John said. "I knew her from my street days. She had a mean streak in her then, but I didn't blame her. It was hard enough being a boy on the street, but being a girl, that would have been so much harder."

"Where did she come from?"

"That's the thing about the street, Danol. Nobody talks about anything other than how they're going to eat on any given day." John lowered his head. "I wish I had been kinder to her, but I was only young and doing what I could to stay alive."

"Why did you run when you saw her?" Danol asked.

"I can only say that it was instinct. I have it good now with Alice. I've asked her to marry me," John said. "Rosie knew me as Teddy White, and we just buried him. If she makes the connection, then everything we did will be gone."

"She definitely recognized you," Danol said. "I'm certain of that."

"I'll try talking to her," said John. "Maybe she can be reasoned with."

"We don't know what she wants yet. I'm sure it's not the children."

"I believe she ended up in a brothel. At least, that's the way she was talking the last time I saw her," John continued. "I had just met Lavinia then, and not too long after that, John

MacDonald and his father. I fared off pretty good. I doubt it was the same for Rosie."

"I'm confused," said Danol. "In order for Rosie Ryan to be Kathleen's daughter, she'd have to be in her mid-forties."

"No, sir, she can't be," John said. "She's closer to my age. For sure, she can't be more than thirty-five."

"So, we know she is not after the children because of some maternal need, and she's not a relation."

"Like the rest of us, Rosie didn't end up on the street of her own accord. She survived there long after we thought she wouldn't. Whatever she left had to be worse, so that would have been pretty bad."

"Understood," Danol said. He'd seen some pretty bad living situations during his policing days in Boston. However, he wasn't naive enough to think that a cornered animal wouldn't do whatever it took to get clear. He'd be careful how he cornered Rosie Ryan.

Danol looked up the hill toward John's Pond. "I'll head back. Mary and Peter should be along pretty soon. Keep the children on this side of the harbour until I come back for them."

"They'll be all right with me and Alice," John said.

"I know," Danol said. He turned and headed for the dory.

By the time he reached the house, he could see the small rowboat crossing the gut. The doctors weren't far behind him. He rushed into the house just as Rosie was opening her eyes.

"Stay there," Erith said. "The doctor is coming."

"Doctors? Way out here," Rose mumbled. She tried to sit up. Erith shoved a pillow under her head and used her hand to keep the woman on the floor.

"They're right behind me," Danol said. "Crossing when I

was coming in." Erith looked at him with knitted brow. "I sent George." She nodded.

Maggie was tending to the dough in the corner. "No need to let a good batch of bread go to waste," she said as she worked the pan with her fists. Danol turned up the corner of his mouth, and she punched the dough harder. She mumbled something he couldn't understand but guessed she was in a sour mood after meeting Rosie.

40

Mary Ro rushed in just ahead of Peter. She knelt by the woman, and Erith got up to stand by Danol. He put his arms around her, and they both watched Mary and Peter go to work. "Everything is going to be all right," he said to Erith.

He saw the shadow in the doorway before he saw John. John glanced at Danol and nodded.

Erith squeezed Danol's hand, and he tightened his arms around her.

Mary stood up. "Can we move her somewhere off the floor?"

"The cot is still set up in the storeroom," Erith said. "We've been meaning to take it down."

"You sure?" Danol asked. "We can take her to the Walshes. I'm sure they'd welcome a boarder."

"She came here, she'll stay here," Erith said. "Mr. Payton can stay at the Walshes' when he's ready."

"Help us move her," Mary ordered.

"I got her," John said. He scooped Rosie up and brought her to the storeroom. Mary followed him, and Danol came to speak to Erith.

"She's frail," Danol said. "I don't think she's eaten in days, by the look of her."

"What about the coughing?"

"Too early to say," Peter said. "We'll know more soon. I'll be back."

Payton had been sitting on a chair by the stove. Danol released Erith and went to the man. "I'd like to have a word with you outside." The man, small in stature, was dwarfed by Danol. Danol could see fear in his eyes as he slowly rose from the chair.

"A word? That's all?"

"We'll see," said Danol.

Danol walked out near the shed and sat on the sawhorse. He picked up the bucksaw that he'd left hanging on the post and sized up the blade. Payton watched him from several feet away.

"What are you doing here, Mr. Payton?" Danol said.

"You heard me in there."

"I did, but that doesn't answer my question. We both know that Rosie Ryan is too young to be the daughter of Kathleen Ryan."

"I don't know that," Mr. Payton replied. He shifted from foot to foot and stared at his hands.

"Well, you do now," Danol said.

"I don't want any trouble."

"You got it just the same."

"Look, Mr. Cooper, I had a few dalliances with Miss Ryan a few years ago. She showed up a few weeks ago and told me that she'd tell my wife if I didn't go along with her scheme."

"What scheme is that?" Danol asked.

"She wants money, that's it. She's not interested in the family. She just knows there's money here, and she wants it."

"But she's not related to the family," Danol said. "She's too young to be the daughter of Kathleen Ryan."

"Thing is, she believes she is," Payton returned. "I don't think she's making that up."

"It's impossible," Danol said. "You understand that, right?"

"I do. But she doesn't. Regardless, it's too complicated for me. I'm going back on the next boat."

Danol brought him to the Walshes and told Mrs. Walsh the man would need a room for the night. Danol paid for it, despite his disdain for what the man was trying to do.

Erith ran to him when he went back to the house. "I was worried about you," she said. "You didn't hurt him, did you, Danol?" He almost laughed until he saw she was serious.

"I brought him to Walsh's. What did you think I was going to do with him?"

"I don't know," Erith said rather sheepishly. "But I worried, anyway."

"Has Mary or Peter been out?"

"Not yet," she replied.

Danol fixed the table and chairs back while they waited. Maggie got the bread ready for the pans, grumbling away to herself about all the work she had to do. Danol smiled at her, and she muttered something back at him that he didn't want to ask her to repeat. He understood Maggie. A threat to Erith was a threat to her. He didn't take that lightly, nor did he take it for granted. Danol was glad he'd asked her to come today. He was sure that Maggie was, too. She was tormented about the children and about Erith.

On impulse, he went over and hugged her. Maggie clung to him for a moment. "Everything is going to be just fine, Maggie. Don't worry," Danol whispered. She pushed him away and then threatened him with the baking pan. He laughed, and she joined in.

Mary came out, followed by Peter. "She's got pneumonia and is undernourished," Mary said. "She could possibly have been in contact with tuberculosis, or TB, as it is commonly known. That's not something to fool around with. She is terribly ill."

"What do we do?" Erith asked.

"First, keep the children out of the house, and then wash down the room after she's gone. You can't be too careful with TB."

"I'd like to help her, Mary."

"We gave her some medicine and will keep watch on her for a few days. She needs some soup to get her strength, and we'll know more after that."

"We can do that," Erith said. "Can't we, Danol?"

"We can't throw her out, which is what she deserves," Danol said. "She's definitely not who you think she is."

"Who is she, then?" Erith asked.

"Oh, she's Rosie Ryan, all right," he said. "But according to Mrs. Patsy, she would be ten years too young to be Kathleen's daughter."

"How do you know how old she is? I couldn't tell."

"John knew her. He knows her age."

Erith stared at Danol but didn't ask anything else. She knew he'd tell her when they were alone. "We can throw some peas on with the ham, but that will take some time to cook. Until then, what can we give her?"

"How about some sugary tea with a slice of toast?" Mary suggested.

"I have blueberry jam," Erith said.

THE LIARS

That commenced the nursing of Rosie Ryan. Danol advised Erith to hide any cash she had in the house. John had told him it would be wise. He told her what John knew about Rosie and what Mr. Payton had said. He believed there was something more to the story than they realized, and he would find out.

41

John waited at the store until there was news of Rosie. He thought back to all the times they had crossed paths. They'd robbed together and eaten together more times than he could count. There was no allegiance on the street. It was an everyone-for-themselves affair, and not everyone was made for that existence. People disappeared and were not heard from again—almost always the few girls who came along and, less often, young boys. Everyone who lived on the street knew that and accepted it as a possible fate. Rosie knew that, too, but somehow she had managed to last. In some ways John admired her for that.

Now, she wanted to talk to Teddy. The doctor said she was pretty weak but insisted on seeing him.

"Teddy, I knew it was you the moment I laid eyes on you," Rosie said. Her voice was hushed and ragged.

"I knew it was you, too, Rosie."

"Remember what I told you the last time I saw you?"

"Can't say as I do, Rosie. It's been a long time now."

"I told you that you'd regret the day you crossed Rosie Ryan."

"You were probably angry about something or other," John replied.

"You've got a nice place for yourself here."

"I don't live here," he said. Stirrings of anger and fear ignited in him.

"You have money, Teddy. I can see by the way you're dressed. All fancy, you are."

"I have no money. Somebody else dressed me," John argued.

"Well, you'd better get me some money from these folks, or I'll get you undressed pretty quick," Rosie snarled. She coughed, and her body trembled.

"Don't get yourself worked up," he countered. "You're a sick woman." John took the cloth from the pan at the side table and wrung it out. He mopped her brow with it, though she weakly tried to brush him away.

"I'll tell these people who you are, Teddy. I'll ruin your life."

Danol spoke behind him. "These people already know about his life on the streets. He's welcome here."

John saw her eyes flick from anger to something akin to defeat. "What do you want, Rosie?" he asked again.

She turned her head to the side to signal she was finished talking.

Danol spoke again. "Rosie Ryan, you are not the daughter of Kathleen Ryan. Her child would be ten years older than you."

Rose turned back to look at John, then at Danol. Her look of disbelief was real.

"That's right, Rosie. Kathleen Ryan died two years ago. She was fifty-seven. She had one child when she was fifteen. That child would be forty-five or forty-six now. It can't be you."

"But Elias told me," she said.

"Who's Elias?"

"He's my brother."

"Elias was wrong," John said.

Rosie put her hands over her face and rubbed her temples. She coughed again, and John lifted her head and gave her a drink of water.

"Why are you being nice to me?" she demanded, her breath coming quickly at the exertion.

"I always liked you, Rosie. I admired how you stayed alive when so many others failed. You were strong. You still are."

"I would have told on you."

"I would have, too, if I were in your place."

Rosie nodded at his sincerity.

"Who's Elias?"

"I told you, he's my brother. Well, he was my brother."

"Tell us about him."

"Elias was adopted from the orphanage. The missus said she couldn't have children. He was about eleven when they adopted me. My father thought it would help his wife if she had a little girl around. But what he really wanted was a replacement for her, if you know what I mean."

"Oh, Rosie, I'm sorry," John said sadly.

"It was okay. Elias helped me until I got big enough to help myself. He always told me I wasn't a Baker—I was a Ryan like him. He brought me back to the orphanage when he left. I was signed in as Rosie Ryan. My father saw me one time, down on Water Street, after I ran away from one home or another. He tried to pull me in the carriage. You helped me that day, Teddy."

"I remember it. I knocked over a cart. Got in a heap of trouble over it."

Rosie laughed and coughed again. He tried to sit her up, but she pushed him away and settled back down. Danol tapped him on the shoulder and beckoned him to come outside.

"I'll be back in a minute," John said.

"John," said Danol, "it's not looking good for Rosie. Mary says she's deathly ill."

"She's strong."

"She's had a poor life, John. She's not that strong. We need to find out as much as we can from her."

"How do I do that?"

"Make her an offer. If she recovers, I'll uphold it." Danol explained what he was thinking.

"What about Erith? Will she agree?"

"She has a good heart. She'll want to do right by Rosie."

John shook Danol's hand. "It's you who has the good heart."

John sat by Rosie again. "How would you like to go to Boston when you're well enough to travel?" he asked her.

"Boston?" Rosie asked. "How will I get to Boston, and what would I do there?"

"The doctor, Mary Ro, she knows a place there where you can get better. She thinks you might have TB, Rosie. You won't get better if you don't look after yourself."

"Boston is a big, fancy, expensive city," she argued. "I can't go to Boston."

"The Coopers will look after your travel and your stay. They're good people. Mary has family there who can help you."

"I can't imagine me in Boston," she said. "Too big for me."

"Nothing's too big for Rosie Ryan."

"I'm glad I got to see you again, Teddy," she wheezed. Her breathing was shallow, and she barely got the words out.

"You'll see me again. I'll come back tomorrow. Tell me about Elias," John continued. "He sounds like he was a good brother."

"He was," Rosie said. She drifted in and out as she told him what she knew.

"Elias was good to you."

"He was. Stay with me, Teddy. I'd like to have a friendly face—" She coughed again. This time she couldn't catch her breath. She wheezed and rattled and grasped his hand. Mary rushed in and laid a stethoscope on Rosie's chest that was connected to a tube that led to Mary's ears. She tilted her head and pulled the thing off and strung it around her neck. As Mary sat on the edge of the bed near Rosie's knees, she held the patient's other hand, bowed her head, and waited. Rosie took two more shallow breaths, and then she was gone.

John laid her hand by her side and got up. Mary touched his arm. "Make sure you wash your hands in the pan by the door."

John nodded and did as she asked. He shook his head at Danol as he left the house. Mary came out. Her voice faded into the distance as she told the others that Rosie was dead. He was sad for her, for her need that was born of desperation. He'd felt that hopelessness before. Lavinia had helped him get off the streets, and Alice had helped him come back to life.

Danol caught up to him before he reached the crossing place. "I'm sorry about your friend," he said.

"I appreciate that," John said.

"Can the children stay with you and Alice at the house tonight?"

"I wouldn't think about sending them back."

"We'll bring food later for everyone."

They walked in silence for a few moments before John ventured, "Seeing as you are captain of the *Angel Endeavours*, would you be so inclined as to marry me and Alice? I don't want to wait. We've waited long enough."

"I'd be happy to do that. Just tell me when."

"Thing is, I don't want Beatrice to know."

"I understand."

"I'd like to do it in the next day or two. I have to tell Alice first."

"I think that's important," Danol said. He clapped his friend on the back. "I have to do something in St. John's in a few days. If you want to go, we can do it then. We can leave the children with Maggie for a few days."

"I'll tell Alice."

"I've got to get back. I just wanted to see how you were faring," Danol said. John stopped and shook his hand. They both eyed each another and shook hands again before parting ways.

42

John returned to the house and told the four of them the plan for the evening. Mary and Peter came in on their way home and suggested the children go to John's Pond with them for the afternoon. Alice and John could come with Danol and Erith for supper, and the children could return at that time.

Alone with Alice, John decided it was time to tell her everything about his life. They sat together in front of the stone fireplace at Danol's house.

Alice held his hand while he told her what there was to know about Teddy White and John MacDonald.

"If you can stomach me after that, I want you to be my wife. If you can't, it's not too late to run away."

Alice started to cry. "John, before I say anything, I want to be sure that you will want to marry me."

"Alice, I love you. I will take you just as you are, and there is no need for you to tell me anything."

"I have to, John. Or it will come between us."

"After what I've told you, I doubt there is anything you can say that will keep me from marrying you. I don't want to know."

"I want to tell you. Please."

"All right," he said.

"You know about Ezra. But you don't know everything," Alice said. She sat back in the chair and closed her eyes. She let her grip relax on his hand, but he didn't let go.

"I ran away from home. My father wanted me to marry some lout in the village. Irene had wed at sixteen, so I went to her in Labrador. I had nowhere else to go, so I married Philip—you know all of this.

"What you don't know is Ezra was persistent, and Philip was all tied up in worrying about his mother, about making a living, and about anything else that could torment him. I was young and wanted some excitement. I wasn't welcomed by the common folk at the Mission. I was an outsider. So, I lay with Ezra. Just one time, but one time nonetheless. I regretted it every day after that, but I couldn't tell Philip or he'd kick me out and I'd have nowhere to go. So, I pretended that it didn't happen and tried to avoid Ezra, but that was next to impossible. Then I found out I was having a baby."

Alice tried to pull her hand away, but John held on tight. Questions were swirling in his mind, but he waited for her to tell him. She had waited for him. She brushed her face with her other hand but didn't open her eyes.

"Ezra thought the baby was his, but to be truthful, I didn't know. I still don't know. The day we left to go to Zoar was one of the best days that I could remember with Philip. He was playful like he had been when we first met. We were having such a carefree day. We left the baby, my son, James, with a lady at the Mission. I swear on that little boy's life that I didn't know Ezra was following us. You believe me, don't you?"

"I believe you, Alice. I know what kind of woman you are."

"When I saw Beatrice that day, needing somebody to love her, I thought about my boy. I clung to her to save myself. I knew she could never replace James, but in my heart, I needed something to survive. Beatrice was that something. Being a mother to Beatrice was like a redemption for leaving James."

"She was my something, too," John said softly. "I'd been empty of every kind of feeling for so long that she was my saviour, too."

"When we got to Zoar, Irene came up with the plan to leave. She was afraid of what Ezra would say. My sister knew what happened between us. She didn't want her husband, Paul, to find out because of what it could mean for their marriage. I was running from more than just Ezra. I was running for my life. She told me she'd get Paul to take the baby. As far as I know, Irene has James, but I don't know that for sure. I don't know where James is. He'd be all grown up now. Best he doesn't know about his mother."

Alice began to cry again, and John pulled her to him. She sat in his arms in the chair and cried until she could cry no more.

"You'll be able to write Irene now. You can get in contact with her again."

Alice told him about the teacher who sent the note for her when Beatrice was in grade one. She knew that's what had led Ezra to them. He had nearly killed Irene, and then whom she believed to be Caddy in Holyrood.

"Thankfully they will both recover," she said. "I won't have that on my mind. So, if you can stomach me after that, I'll marry you."

"How about the day after tomorrow?"

"Oh, John," Alice said. She threw her arms around him. "We've waited long enough."

43

Erith and Danol had one final thing to sort out before returning to the *Angel Endeavours*. "You're sure about this?"

"As sure as I'll ever be," she said.

"Constable Jeffries made the arrangements for 2:00 p.m. That will give us time to walk there if you want."

"I'd like that," Erith said.

"Are you nervous?" Danol asked.

"Just a little. But I'll be fine as long as you're with me." He kissed her cheek, helped her with her coat, and they set out for the St. John's Penitentiary near Quidi Vidi.

The day was warm and breezy. They walked the cobbled streets arm in arm, chatting about the children and everything that had happened over the last few days.

"Alexander MacDonald seems like a nice man."

"I thought so, too," Danol said.

"I can't believe how easy it was to convince him to come with us."

"Well, he wanted to see his son get married."

"John and Alice were happy enough to postpone their

wedding by a few days when they found out he might be able to come."

"Walsh and Hearn are gone to help him take what he wants," said Danol. "They'll be on board before we get back."

"Did you talk to John yet about Mount Carmel and the mill?"

"No, not yet. I think he'll agree to run it for me. John's not happy accepting charity, as he calls it. He's grateful but says he wants to work."

"So, you'll be building boats," Erith teased.

"After I finish the house."

"But it's finished."

"Not the way I want it. It was finished when I was a bachelor. Now I'm a married man, and I have needs," he said and squeezed her arm. They both laughed.

"Needs. Well, now, I can't wait to find out what those are," Erith said, pushing him off his stride.

They continued to banter back and forth until the large stone building came into view. "There it is, my dear," Danol said. "It's not too late to go back."

"If you're going, then I'm going," she said. "And I know you're going."

They wound their way along the gravelled path that led to the front of the building that backed onto Quidi Vidi lake.

"I don't see a door," said Erith.

"Jeffries said to go down to the right, and the entrance was there. Almost like it's under the hill."

"It must be there where the guard is," she said as she pointed toward a man in a black uniform. As they crested the small rise, they noticed stables to their far right separated from the main building. They couldn't tell if the huge stone structure was three or four storeys high. There were no windows to be seen, but there were indents that were either placed for show or were intended to be glassed at one point in time.

Danol spoke to the guard. The man eyed Erith and asked if he was sure she wanted to go in. Danol assured him that she would be fine. They passed through a large iron gate and entered a stone-covered porch. The guard rapped on the wooden doors, and a small shutter, not much bigger than a peep hole, opened. The guard gave his permission to open the doors. The shutter closed, and the latch creaked before one of the doors swung wide. They looked to be almost a foot thick.

Two guards stood inside, one behind a table directly in front of them and one near the door. The one closer motioned for them to go to the desk. Danol told him the name of the prisoner they were there to see.

The man who stood by the door secured the latch and then strode down the long corridor to another a set of bars. He unlocked them, a portion swung inwards, and he went inside. The remaining guard told them to wait on a bench that had been partially hidden by the open door. They sat in silence until they heard the guard call to them from the end of the corridor. They followed him to a small room through a maze of walkways that overlooked the pond and a grassy area enclosed by a stone wall. They entered the room, and the guard stood by the door. Danol and Erith sat on one side of a long, narrow table that divided the room.

A door on the opposite wall opened, and a guard and a man in a white striped shirt and pants entered. The prisoner was brought to the table and seated, and the guard backed up to the brick wall.

"What can I do for you, Mr. Cooper?"

"Elias Ryan, or should I say Captain Baker, have you met my wife?" Danol kept his voice low so the guards wouldn't hear him.

"Can't say as I have. Mrs. Cooper. Pleased to meet you, ma'am," the prisoner said.

"We know who you are," Erith said, her face flushed at her whispered outburst.

"I know. Your husband knew me on the boat."

"No, I mean we know who you *are*," she said.

The man studied her for a moment. "Tell me more," he said.

"We came to bring news of Rosie," she said. "I'm sorry to have to tell you that Rosie died at my home a few days ago." She couldn't tell by his face if what she was saying registered with him.

"The doctor tried to save her, but she had a lung infection that was left untreated for too long," Danol put in.

"We gave her a proper burial," Erith said rather quickly.

"Thank you," Elias said. "I knew this would come to Rosie sooner rather than later."

"She died peacefully. If that's any comfort to you," Erith said.

"I'm sure you didn't come here to tell me Rosie was dead. Although I appreciate it, why are you here?"

"Your mother reared me," Erith said. He didn't blink. Elias showed no sign that her words meant anything to him. Erith went on to tell him what Mrs. Patsy had told her.

"What was she like?" Elias asked.

"I won't lie," Erith replied.

"I don't want you to."

Danol held her hand beneath the table as she described the

dismal life she'd had with Kathleen. The sadness came through in her voice. "The only good thing that came out of that was my getting to meet those three precious children whom I now call my own. They're your kin. We have both adopted them."

"I think you already know this," Danol said.

"What if I do?"

"Nothing, really," Danol said. "But I also think that what happened to the children and to Erith a few years ago had something to do with you, Elias."

Erith squeezed his hand beneath the table and hung her head.

"It had to do with the children, I'll admit," Elias said at length. "And what happened to your wife was an unfortunate consequence for which a harsh message has been sent."

Erith gasped. "You mean . . ."

"A very harsh and final message, Mrs. Cooper," Elias said with emphasis. "We are brigands. We are not beasts. I don't tolerate that behaviour."

Danol rubbed the back of Erith's hand, hoping to provide a little comfort as she endeavoured to comprehend Elias's words. He felt her shift just a little as she tried to lean closer. He suspected she didn't want to call attention to her discomfort, nor to show any weakness in front of Elias. Danol pulled her hand over to rest on his leg and covered it with his own.

"What was the recent attack about?" Danol asked. "You had spies on my boat."

"In some ways, coincidence, Mr. Cooper. I also have a debt to settle with you for interrupting my lucrative rum-running. You cost me a boat. But you also have care of my kin, although few people know that. I had planned to take your cargo, keep you and your crew for a few days, then let you go. Unfortunately, you interrupted that, so the price still remains and has doubled."

"And what was the coincidence?" Danol asked him.

"Let's just say we had an accident a few years ago on the Labrador. One of my men, dare I say . . . got a little too fervent. He murdered some crew on a vessel and left one alive. Although I didn't agree with what had happened, nor was I present at the time, I take responsibility for the actions of my men. The one who was killed on the boat, he can no longer give witness against what happened, so, thanks to that boy, I no longer have that problem. How is the boy, by the way?"

"He's just fine. He's not one of your kin," Danol said.

"I know that. He's a little too old."

"I need to know my family is safe," Danol said. He squeezed Erith's hand beneath the table.

"I have respect for you, Mr. Cooper. You're a smart man. Have you ever considered becoming a pirate?"

Danol laughed without smiling. "You haven't answered my question. You seem like a smart man. Have you ever considered going into a legitimate business?"

"You answer my question first," Elias said. "Why didn't you turn me in on the ship? You knew who I was. You were a man of the law, and I believe you still are."

"That's hard to answer, because I honestly don't know. Maybe something came over me. Nothing had really happened beyond some threats." Danol paused and regarded Elias. "I wanted you to have a victory, of sorts, in the eyes of your men. I believe it is something of a point of honour among captains. I may have made that up from a dream, or I may have heard that somewhere, sometime. Very vague, I realize, but yes, I did know it was you, and honour is important to me."

"We are not so different," said the prisoner. "Honour is important to me, too. I appreciate your efforts. Your family is safe. You have my word."

The tension Danol felt in his belly slowly ebbed, and he almost sighed aloud. "But my ship is not. Do I have that correct?"

"There is a price to be paid. My men must see that," Elias replied. "However, your ship will not be harmed, your crew will not be harmed, and I believe you carry insurance for your cargo. Am I really hurting you? And just so you don't lose any business, I'll make sure there is at least a year in between."

Danol chuckled. "And if I try to avoid such encounters?"

"The price will go up."

"At least I know how things are. I'm holding you to your word on my family," Danol said. "That's what's important to me."

"I consider myself held," Elias said with a nod. He turned to Erith. "I am truly sorry for what happened to you. I do feel responsible in many ways. Thank you for taking care of Rosie, and thank you for taking care of the three little ones. I have no children myself, so I consider them my kin. That includes you." He turned to Danol and grinned. "I guess, by circumstance, that means you, too."

"Constable Jeffries tells me you will be out by next week, at the latest. He was intrigued by my request to see you but didn't pursue it."

"It's not so bad in here," Elias said. He shrugged. "A bit of a rest, actually."

"If it will help pay my debt earlier, I got the *Seafarer* for a pittance as salvage. She'll be at the dock here for at least a couple of weeks before I move her."

"I'll take it under consideration. I have a week to think about it."

Danol led Erith back the way they came, following the guard. She hadn't said much, and he hoped he wouldn't regret bringing her along. It was troubling him. He didn't want to keep secrets from her, but maybe this could be an exception.

When they got outside and away from the prison, he stopped on the path before they reached the cemetery. Erith was silent as she clutched his arm. He pulled her around to face him. "I shouldn't have brought you in there," he said. "I'm sorry."

"I'm fine, Danol," she said.

"You're not. Before you went in, you were talkative and happy. Now you are quiet and seem so sad."

"I'm just thinking about what he said."

"Which part?"

"When he said the people had paid for hurting me. He meant those men were killed, didn't he?"

"I believe he did, yes."

"That's what I'm thinking about," Erith said. "I was happy when I heard those men had been killed. Does that make me like Elias?"

"Oh, Erith, not at all. That makes you who you are. I was ready to kill them myself when I found out. Only for Peter stopping me, I might have done it. Don't feel badly for those men."

"I don't." Erith paused and pushed away from his embrace. Her eyes were big and wet. "When I heard they'd been killed in prison before the trial, for a time I felt like I didn't get justice. They were still dead, but I felt like I had somehow been robbed. But now that I know they were killed because of what they did to me, it makes me feel different—like I was avenged. Does it make me a bad person for being happy about that? Not really happy—more like satisfied."

"Erith, my love, that makes you the most beautiful person I know." Danol pulled her to him once more and kissed her. "I can't believe how much I love you and how lucky I am to have you by my side."

He led her along beside the cemetery and glanced at the spot where they had supposedly buried Teddy White. Tonight, after they set sail, he'd officiate and marry John MacDonald and Nancy Alice Martin to fulfill their wish that Beatrice would not know about their complicated relationship.

As they strolled past the stores on Water Street, something caught Erith's eye in the London, New York and Paris store on the corner of Baird's Lane, and she dragged Danol to a stop.

"I don't remember this store being here," she said.

"It's been here a couple of years, I believe. We probably wouldn't have passed it, though, as we usually came down Duckworth Street. Is there something you want?"

"Do we have time?" she asked.

"As long as we're back before supper," said Danol. "Do you plan on being in there that long?"

"No, I just want to get that," she said as she pointed at the window display.

"What? I only see that white thing with wheels. Is that what you're looking at?"

"Yes," Erith said. She looked at him and searched his face.

Danol was confused. He didn't know what the thing was. It looked like a tea cart of some sort, but he didn't know Erith to want for fancy things. "Do you want me to go in and get it for you?" he asked. "I have no notion of what it is."

"Danol, surely you've seen one before," she said as she continued to stare at him. "It's a pram. A baby carriage."

"A baby carriage? Who do you need one for?" he asked.

"For us."

"For us," he repeated. Then it struck him. "For *us*?" She nodded as she continued to stare at him. "For us!"

He grabbed her and spun her around and shouted, "For us!"

"Danol, put me down," Erith cried. She giggled, her face turned red, and she made a swat at him to set her down.

"Oh, did I hurt you?" Irrational fear seized him.

"No, you didn't hurt me."

"Did I hurt the baby? Erith, we're having a baby? When? How do you know?" His emotions went from one extreme to the other. He couldn't control them.

"Mary Ro says I am."

"Mary knows?"

"Yes, Mary knows. She examined me when she was over two days ago," Erith said. "I didn't want to tell you until we had finished up with everything today. Then our conversation took us somewhere else, and I was going to wait until tomorrow. Then I saw the carriage. Are you happy, Danol?"

"I don't know. I think I am. I don't know what I am. This is a shock. I know that's what happens when, you know . . ." he said. "But I hadn't thought about it. But I *did* think about it. I'm building a nursery on the third floor for us and for babies."

"Oh, Danol, a nursery?"

"Yes, and the first thing that I'm getting is that thing in there. What did you call it?"

"A pram."

"A pram. That's the first thing I'm getting for it." He laughed and was about to pick her up again, but he stopped himself. He had to try to keep better control over his impulses when he was around her.

Erith laughed. "It's okay, Danol. You won't break me."

"Oh, Erith, a baby! With you!" He kissed her soundly in the middle of the street before entering the store. He purchased every baby item that was for sale.

44

One year later

The *Angel Endeavours* tapped off the dock in Mount Carmel, and Mary Ro, standing on the gunwale and with one hand gripping a wooden rail on the house, was first to spring onto the wharf. This urgency was familiar to her, but not to Erith. John's grimace and furrowed brow worried her. He was waiting to carry Mary's doctor's bag.

Danol signalled for Erith to follow them as they rushed to the edge of the beach and up over the embankment to the two-storey house in the meadow. Not as sure-footed, the gravel skittered beneath her feet and she had to catch herself to stay upright.

Beatrice waved from the gallery. Mary and John darted past her into the house. A few steps behind, Erith held out her arms to the child as she came up the steps, and Beatrice pressed herself into Erith's embrace. Beatrice bawled while Erith, grappling for breath, led her to the wooden chair beneath the window on the covered deck.

Erith pulled the girl into her arms and hugged her tightly until the child was spent. John came out moments later and sat on a stool near the step. He put his palms to his face and rubbed them around his temples while he bent to rest his elbows on his knees.

"Daddy."

He straightened and looked at Beatrice. "Mommy will be fine," he said, sounding more confident than he looked. "Dr. Mary is with her now."

John locked eyes with Erith. He was searching her face for some sort of reassurance, and she smiled. She reached out and patted his arm. "Mary knows what she's doing."

"She's in so much pain. It's been so long. How much can she take?"

"That's not unusual, John. Alice is strong and healthy. Mary was happy to come."

"I'm sure glad to have her. She threw me out as soon as she went in the room."

Erith laughed as she remembered that Mary had done the same thing with Danol only a few months before.

"You go on to the mill with Danol. I'll stay here with Beatrice."

John stood and patted his daughter's back. She looked at him and then quickly buried herself again in Erith's neck. Erith hugged her more tightly and murmured words of comfort.

"Mommy told me you were my 'before mother,'" the little girl said as she pulled back from her shoulder and gazed at Erith's face through tears.

Erith blinked. Where had that come from? Her breath caught somewhere deep in her throat. She glanced quickly at John. He nodded. Were John and Alice returning Beatrice to her now that they were having a new baby? That didn't make sense.

"Alice was scared something would happen to her," John whispered. "She thinks there is something wrong."

Erith gulped. For an instant she was sad, but she shook it off. Poor Alice was preparing for the worst. She settled her gaze on Beatrice. "Do you know what that means?" she asked softly.

"I'll be going," John said as he scurried off the stairs and headed toward the wooden structure that stretched along the river below the hill. Erith guessed he was going to seek solace in the place he knew: the mill.

"Annie told me she had a 'before mommy' and she went away. She said you became her new mommy," Beatrice said. "Annie only remembers you, not the 'before mommy.'"

"That's right," Erith said. "Her 'before mommy.'" She paused as she searched for the right words. "Her 'before mommy' had to go away. She didn't want to, but she had to."

"That's what Mommy said. She said that you had to leave me, but you didn't want to. She said I was like Annie."

Tears sprang to Erith's eyes. With every ounce of courage she could muster, she held them in and took a deep breath. She nodded at Beatrice, softly held her cheeks in her palms, and kissed her forehead. "That's right, I didn't want to leave you. I was very sad about it."

"Mommy said that you looked and looked for me but couldn't find me. She told me that you found Annie and George and Tommy and that they needed a mommy."

Erith smiled. "I did, and I love them so much, just like your mommy loves you."

"Mommy said that if she has to go away, you will be my mommy again. But I don't want her to go away."

Erith hugged her. "I know you don't, sweet child. I know

you don't. Dr. Mary is here to help her stay with you. Your mommy will try really hard not to go."

A window slid open somewhere about the covered porch. "Erith, are you there? I need your help."

"I'm right here, Mary," Erith called out. "I'm coming."

She lifted Beatrice off her lap and stooped in front of her. "You run down to your daddy and Danol. I'll come get you as soon as I can."

Beatrice nodded and moved slowly toward the step.

"Go on now," Erith said. She peered toward the mill. John and Danol were sitting on a pile of logs. She shouted to them, told them Beatrice was on her way, and watched the child until she was in view of the men. She bolted into the house and followed the noise of a labouring Alice.

Alice's brow was soaked with sweat as her body contracted violently before being momentarily released. She motioned for Erith to come to her side. A grey-haired woman, the midwife, was tearing strips from a bedsheet and soaking them in a pan of steaming water. Bloodied bandages were piled at the foot of the bed. Mary Ro didn't meet her gaze.

"You have to take Beatrice," Alice whispered.

"I'm not taking her," Erith said through gritted teeth. "There won't be a need."

"You promise me," Alice moaned as her body wrenched once again. She grabbed Erith's hand. "Promise me."

Erith sat on the side of the bed and squeezed her hand. "Hold on, Alice. You'll be just fine," she said. "No matter what happens, you don't have to worry about Beatrice."

Mary came behind Erith and looked down at Alice. "The baby is legs first, Alice. I need to turn him. Erith and Clara will hold you. After the next contraction. You won't last like this if I don't turn the baby, and it is too late for surgery." Mary clasped their joined hands. "Hold on for another few minutes."

Mary looked pointedly at Erith and Clara. "Whatever you do, hold her down."

When the next contraction seized Alice, Erith and Clara pushed her shoulders into the bed and held her there. Alice screamed as Erith bent over her and whispered words of encouragement.

In a loud voice, Mary kept repeating, "Almost there, Alice! Almost there."

The spasm subsided, and Alice loosened her grip. Erith moved back to look at her. The woman was exhausted.

"You're ready, Alice. Next one and the baby is here."

"I can't," said Alice as she slowly shook her head from side to side.

"Yes, you can. Erith and Clara are going to help you."

Alice cried out again, and Erith and Clara lifted her shoulders as her body tensed. Alice's face turned blue as she gave one final shriek.

Erith cried out with her and stroked her hair. Was it only two months before that Mary was with her when little Charlie was born?

She eased Alice back onto the soaked pillows, and Mary handed the baby off to Clara. "You're not done yet, Alice. Just a little while longer."

Erith glanced at Mary with a raised eyebrow.

"She's having twins," Mary said. "That's why she's early." Mary Ro had been here months before, when Alexander MacDonald took sick. She had stayed for a few days until he died. At that time there would have been no way to know that Alice was having twins.

Erith hadn't been able to come then. She was too far along, and a few days after Mary got back, she had given birth herself. Now her jaw dropped at the news of twins. Alice moaned. Erith wedged herself behind Alice and propped her up in her arms.

"Don't give up, Alice. Your babies need their momma."

Alice's body shook once more, and Erith, using her own body as support, pushed her toward Mary. Mary grabbed Alice's hands and pulled her forward. They both shouted encouragement at the fading woman. Alice shuddered and moaned before collapsing back on Erith when the pain had passed.

Erith reached for the pan and took out a wet piece of cloth. She dabbed it along Alice's hairline and wiped her face.

"Once more, Alice," Mary said.

"No. No," Alice panted. "I can't." Her breathing was shallow. Erith's eyes met Mary's. She saw the uncertainty on her face.

"Yes, you can," Erith said forcefully. "Yes, you can. For Beatrice."

Alice's body flexed, and Erith moved with her as she pushed her toward Mary once again. Mary shouted encouragement at Alice while Erith kept her from sinking back onto the bed.

"That's it. That's it. That's it," Mary said.

Alice's body contracted and squeezed and trembled all at the same time. She let out a mournful cry before collapsing on Erith.

"You did it," Mary said. She handed off the second baby to Clara, then waited for the next tremor to finish the birth. She tapped Alice's legs several times with the tips of her fingers to make sure she was awake. Alice groaned a pitiful protest in Erith's arms. Erith pulled herself out from underneath Alice and set the pillow beneath her head. "Let her rest for a bit," Mary said without looking up. Erith clapped her on the back as she went around her to see the babies.

"We would have lost them all," Clara whispered as she washed the two infants. "Alice was frantic that you wouldn't make it in time."

Erith swaddled one while Clara finished washing the second one. "Why was she so afraid?"

"She couldn't be consoled," said Clara. "She wanted you here for Beatrice if . . . you know."

They quickly cleaned the room and fixed Alice in the bed. Erith pulled open the window to let in some fresh air. She could see the men, and when Mary was finished tending to Alice, she went downstairs to call them.

John and Beatrice raced toward the house with Danol close behind. Erith smiled at John, and he lifted Beatrice and swung her around. "You're going to be a sister!"

Beatrice squealed as John carried her up the stairs, taking them two at a time. Erith followed. Mary and Clara came out to give them privacy. Erith watched John's face as he realized he had two babies, one perched on either side of Alice, who was propped up on clean pillows. Though she was weak and pallid, she was smiling. Beatrice ran to her mother and hugged her. Erith left to find Danol.

"They have a boy," Erith said to her husband.

"A son for John," Danol said.

"And a girl."

Danol's eyes widened when he realized what she had said. "A son *and* a daughter?"

"A sister and brother for Beatrice," Erith said. She smiled and threw her arms around him.

He laughed. "Let's get home to Charlie."

"Yes, let's," said Erith. She was sure her contentment mirrored his.

"John mentioned that Alice's sister and her family are coming for a visit in the next month or so," Danol told her.

"That will be good for Alice. Clara will stay with her for a few weeks until she is well."

Epilogue

St. John's
Ten years later

"What do you think of that, Mrs. Cooper?"

"It's beautiful. She's beautiful, Mr. Cooper."

"Then you approve?"

"Well, it's too late now, really, isn't it?"

"We could change the colour if you want," he said.

"No, yellow's my favourite. This one is truly a beauty."

Erith's Quest would be launched the next day from the St. John's dockyard. The finest vessel they owned—and the largest. Today, Danol wanted to show her the completed ship before the fanfare of the christening. They finished the tour in the master suite, the main cabin, where he had a surprise for her.

"Danol, it's a big boat. Are you sure we want something this big?"

"Well, I need to talk to you about that."

"Really?" Erith asked.

"Yes. I spoke to Peter, and he agrees that we can find somebody in North Harbour to skipper the *Angel Endeavours* this year. George will skipper the *Beatrice Annie* and do all the freight runs while we're gone. Tommy will look after the business for us."

"And where might we be going, Mr. Cooper?"

"Well, I heard there's this little town in England . . ." His voice trailed off as his words sank in.

"What?"

"You heard me, Erith. We're going to find your mother's family."

She flung herself into his arms. "Danol Cooper, I had no idea you were planning this! How did you keep this a secret?"

"It was easy. Nobody knows except Peter Sr., George, and Tommy. Oh, I mean Tom."

"Yes, don't forget, it's Tom now. He's too grown up for Tommy." They both laughed. Tom was, after all, twenty-four years old. When he came home from college the year before, he told them he sounded more professional as Tom. Danol had helped him start an accounting firm in St. John's, and he was prospering.

"Well, who's going? Give me some details."

"We'll set out in about two months. *Erith's Quest* will have her sea trials by then."

"I'm going to ask Annie and Eddy if they want to join us." Annie Ryan and Edward Nolan had been sweethearts from childhood and married as soon as Annie came of age. They had two children. Despite Danol's belief that Eddy was going to be a sailor, Eddy followed in his father's footsteps and became a doctor. Their Annie became a nurse and worked alongside her husband. "If they can't get away from their practice, then maybe the children can come. Of course, we can't leave without the other six."

Danol and Erith had six children since they married. She

had given up the store in favour of living on the south side of the harbour in the big yellow house with all the windows and the two staircases. George and his wife took over the store. George became a seafarer like Danol, and his wife managed the business.

Danol built a third floor in the attic, with fancy glass windows in the nursery, then took to building boats and hiring them out—and selling some as well. He liked his life on shore with his wife and children. He commissioned the St. John's dockyard to build *Erith's Quest* but had designed it himself.

The *Beatrice Annie* was the first boat he built from the MacDonald Lumber Yard in Mount Carmel. He built that one for her baby girls. Erith thought she couldn't love him more.

Beatrice spent several summers with them. Erith funded her education, and Beatrice was now a journalist and living in Toronto, Canada. She wrote to them often. Erith loved Beatrice and was happy to have shared her life along with John and Alice.

She was truly spoiled. Danol was giving her a chance to meet the family she hadn't known. Her mother's people were in Erith, England. Her mother had given her the most precious gift, the name "Erith," which had mapped a course that led her to Danol. And now, even further, with the man she loved.

"Did you say the other six?"

"Yes, why?"

"You may need to count again. There'll be six and a half on this journey."

She beamed at Danol and watched his face as the realization set in that there'd be a seventh Cooper in North Harbour before the end of the year.

"Do I need to get another pram?"

He kissed her tenderly to finish the tour.

Afterword

There is such a rich and fascinating history attached to New-foundland and Labrador and her people.

Very rarely did a news story pertaining to crime in Labrador make it to the papers on the island of Newfoundland. However, a couple of articles that led to this novel's beginnings were among the few.

I came across the story of Ephraim the Esquimeaux's escape in Harbour Main while I was researching the provincial history of the late 1800s. I filed it away, and it helped spawn the sequel to *The Promise*.

I found several articles and Moravian journal accounts that followed the capture, escape, and recapture of Ephraim (sometimes spelled Ephriam) the Esquimeaux or Esquimo. During the trial in St. John's, he was referenced as Ephraim Taktos. From careful research I was able to determine that Ephraim killed his first wife (Ruth Taktos) by throwing her into the sea. Within a few months, he married a woman who was almost twice his age and murdered his stepson, Philip, in part due to a relationship with the stepson's wife, Nancy. Ephraim was taken into custody by the Moravian Brethren after the second murder. Having nowhere to keep him over the winter, he was sent to St. John's. He escaped in Harbour Main and was recaptured. After trial he was sentenced to be hanged, but the sentence was commuted to life in prison. Ephraim died a few years later from complications of tuberculosis.

Additionally, part of our fishing history is attributed to the green fishermen—those who stayed in Labrador and returned to their Island homes in the fall, as well as the floater fishery—those who prosecuted the fishery from a base on the Island of Newfoundland, where the boats were registered and the fish processed. The floater fishery employed women servants to cook and "ready" the fish. The women were paid less, worked hard, and had no privacy, until the mid-1880s, when enterprises were fined for not keeping separate accommodations for females. Enterprise owners often hung a curtain between both genders in order to meet regulations.

Both these pieces of history led to the characters known as Ezra Shawe and Alice Martin.

Another fascinating story is related to a mystery surrounding George's Island in Labrador. A man showed up in a small community several miles away claiming to have been the sole survivor from the *Walrus* when she was wrecked on the island during a windstorm. Upon investigation by local fishermen, several headless bodies were found lying together on the beach, another some distance farther away, where the head had been cleaved with an axe. A campsite was discovered, as well as papers, books, and the black and white photo of a woman stuffed in the rocks. To this day the mystery has not been solved, nor did it make it to the newspapers on the Island of Newfoundland until the following year.

Another story is related to events surrounding Lieutenant Colonel John Moody and a charwoman's death while in service to John Jackson's daughter, Margaret. Although this took place in the eighteenth century, I believed it was worth mentioning and led to the character Lavinia.

These two scenarios played a crucial role in the development of Teddy White and his transformation into John MacDonald.

The novel is in no way intended to represent these stories disrespectfully. It is merely meant to highlight some of the not-so-pleasant histories that make up the foundation of our beautiful province, Newfoundland and Labrador.

The following entry was posted in *Archival Moments* and tagged "domestic," "Emily Day," "girls," and "servants" on July 16, 2019, by Larry Dohey.

Females engaged as servants in the fishery
Archival Moment, May 5, 1884
An "apartment" for the females engaged as servants in the fishery

The women of Newfoundland have long had a place on the fishing boats that have gone to the sea. These fishing boats were often small vessels, with limited space, that allowed for little privacy for the crew, especially for the women.

On **May 5, 1884**; A. J. Pearce, Sub collector at the Custom House in Twillingate responsible for recording the arrival and departure of all vessels, inspecting the cargo of the vessels and insuring that all paid the required duties and taxes made it known that he wanted the privacy of women aboard vessels protected.

Under the headline "Notice to Schooner Holders" he posted in the local newspaper an announcement that read:

> *"Sailing Vessels carrying females engaged as servants in the fishery or as passengers, between Newfoundland and Labrador shall be provide with such separate cabin or apartments as will afford at least, fifty cubic feet for each of such females and the owners of such vessels shall provide for such females sufficient accommodation for sanitary purposes." (Section I and V of the said act)*

Captains of the vessels were warned that if they did not conform to this new regulation they could face *"a one hundred dollar fine."*

The regulations were largely put in place for the women involved in the Labrador fishery, especially those involved in the "floater fishery." The Labrador fishery consisted of "floaters," those who lived on their boats and fished along the Labrador coast. Floaters brought their catch back to Newfoundland for processing. Women involved in the floater fishery were typically young and single, and their primary responsibility was cooking for the fishermen.

The regulations that were introduced describing the space to be provided as *"a separate cabin or apartment"* were somewhat exaggerated. The reality was that the small space (fifty cubic feet), below deck, tended to be just large enough to curl up and sleep. The wall of this so-called apartment would be an old wool blanket.

In 1900, approximately 1,200 women—one-third of the

fishing crews—travelled in small schooners from the communities of Bay Roberts, Brigus, Carbonear, Harbour Grace, and Western Bay to work as hired "girls" in the Labrador fisheries.

Captain Alexander Ploughman of Ship Cove, Trinity Bay, in describing the space allotted for women, wrote:

> *"In most cases the accommodation is very meager being merely a screen dividing the female compartment from that of the men . . . in many cases they [women] are lying around like so many cattle."*

No matter what the cost of making the space for the women, Captain James Burden of Carbonear was determined to provide separate accommodation. He wrote:

> *"I cannot think of prohibiting females as we have to make our fish on the Labrador. Two females are better than two men in many cases, and not half the expense."*

Dictionary of Canadian Biography—John Moody
MOODY, JOHN, lieutenant-colonel; deputy-governor of Placentia; b. c. 1677; d. 1736.

Moody was appointed lieutenant in Captain Michael Richards' Independent Company in Newfoundland, 18 Feb. 1703.

Trouble had always arisen between the residents at St. John's and the military commanders, because the latter regarded themselves as entitled to certain perquisites and privileges. Although prohibited by orders from so doing, every military commander speculated profitably in trade in provisions, fish, and oil on his own account. As the commander's position gave him special advantages, the residents strongly objected. It was not long therefore before accusations similar to those against Lloyd were levelled against Lieutenant Moody. But the winter of 1704–5 was to provide grounds for more precise and spectacular accusations against Moody. In December Moody ordered that Christian, a charwoman employed by John Jackson's daughter, Margaret, should be whipped—allegedly for the theft of some rum and brandy. The exact details of the case are lost in a mass of contradictory reports, but it may well be that Christian's real crime was that she knew too much about Moody's private life. At all events, she died a few days after her ordeal, and a number of the inhabitants accused Moody of causing her death. The following summer Moody demanded a trial, which was presided over by Commodore Bridges. The court found that the allegations were "malicious and unfounded"; the woman—according to the court—had died from venereal disease.

In October, Lloyd returned as commander of the land forces, and on 21 Nov. 1705, Moody sailed for England with Commodore Bridges in the Looe. In the same convoy went John Jackson with whom, despite the episode with Christian, Moody had maintained a steady friendship. The Looe was wrecked on the Isle of Wight, with some loss of life, but Moody and Bridges survived.

Article #1: The Mystery of George's Island, Labrador
ALLEGED TRAGEDY ON THE LABRADOR COAST.
Monday, December 17, 1877 – The Patriot and Terra-Nova Herald
[From the Harbor Grace Standard.]

THE LIARS

For some time past, very ugly rumors have been rife among certain of bur Labrador fishermen with reference to the manner in which, it is conjectured, the captain and part of the crew of the Hudson Bay Company's schooner Walrus came to their untimely end.

Not to mention reasons arising from the case itself, the assumed Basset murder and other similar instances admonish us to be careful not to speak dogmatically. We wish it to be distinctly understood, then, that we give the subjoined details just as we have learned them (after careful enquiry) from the lips of several respectable planters— one of whom had a conversation with the green fish catchers mentioned below, another heard the whole story from Mr. Pottle himself, who, our informant added, was convinced that the men did not come to their death by fair means.

The Walrus, it will be remembered, left Rigoulette on the 15th October of last year for Gyady on route to Montreal, with a cargo of salmon, trout, oil, etc. There being no wind, and a heavy sea on, she anchored for the night off' George's Island.

On the following day a gale of wind springing up, the captain with his crew attempted to land, but were upset in the surf, and (with the exception of one man) drowned.

After being on the Island for five days, the solitary survivor, by plugging the holes in the boat with his jacket, succeeded in again boarding the vessel. Slipping her cables he ran her ashore at Black Island, where she became a total wreck.

Such was in effect the story told by the survivor. But now it turns out—(if we can credit the statements of our fishermen) that instead of being drowned in the manner described, the captain and crew of the hapless vessel were cruelly murdered. It appears from all we can glean on the subject, that a crew of green-fish catchers whilst searching for bait early last season, had occasion to land on George's Island, and were horrified to discover lying on the strand the bodies of three men, with—strange to say—their heads off. As their other limbs, as well as the clothes they had on, were intact, it was seen at a glance that this could not have been caused by the action of the sea, the bodies, moreover, being beyond high water mark. About sixty yards farther west, another body was discovered, the head of which was cleft in four pieces. The suspicions of the men being aroused, they began to make further search. Their efforts resulted in finding the remains of two large canvas tents which—judging from their size and the trampled state of the ground all around them—they believed must have been erected by more than one man.

Covering the bodies with sand, the green fish catchers made their way to the opposite side of the Island. Here they fell in with a man by the name of Williams, to whom they related all that they had just discovered, Williams at once proceeded to the place indicated, and found that the story told him by the men respecting this horrible affair was correct in every particular. Taking with him the canvas of which the tents had been built, Mr. Williams immediately Set on for Fish Cove, a place some miles farther west, where resides a Mr. Pottle, whom he made acquainted with the particulars of this mysterious affair. A short time after, Mr. Pottle, with some of his men, visited the Island, and proceeded to make a thorough investigation. Uncovering the bodies he found them just as has been described. He also discovered in a small crevice in the rock near which one of the tents had been erected, a number of half-decayed books, papers, etc., as well as a woman's photograph and a small quantity of tea—the presence of which proved pretty conclusively that the boat was not upset in the surf as was alleged by the survivor.

Walling the bodies round with stone, and once more placing the sand over them, Mr. Pottle and his men left George's Island, with its ghastly occupants, and returned to their homes.

*T*HE *LIARS*

Article #2: The Twillingate Sun, Thursday December 2, 1880
The Esquimo Murderer
His Career of Crime as Narrated by To-Day's "Newfoundlander"

We remarked on Friday that the Esquimo charged with murder at Nain as just been captured. He would have been brought here from harbour Grace yesterday if the steamer had crossed, but the weather was rough, and he will probably be sent over to-day instead.

The story of the later years of the man's career, as far as it is yet told, exhibits a singularly vicious nature. Of course we only give the narrative of his deeds as we learn it, and without any prejudgment upon allegations which have yet to be tested by law.

He was born at Nain, Labrador, his name is Ephriam; and his age is thirty six. Nothing more is said of him till the time of his marriage in 1865 to a woman named Ruth. Ten months after their marriage she fell from a height into the sea and was drowned.

In 1868 he married a widow with three sons, his second wife being by 24 years his senior. His violence to her sons was such that it drove them all from the house, and his treatment of their mother was exceedingly cruel. He is also charged with savage conduct towards his parents. On one occasion when thep (he) and one of his step sons named Paul were working together, a dispute arose and as they left the place he fired a gun at them and the ball barely missed killing his father. His temper was at all times fierce, and he frequently uttered threats against the members of his wife's family.

In September last, Ephriam and his step-son Philip travelled from their fishing place up into a creek. Soon after they began to move, Philip was shot through the neck and died on the spot. Ephriam's first story was that Philip stumbled and fell and in the fall the gun got discharged; and Philip's wife Nancy, who is said to have been Ezra's paramour, confirmed the statement. She afterwards however told Philip's brother Paul that this statement was untrue and that she was afraid of Ephriam to tell the truth, which was that Ezra himself had committed the murderous act. She added that he had threatened her own life and that of her child if she did not confirm his version of the cause of Philip's death. The Moravian missionaries on hearing of the case sent some of their body with a company of Esquimos to the place where Philip's body lay. Meeting Ezra on the way they apprehended him. On examination he adhered to his first assertion that the cause of death was accidental; and persisted in this even when confronted with Nancy who now made a contrary statement. She said that as soon as Ezra came back after Philip's death he told her that he had shot him. Ezra still denied; the missionaries and their party then made him go with them to the scene of the blood.

As they went, he uttered threats that something worse would yet happen. Soon after and before reaching their destination, Ephriam voluntarily confessed to the party that he was guilty of the crime. He said he had gone out hunting with Philip, that they were disputing about Nancy, that Philip said something which Ezra though disparaging of her, and that a struggle ensued; that Philip seized his gun, and Ezra also laid hold to it and threw Philip down; he then shot him from behind in the nape of the neck.

When the missionaries arrived at the place they found Ezra's gun hidden in the bushes, and near it Philip's body wrapped in a reindeer skin, partially buried and covered with turf and wood. The place where the ball had gone through was distinctly seen. They there and then made a grave and interred the body.

The missionaries lost no time in ridding the locality of Ezra and sending him on here to be dealt with as the law shall adjudge—St. John's Evening Telegram, Nov. 23.

Article #3: From the Harbour Grace Standard

About a quarter to eight o'clock last night, Police Inspector CARTY received a telegram from Brigus stating that the Eskimo charged with the murder of his son at Nain, Labrador, and who escaped at Scrammy, from custody, on board the SS Panther, had arrived at Harbour Main from HANNON, and that while being conveyed by the said HANNON from Harbour Main to Brigus, to be handed over to the police authorities there, he made his escape at Gasters, Salmon Cove. On receipt of this information, the Inspector immediately sent dispatches to the police in Holyrood, Brigus, Bay Roberts, and Harbour Grace, instructing them to leave nothing undone that would be likely to lead up to his apprehension. At eight o'clock, some of the horse police were sent from St. John's in search of the fugitive, followed shortly after by a detachment on foot. Up to the time of our ongoing press, his recapture had not been effected. -Ibid 12.

*I*DA LINEHAN YOUNG

Periodical Accounts Relating to the Missions of the Church of the United Brethren; (subtitled) Brethren's Society for the Furtherance of the Gospel among the Heathen

Volume 33, page 209 states: . . . *tidings had recently come of the death of Ephraim the Eskimo, in prison, in St. John's. . . . Before his death he confessed, what long had been suspected, that he was also guilty of the murder of his first wife, whom he had pushed off some rocks into the sea.*

First and foremost, Ida Linehan Young is a grandmother to the most precious little boys, Parker and Samuel, a mother to three adult children, Sharon, Stacey, and Shawna, and a wife to Thomas. In her busy daily life, Ida works in the information technology sector of the federal government of Canada, and she volunteers her time in the community of Conception Bay South with the Kiwanis Club of Kelligrews.

Ida had a fascination with writing in her high school days, when she dabbled in poetry and essays. In 2012, she became serious about her writing with a story to tell, and that led to her memoir, *No Turning Back: Surviving the Linehan Family Tragedy*, in 2014. Having found a passion for writing and with a love of local history and lore, she published several historical fiction novels, *Being Mary Ro* (2018), *The Promise* (2019), and *The Liars* (2020). (*continued*)

With strong influences of the familial art of storytelling passed down by her father, Ed Linehan, and her maternal grandfather, Frank Power, Ida writes stories about her beloved province, Newfoundland and Labrador. She enjoys researching events of the late nineteenth century and weaving fictional characters through historical tales that complement that cultural richness and renews and regenerates interest in our storied past.

Follow Ida on Facebook, Twitter, or Instagram:
@idalinehanyoung
Or on her website:
www.idalinehanyoung.ca